ALSO BY KATEE ROBERT

Court of the Vampire Queen

Dark Olympus
Stone Heart (prequel novella)
Neon Gods
Electric Idol
Wicked Beauty
Radiant Sin
Cruel Seduction
Midnight Ruin
Dark Restraint
Sweet Obsession

Wicked Villains
Desperate Measures
Learn My Lesson
A Worthy Opponent

Black Rose Auction
Wicked Pursuit

TENDER CRUELTY

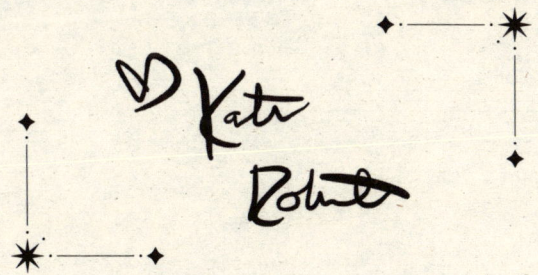

TENDER CRUELTY

KATEE ROBERT

Copyright © 2026 by Katee Robert
Cover and internal design © 2026 by Sourcebooks
Cover design by Sourcebooks
Cover illustration © good_mood/Shutterstock
Internal art © Anna Moshak

Sourcebooks and the colophon are registered trademarks of Sourcebooks.

All rights reserved. No part of this book may be reproduced in any form or by any electronic or mechanical means including information storage and retrieval systems—except in the case of brief quotations embodied in critical articles or reviews—without permission in writing from its publisher, Sourcebooks.

No part of this book may be used or reproduced in any manner for the purpose of training artificial intelligence technologies or systems.

The characters and events portrayed in this book are fictitious or are used fictitiously. Any similarity to real persons, living or dead, is purely coincidental and not intended by the author.

All brand names and product names used in this book are trademarks, registered trademarks, or trade names of their respective holders. Sourcebooks is not associated with any product or vendor in this book.

Published by Sourcebooks Casablanca, an imprint of Sourcebooks
1935 Brookdale RD, Naperville, IL 60563-2773
(630) 961-3900
sourcebooks.com

Cataloging-in-Publication Data is on file with the Library of Congress.

The authorized representative in the EEA is Dorling Kindersley
Verlag GmbH. Arnulfstr. 124, 80636 Munich, Germany

Manufactured in the UK by Clays and distributed
by Dorling Kindersley Limited, London
001-355605-Dec/25
10 9 8 7 6 5 4 3 2 1

To every single person who cursed me for Zeus and Hera being book nine instead of book three.

Tender Cruelty is an occasionally dark and very spicy book that contains pregnancy, abuse (child, historical, referenced briefly throughout), violence, blood, murder, and explicit sex.

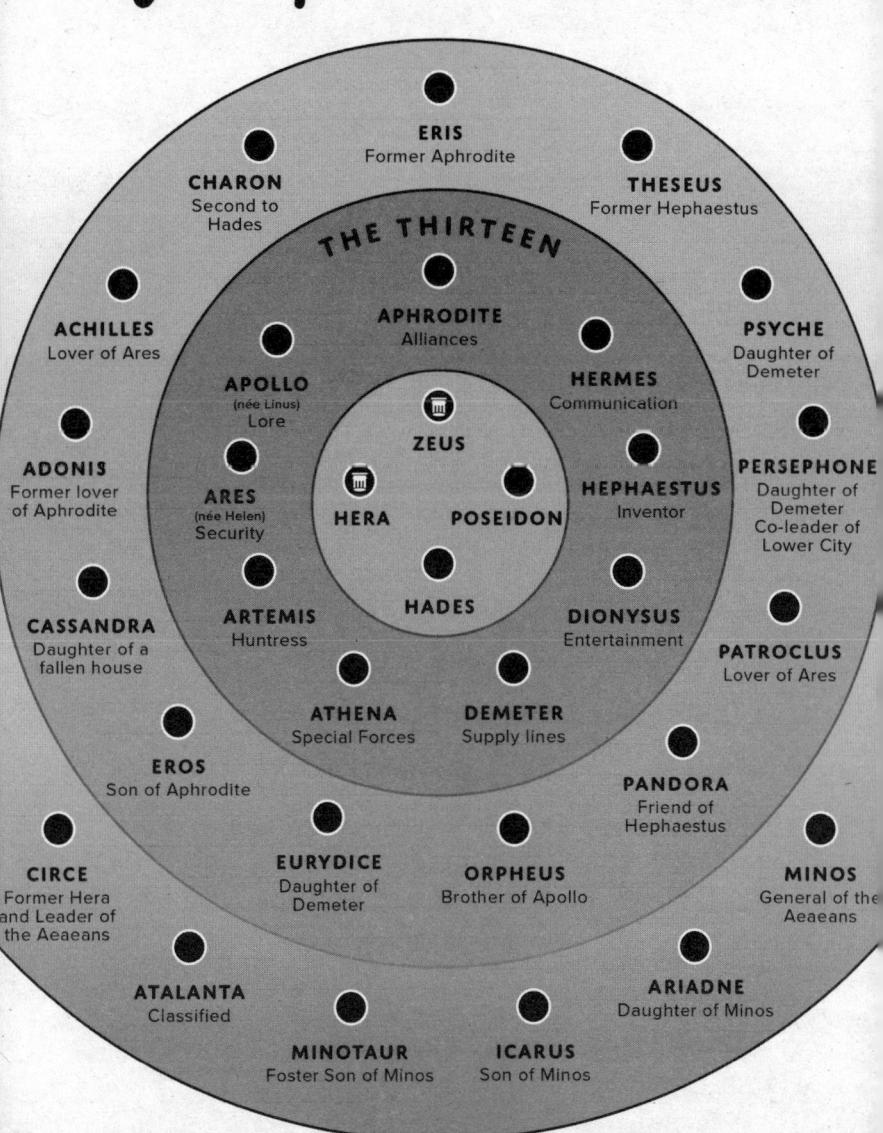

MUSEWATCH

Previously in Olympus...

OLYMPUS'S SWEETHEART GONE WILD!

Persephone Dimitriou shocks everyone by fleeing an engagement with Zeus to end up in Hades's bed!

ZEUS FALLS TO HIS DEATH!

Perseus Kasios will now take up the title of Zeus. Can he possibly fill his father's shoes?

APHRODITE ON THE OUTS

After a live stream in which she threatened Psyche Dimitriou for marrying her son Eros, Aphrodite is exiled by the Thirteen. She chooses Eris Kasios to be successor to her title.

ARES IS DEAD!

A tournament will be held to choose the next Ares… and Helen Kasios is the prize.

…LONG LIVE ARES

In a stunning turn of events, Helen Kasios has chosen to compete for her own hand…and she won! We now have three Kasios siblings among the Thirteen.

NEW BLOOD IN TOWN!

After losing out on the Ares title, Minos Vitalis and his household have gained Olympus citizenship… and are celebrating with a house party for the ages. We have the guest list, and you'll never guess who's invited!

APOLLO FINDS LOVE AT LAST?

After being ostracized by Olympus for most of her adult life, Cassandra Gataki has snagged one of the Thirteen as her very own! She and Apollo were looking very cozy together at the Dryad.

MURDER FAVORS THE BOLD

Tragedy strikes! Hephaestus was killed by

Theseus Vitalis, triggering a little-known law that places Theseus as the new Hephaestus. The possibilities are…intriguing.

HEPHAESTUS AND APHRODITE ARE OUT!

Our new Hephaestus and Aphrodite have stepped down unexpectedly! But can a leopard really change its spots? We don't expect Eris Kasios and Theseus Vitalis to fully turn their backs on Olympus politics… even for the love of Pandora and Adonis.

THE WAY TO THE LOWER CITY IS BLOCKED

After a series of attacks in the lower city, Hades has strengthened the barrier along the River Styx! There's official word on the reasons why, but an inside source says that he won't lower the barrier until the Thirteen present a unified front. We hope he's prepared to wait…

THE BARRIER HAS FALLEN!

The unthinkable has happened: for the first time in Olympus's history, the protective barrier keeping us safe from the outside world has fallen. Newly vulnerable, all Olympus can do is wait and hope…

OLYMPUS UNDER ATTACK!

A squadron of enemy ships have been spotted forming a blockade in Olympian waters. Rumors say they are led by Circe, who was once our very own Hera, long presumed dead. Has this ghost returned to burn Olympus to the ground in revenge?

MINOS KILLED IN DARING ESCAPE

Minos and his children may have managed to tear down Olympus's barrier for their ally Circe, but not all went according to plan: while Ariadne and the Minotaur escaped, Minos was killed and Icarus captured. We can only hope our own Poseidon means to bring the full fury of Olympus down on this enemy of the state…

WAR COMES TO OLYMPUS!

Our great city is under attack! Citizens evacuate to the countryside under Demeter's watchful eye while all of Olympus holds its breath.

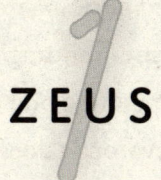

ZEUS

IT'S ALL COMING APART. TONIGHT SHOULD HAVE been a victory that cemented my reign as Zeus and eliminated the threat against Olympus once and for all. Instead, four out of five Aeaean ships sailed off into the night, possibly about to turn around and attack us the moment we aren't looking—and Circe has once again slipped through our grasp.

My father must be rolling over in his grave. The bastard might have been a monster of the most dangerous variety, but he reigned as Zeus for nearly fifty years of peace. More or less. I've held the title for less than a year, and during that time, the assassination clause has become public knowledge, resulting in unprecedented violence against the Thirteen, we're facing an external enemy for the first time in Olympian history, the barrier that protected our city from the outside world has come down, *and* I've staged a coup with the other legacy titles, betraying everything Zeus is supposed to be.

Truly, a spectacular failure all around.

I sit in my car in my building's parking garage for long enough that I start getting odd looks from the guards positioned near the elevator. It doesn't matter how long I take or how deep and slow my breathing; there's no banishing my father's derisive voice from my head. He might be dead, but he haunts me still, even though this is all his damn fault.

There isn't a neat solution to the Circe problem, and she wouldn't even *be* a problem if my bastard of a father hadn't kidnapped her off the street, marched her down the aisle, and then attempted to murder her on their honeymoon. Up until very recently, we all assumed she was dead—another Hera fallen at the hands of a violent Zeus.

The worst part is that I don't blame her for her determination to get vengeance. She was horribly mistreated by both my father and the rest of the Thirteen at the time. Not a single person tried to step in to help her.

But my father is dead and gone—at least to everyone who didn't spend their entire lives being trained to become the next him. Of the Thirteen who held the positions when she was Hera, only three remain—Poseidon, Athena, and Hades. Even if there were more left, no one stands against Zeus. At least the Zeus my father was. She's striving for vengeance against people who hold no blame in her pain. More than that, she's endangering the civilians of the city.

What the fuck am I doing? I have all this power, and all I've managed to do with it is stumble around in the dark.

I sigh. I'm not going to solve this problem by sitting in my car and berating myself in my late father's voice. There will be no peace up in the penthouse either, not with *my* Hera swishing about, plotting my death. She wasn't successful in her most recent plans, but she's not a woman to give up easily. Sleeping peacefully at her side should be out of the question.

And yet it's the only time I get any rest these days.

I shove out of the car and stalk past the guards, forcing myself to nod at them in greeting, and take the elevator up to the penthouse. It's late enough that dawn is a short time away, so I don't expect Hera to be awake. I sure as fuck don't expect her to have company.

But as I walk through the door, there's a deep voice intertwined with her more musical tones.

One of the first lessons my father taught me was that emotional reactions are handing a weapon to your enemy and exposing your throat. *He* was the enemy back then, but the lesson remains. No matter how Hera strives to incite my fury, I don't react. I will *not* be my father and terrorize those in my household. The more my wife acts out, the thicker the ice I use to keep my temper under control.

I find her sitting on the couch with Ixion, one of the new guards who follow her everywhere. She acquired him and the other two from Ares at some point in the last two months. I approve of her keeping herself safe. I sure as fuck do *not* approve of the way Ixion allows his thigh to press to hers.

They look up as I stop in the doorway. Hera gives me nothing, but that's to be expected. People accuse me of being an ice king, but she's all blades and no softness. She has one reaction to any given situation—strike first. She leans back and crosses one long leg over the other, which is right around the time I realize she's wearing a robe and nothing else. Her dark hair is mussed a bit, too; she must have run her fingers through it recently.

Or *Ixion* ran his fingers through it.

Ixion gives me a smirk as if *he* has a better claim to the woman I married than I do. The fact that he might be right nearly has me reaching for the gun in my shoulder holster. I can even see what she finds attractive about him—he's a white man with short blond hair, a neatly trimmed mustache, and the kind of muscular body that one gets from a life of work. The mustache alone should write him off, but he's a handsome fucker and charming enough to make it work for him.

I hold his gaze for long enough that a bright pink takes up residence in his cheeks. Only then do I speak. "Get out."

Ixion doesn't immediately obey. He looks to *her* first,

waiting for her nod, then rising easily to his feet. "I'll see you tomorrow."

"Bright and early." She even manages a smile for him, which is more than I ever get from her. "Have a good night."

"You too." He doesn't shoulder check me as he walks past, but he clearly wants to. I let him have my back as I listen to him walk down the hall to the door. When Hera acquired her trio, I had Apollo look into them. They all held exemplary records with Athena before they resigned and came to Hera. There was literally nothing to criticize, no good reason to step in and demand she retain the guards *I* handpicked for her instead.

It irritates me deeply.

"Zeus." I hadn't realized there was warmth in her tone for him until there's none for me. "You're home late."

If I were a better man, I wouldn't relish the thread of jealousy beneath her question. It's faint enough that I'm not entirely certain it's real, but I *want* it to be real. I want Hera to care enough to worry about whose bed I might be spending time in. Because of that weakness, I can't bring myself to address it directly. "And you had Ixion here late." I make a show of looking at my watch. "He must be costing a fortune in overtime."

"You have no idea." Her hazel eyes flash. "Take a shower. You're not coming straight from someone else's bed to mine."

"You first, *Wife*."

"Gladly." She's off the couch and across the room in seconds, disappearing through the doorway leading deeper into the penthouse.

Hera represents another failure in my year as Zeus. Marrying her accomplished my goal of getting Demeter and her formidable alliances on my side, but if I had tentative hopes of this marriage being a true partnership—let alone something more—they died on my wedding night. My home has since turned into a battleground *again*, each interaction another fight in an ongoing war. Sharing a bed? It's just another facet of that.

I should deny her. She's actively trying to orchestrate my death and I highly doubt that the most recent failure will set her back for long. Letting her be close enough to access me when I sleep is foolhardy to the point of being suicidal. Having sex with her is even worse. Even knowing exactly how intensely she wants me dead, I…forget myself.

Knowing that doesn't stop me from walking to the spare bedroom and taking a quick shower. It isn't enough to keep me from pulling on a pair of shorts and padding barefoot across the hallway to the primary bedroom. Opening the door allows a sliver of light into the darkness. Hera has pulled the curtains already; can't entertain even the slightest possibility that someone might see what happens in our perfect darkness.

She steps out of the bathroom, a silk robe wrapped around her lithe body. She meets my gaze boldly and reaches without looking to shut off the light. My breathing feels unnaturally loud as I move unerringly toward the bed. Toward Hera. The faint slither of her robe dropping down her body to the floor makes me so hard it's difficult to think. It's always like this. No matter how cold we are in the daylight hours, no matter what violence her plots entail, in the dark all I can think about is the feel of her, the way she tastes on my tongue.

It's because of that desperation that I hold back. That I *have* to hold back. I have to be sure. "Hera."

"Gods, you are *unbearable*."

I ignore that. "Say yes."

"I'm naked and waiting in your bed, you utter bastard. Get over here and do your husbandly duties so I can get some sleep."

When we were married, we signed a contract explicitly spelling out that an heir and a spare are required, but she demanded a full twelve months before actively attempting to get pregnant. I was more than happy to oblige that particular demand. Hades already has an heir on the way, which creates pressure for me to do the same, but there are few horrors I can imagine beyond forcing a pregnancy on a person, so even after the year is up, I'll wait for Hera to decide for herself that she's ready to stop taking her birth control.

That year *should* mean we aren't fucking, but that small detail got lost somewhere in translation. Every single night, when the lights go out, we find each other in the dark. And every single night, I refuse to touch her before getting verbal consent. "Say yes."

She curses. "Yes."

Hera. My queen. The person in Olympus who hates me the most.

But when my fingers brush her hip, she grabs my wrist and pulls me down to her. No hesitation. No ice. Just a heat so intense *I'm* certain it will burn us both away to nothingness. She's not sharp as I pull her close and kiss her. She's soft and fiery and full of need. Her fingers dig into my hips, urging me to line up with her, to *get this over with*.

Despite everything, stress and rage and a deep sense that I'm fucking things up beyond all repair in every facet of my life, I smile against her lips. "Say yes."

"I *hate* you."

It's the truth. But not in this moment. When she's moving against me, a battle of wills where we both win, I can almost see the partnership we could have if we'd just get out of our own ways. If she wasn't Hera, determined to stand apart from her predecessors and survive. If I wasn't Zeus, trapped in a long shadow of all those who have held the title before me. We would be unstoppable. We might even be happy.

But we *are* Zeus and Hera, and I can't afford to forget

that. I drag my mouth along her jaw to speak directly in her ear, as soft as a secret. "Say yes, Hera. Spread your thighs and let me taste you."

Her nails prick my hips, but when she speaks, she's the same cold creature I married. "I already said yes, Zeus. Don't be a bastard and try to make me beg. You'll fail."

We both know that's a lie, but I allow her the illusion that it's not. She always begs in the end—for me to go harder, deeper, to not stop. Tonight, I don't test the limits of her patience. I never do. Instead, I kiss my way down her body and settle between her thighs.

Here is where Hera is sweetest, and she proves that to be true yet again at the first slow drag of my tongue through her folds. Instantly, her legs fall wide open. She laces her fingers through my hair and lifts her hips to meet my mouth.

These stolen moments of peace never last. They're a fantasy I can't help engaging with, an alternate reality that I only allow myself to entertain when there is nothing to illuminate the lie. Dawn will come soon enough to pierce the illusion that I have a wife who actually wants me.

But for now, we have this.

HERA

I *HATE* ZEUS. I'VE HATED ZEUS SINCE I WAS A LITTLE girl and realized exactly how much power he holds over Olympus—over my family. It doesn't matter that *this* Zeus and that one are two different men. Zeus may be a title passed down from parent to child since the beginning of Olympus, but they're all monsters.

This particular monster currently has two fingers inside me and is licking my clit in a rhythm that has my toes curling almost painfully.

It only makes me hate him more, yet it doesn't matter how little I like the man between my thighs. When the lights go out, I can almost pretend he's someone else, someone whose pleasure I can accept without choking on it.

It's unfortunate I've never been all that good at playing pretend.

Zeus crooks his fingers inside me again and again, driving me into an orgasm so strong it almost wipes away the bitter taste of failure. If I'd gotten my way, I'd be a widow by now, my husband crushed in a truly unfortunate *accident* in that eyesore he calls a workplace. Instead, I'm shoving him onto his back and straddling him, taking his ridiculously large cock into me.

I don't *need* to fuck my husband any more. I got what I came for—an heir to take his title, a clear path into a future without him in it. I'm months along at this point and all signs indicate that the little parasite in my stomach is perfectly healthy and will continue to be until the moment they come barging into the world, no doubt to grow up to be a monster just like every Zeus before them. But they'll be *my* monster.

We have no shortage of those in my family.

So, no, I don't need to keep having sex with Zeus. Every night, I tell myself that this will be the night I'll go sleep in the spare bedroom, or will at least resist telling him *yes* the way he keeps insisting before touching me.

And every night, I'm back here again, riding his cock and letting pleasure sweep over me until this entire interlude hardly feels real.

In the morning, I'll wake up to find him gone and I'll hate him all the more for his absence. And maybe I'll hate myself a little for the sliver of disappointment I can't quite banish. I've always had more than my fair share of hate to spread around.

He grips my hips, pulling me down in a grinding motion while he presses against the sides of my mound with his thumbs. The squeeze isn't direct contact to my clit, but after coming so hard from his tongue, I'm sensitive to the point of pain. It's as if Zeus has a map of my pleasure in a way that no one else ever has. He's so fucking methodical that I think he clocked me on our wedding night. He's only gotten better since then.

Bastard.

Through it all, he never says a word. Not even when I lose control and dig my nails into his chest. "More!"

He gives me more. He always gives me more. Until I overflow with it, my body going tight and hot and *gushing* all over him. Normally, it's enough to pull him over the edge with me, to end this awful, wonderful moment where nothing makes sense. Then we'll clean up and retreat to our respective sides of the bed and sleep. Or he sleeps. I lie there, filled with loathing for him, for this city, and for myself.

Not tonight. He rolls us and shifts back to kneel between my legs, pressing my thighs wide until I'm bent in half. Then he's inside me again, fucking me in long, punishing strokes that rub deliciously inside me. I don't mean to reach for him. I sure as fuck don't mean to grab his hips and pull him deeper yet. "Harder," I gasp.

He doesn't hesitate to give me exactly what I ask for. It should be enough to make me feel in control, but I'm the one unraveling and he's still the perfect ice king. He fucks me like he's mad at me, like he's punishing me, but that doesn't make any sense because who punishes with pleasure?

My orgasm has barely faded and it's already building again, even stronger this time. If I were more in control, I would shove him off and walk away, leaving him with only his hand for comfort. But I'm too greedy. Instead of pushing him away, I pull him closer and then it's too late—I'm coming again, and this time he's coming with me.

In this one perfect moment, my mind is still. I'm not a peaceful person by nature, but I can almost wrap my hands around the concept of it. The fact that *my husband* is the source of the sensation is beyond my ability to reconcile. So I don't. I've lived with plenty of dichotomies in my life; what's one more?

Zeus's hands flex on my thighs, holding me open even as my body pulses from the strength of the orgasm, drawing me back into the present. "No more, Hera."

I blink into the near-perfect darkness. I can't even see his outline above me. Why is he talking to me? We don't *talk* in bed. "What?"

"You're discreet enough that not even MuseWatch has caught wind of your lover, but I don't give a fuck. I don't want him *here*."

My...lover.

It takes my pleasure-drunk brain a beat to catch up. He

means Ixion. He's *jealous* of Ixion. The thought would make me laugh if I had the breath for it. I'm not fool enough to sleep with anyone except Zeus, not when the parentage of my parasite is so vital to my plans and, by extension, the safety of my family. That's why I accepted this marriage, after all—to protect my sisters.

But admitting that Ixion and I aren't having sex feels like giving away a piece of vital information—and power with it. Especially when I'm sure Zeus's late nights at the office aren't spent alone. I see the way people watch him. Even though he's not charismatic like his father, he's got power and that's enough to make him attractive to a certain type of person. Ganymede missed becoming Hera and now he practically throws himself at Zeus every chance he gets. And he's just one person. There are a dozen more young, beautiful things willing to play paramour, and those are only the ones I know about.

Not that I'm jealous. I'm not. I don't care what my husband gets up to as long as it keeps him distracted from what *I'm* up to.

"Hera," he growls. "I don't demand much of you, but I'll be damned before I let you make me a cuckold in my own home."

It's on the tip of my tongue to tell the truth, but that's just the endorphins from sex clouding my thinking. If Zeus believes the reason I'm sneaking around is because I'm fucking the head of my bodyguards, then he won't be worrying about what I'm *actually* doing. Mainly: plotting his death.

"I will keep my extracurricular activities outside the penthouse," I finally manage. It's a good idea to leave it there, but I can't quite help myself. I grab his shoulders and pull him down until I can feel his harsh breathing against my lips. "And *you* will give me the same courtesy. I don't want to find someone else's underwear in our bedroom."

Zeus is silent for a beat. Then he thrusts into me, his cock already hardening again. We don't do this. We don't have sex more than once a night. I open my mouth to remind him of that, but he kisses me before I can get the words out. He nips my bottom lip. "Are you jealous, Hera?"

"No." And I'm not. It's about respect, *not* about wanting him all for myself. I don't want him at all. The words feel a little insubstantial, so I shove at his shoulders. "We've met our requirement for the night."

Instantly, he retreats. I tell myself that there's no regret in my traitorous body as I sit up and scoot toward the edge of the bed. "Now you got me all sweaty. I need another shower." The words are harsh with recrimination, but I'm not sure if I'm more pissed at him…or myself.

Shutting the bathroom door between us doesn't offer any clarity. Strategically, it makes sense to keep having sex with him. He doesn't know I'm pregnant, and I have no intention of telling him. My parasite is the path forward into the future. One where I'm set up as regent of the Zeus title until the kid comes of age. There's no space in that future for *this* Zeus. If he knew what I intended, he'd stop me. It's best he suspects nothing.

The logic is solid enough. It's the smart move. If I also get extreme levels of pleasure out of the bargain? Well, Zeus is a giant pain in my ass and being his wife is downright torturous most days. We essentially have a business partnership with a side of fucking, except neither one of us would have chosen the other if there were any other option.

He *didn't* choose me. He was in negotiations with my mother for Psyche's hand in marriage when that shit with Eros and Aphrodite hit the fan—two Aphrodites ago, which defies belief when titles usually shift once a generation. My sister married Eros in a truly reckless effort to live, and that left only me and Eurydice as candidates for our mother's ambition. I couldn't let Eurydice take that hit, so I stepped forward to do it instead. Zeus needed Demeter—and her allies—at his back, so he wasn't in a position to refuse my offer.

I turn on the shower and step in before the water has a chance to warm up. The shock of cold clears my thoughts and shatters the strange spell Zeus wove around me in the bedroom. I duck under the spray and make myself hold that position until the persistent desire to go another round disappears. It takes longer than I want to admit.

I don't rush through drying off and braiding my hair back. With any luck, he'll have fallen asleep by the time I return to the bed. As the racing of my heart finally slows to something more normal, I can't help wondering at what happened tonight to cause him to break our silent rules.

He's been coming home later and later in the evening, and even with Ixion and the others doing their best to keep track of his whereabouts, he slips away every time. Either he's meeting with a lover—multiple lovers, even—or he's up to something in relation to Olympus. Possibly both. Probably both.

But I don't know what, and so I can't bargain that information to Circe in return for my family's safety. I'm not even certain where she is right now, if she's still on that ship in the bay or if she'd already moved forward with whatever her plans are. I deeply resent not knowing.

Exhaustion rolls over me in a wave. Before the parasite, I could operate on little sleep for weeks on end without issue. Now, I need to be in bed by midnight or I'm weaving on my feet. I'm well past that time tonight…or this morning, more accurately. I should have sent Ixion away and tried to get some sleep, but I can't stand the thought of being in that big bed and being surprised by Zeus coming home unexpectedly. That's all.

I scrub my hands over my face, apply my lotion, and pad out to the perfect darkness of our bedroom. Or near-perfect.

Dawn is making itself known in between the cracks of the curtains. Really, I should skip sleeping entirely and go about my day, but my body has other ideas.

The sheets are cool against my skin, the heat from Zeus's sleeping body not reaching my side of the bed. I settle into place, moving gingerly to avoid waking him and potentially starting another conversation I don't have capacity to deal with right now. Or ever.

A few hours. In a few hours, I'll be able to think again, to plan, to find the angle needed to see us through the coming conflict…

HERMES

"THIS IS A PROBLEM."

I lower the binoculars and sigh. "Problems are nothing new. Every step of this has gotten more complicated for no damned reason. We'll deal with it." I almost interfered with Zeus's cute little coup's attempt to sink our enemy's small fleet, but ultimately the ships were *another* problem that needed to be taken care of. Olympus has done nothing but hurt those it's meant to care for, and evacuating the civilians to the countryside—even though Demeter had the foresight to purchase land specifically for this purpose from one of my many shell companies—will put pressure on our food supply sooner rather than later. We needed that blockade gone.

Of course, now no one knows where our enemy is—not even me—and *that* is a larger problem.

Atalanta shifts next to me and bumps her shoulder

against mine. "Normally me pointing out problems has you giddy with the opportunity to fix them."

"It keeps life interesting," I say absently. She smells good—*really* good—like coconut or something tropical that makes my mouth water. Unfortunately, pressing my nose to her skin or, gods forbid, *tasting* her is out of the question. She's the only true friend and ally I have left in Olympus, so I'd be a damn fool to complicate things by crossing that line. It's something we've both mutually—silently—agreed to talk about *after*.

After this plan that's been years in the making either fails spectacularly or, more likely, gets pulled off even more spectacularly. Yes, there have been hiccups. Atalanta had a better than stellar shot at the Ares title, and if she'd won the competition, it would have made everything so much simpler. But no one could have anticipated Minos—or the news he brought with him to Olympus. That Circe is alive and well and bent on revenge.

Circe.

I shiver. No use thinking about her. Not now. Not ever. "You should get going. Athena will be looking for you."

"Not for a bit." Atalanta shrugs, her gaze distant. "Since they didn't find *her*, I'm about to be up to my eyeballs in a wild-goose chase. I don't suppose you have any information about where she is so I can just cut her throat and be done with it?"

We're perched on the roof near the shipyard, watching Poseidon return without hostages—*or* Icarus. At least one person in Olympus can be trusted to act true to form. He's honorable to a fault, and sending Icarus away buttons up a loose end that someone would have taken advantage of.

None of that explains *where* Circe is.

"I don't know everything, darling." It's the truth. If it wasn't... I want to believe I'd hand that information to Atalanta willingly. If we knew where Circe is, Atalanta would have a better than average chance of killing her. She's very good at what she does, and *she* has no messy, complicated emotions when it comes to Circe. Not like I do.

It's a good thing I don't know where Circe is, because I can't say for certain I would give the information to Atalanta. And then I'd have to face some feelings I've been purposely avoiding.

"Shocking," she murmurs, her brows drawing together into a beautiful frown. "Would you tell me if you *did* know where she is?"

I know the proper response. Press my hand to my chest and swear with all apparent sincerity that, of course, I would convey Circe's location to Atalanta and, naturally, I want her dead as much as the rest of the Thirteen. It *should* be the truth. I might be enacting a plan that hatched many, many years ago with Circe herself, but our methods vary wildly. We are not in alignment. Not anymore. Never again.

"Hermes." Atalanta grips my shoulder, her strong fingers anchoring me in place even as her dark-brown eyes see far too much. "I know better than anyone the kind of history you have with her..."

History. It's such a trite way of putting it. There was a season in my life when my sun rose and set on Circe's smile. A simpler time, yes, but all the crueler for it. Olympus has never been the utopia the Thirteen and legacy families pretend. Someone has to pay the price for their ambitions, and it falls to the civilians who might as well be nameless as far as those in power are concerned. For the first third of my life, I lived in the countryside and worked in one of the farms that feeds the city, Circe by my side.

And we dreamed of a better world. One that was *fair*.

Ironic, that. Nothing in life is fair. If it was, Zeus never would have seen Circe on her trip into the city to buy me a gift with her hard-earned money. He never would have taken her, married her, and murdered her on their honeymoon.

To find that he *didn't* murder her...

I clear my throat. "Yes, we have history. Ancient history." Losing Circe broke something in me that will never be repaired. It was only finding Atalanta and having her there to pick up the pieces that saved me. Saved, but never healed. Not fully. Even if Circe isn't dead like I believed for damn near twenty years. I attempt a smile, though it falls flat. "It's a nonissue."

Atalanta snorts. "You can lie to everyone else with aplomb. Don't lie to me. I know better. It's an issue."

Damn it, I hate when she perceives me. I sit back and kick my feet out over the drop to the street. "It won't be an issue in the way you mean. It will hurt to see her again, but you and I have been working for damn near fifteen years to give Olympus a chance to fix itself. Having my ex show up to blow the place to smithereens is not the distraction you think it will be."

"Yeah. Sure. I'll believe it when I see it." Atalanta sighs and hefts herself to her feet. She looks particularly fetching in her black fatigues. I never thought I'd have a thing for pseudo military types, but who *wouldn't* have a thing for Atalanta? She's gorgeous with her medium-brown skin, her curls styled back into a mohawk, her scars cutting through the lines of her face in a way that feels like staring into a mirror sometimes.

She gives me a severe look. "We can't afford to drop the ball now. They're scrambling, but not enough."

"I know." I don't lift the binoculars again. There's nothing new to see. Circe might have offered the perfect distraction, but her arrival also gave the Thirteen a chance to unite for the first time ever.

They didn't, of course. Instead they bickered and backstabbed and talked and talked and talked. But they *could* have. Zeus being wicked enough to unite the three legacy titles and engage in a coup—even a limited one—wasn't on my radar, either. He normally plays things by the book, and it's a testament to everyone's desperation that formerly steady people are acting wildly out of character. Which is good. I want them desperate. What I *don't* want is for any alliance to stand strong.

Now Atalanta and I have to ensure it doesn't happen. "You have Athena's ear." In hindsight, we should have placed her with Athena from the start; Atalanta's skill sets certainly fit there better. But we needed eyes on Artemis—and Hephaestus, by extension—because those two were reckless and selfish and unpredictable. Athena, on the other hand, will always be one step behind Zeus, will always be steadfastly serving Olympus in the best way she can. There are no surprises on *that* front.

"No shit. I'm charming and logical." She grins. "I've already started poisoning the well between her and Zeus. He helped loads when he orchestrated that cute little coup without discussing it with her first. She's one minor inconvenience away from dropping a building on his head and taking her chances with... Well, I guess it would be Helen who would claim the Zeus title as the next eldest Kasios? Which leaves the Ares title hanging, and no one has time to put together another tournament to get a new person in there. So, yeah, it's going swimmingly."

I want to pretend I don't have a conscience, but it tends

to rear its goofy little head at the most inopportune of times. Like now, contemplating Zeus's death. It was a lot easier to do with the last one. *He* was evil, and murdering him was a blessing for everyone in the city. His son, our current Zeus, is still in his fledgling monster stage. It's possible someone could pull him out of it...

"I'm worried about Hera," Atalanta says abruptly. "She's got too many connections. She might be able to pull them out of this death spiral."

I shake my head. "She hates the Thirteen. She's more likely to set them on fire than lend a helping hand."

"Hermes." Atalanta puts an emphasis on my title. I am one of the Thirteen, too, after all. "Hera is daughter of Demeter, married to Zeus, and sister-in-law to Hades. Not to mention she's got connections to Eros through Psyche, and he's one scary motherfucker."

"He's a pussycat." I wave that away and keep going before she can snap at me. "We're not threatening Psyche, so he won't bother with us. Easy-peasy."

"We have different definitions of *easy-peasy*."

I laugh. "If it makes you feel better, I'll keep an eye on Hera—and Zeus—to ensure they don't make any more progress trying to bring the gang together."

"That *does* make me feel better, actually." Atalanta leans down and presses a light kiss to my forehead. She's gone before I have a chance to react, the little asshole, striding away to the edge of the roof. A few seconds later the ladder on the other side creaks as she climbs down.

As the warmth of her presence leaves me, I can't help wilting a little. It's so much easier to keep up appearances when feeding off the energy of others. We're close to realizing the goals we've been working toward since the moment I met Atalanta and realized we were in alignment. The goals that started even before then, with Circe.

The Thirteen have to fall. I would prefer not to line them up and put a bullet in each of their brains, one after another. Better—smoother—if they can be convinced to step down. Then we can move forward with the plan to bring true democracy to this shit show, nominating and voting three delegates from the three main parts of Olympus: lower city, upper city, and countryside. The *people* will decide. More than that, if the leaders the population chooses fuck up and don't represent their interests, there will be checks in place to force them to step down.

I'm not a fool. I understand that there aren't any known governments in the world right now that are fully free of corruption. That doesn't mean we can't strive for something better. And that something better is *not* a dark queen to take the place of thirteen corrupt assholes—myself included.

Exhaustion weighs heavy on my shoulders. It's been so long… But with the finish line in sight, I can't afford to flag. There's still plenty of work to be done. First step being trying to talk some sense into Zeus now that the stakes are clear. He won't be happy to see me, but people rarely are these days. I heft myself to my feet and head toward the ladder leading down to the street.

Olympus has to fall, and I still have some key support beams to kick out to make it happen. Time to get to work.

ZEUS

I WAKE ALL AT ONCE. IT'S A TRICK I LEARNED AT TOO young an age; there's no use dwelling on *why*. I reach over without thinking, touching the empty side of my bed where my wife normally sleeps. Cold. She's been gone for some time. Whether she woke early or barely waited for me to fall asleep before she left... It's better not to think about that.

Because then I'll start wondering where she went, and who she's with. If she left my bed to go straight to Ixion's. There's nothing I can do to stop her. Trying would be the height of foolishness and would only serve to make me look weak. A man who can't control his own wife. I climb out of bed and start the process of putting myself together.

It's all unraveling. Everything I've worked for, everything I've fought and bled and suffered for. Olympus. My city, my people, my place in this world.

I've never felt more like a pretender than as I shove out the doors of my building and stalk down the street toward Dodona Tower. On a normal day, the sidewalks would be filled with people heading to work or running errands. Now, it's a ghost town. The vast majority of the city has evacuated to the countryside in an effort to keep civilians out of the way of Circe's threat of attack. An attack that never quite manifested. I want to believe it's because we moved fast enough to thwart her, but there were days between the start of her blockade and the moment I boarded the *Penelope* to find she wasn't there—hadn't been there in some time.

We have to find Circe.

It's only a matter of time before the rest of the world realizes the barrier that kept us separate and safe is down. I doubt it can be repaired, even with the part Circe stole all those years ago. She ensured it would fail eventually, and then she went on to make sure of it with a bomb that took out what was left of the machinery keeping it up.

The outside world will come, first with curiosity and fascination, and then with force. We have a small window to prepare for it, and we can't very well fucking do that with Circe remaining an active problem. More than that, I have no faith that the Thirteen will be able to come together to protect Olympus from the next threat. They wouldn't even vote to take down the blockade, and that was a clear and present danger to the city.

I whip out my phone and call Apollo, barely waiting for him to answer before I bark, "Update."

"There's nothing." He sounds exhausted. "My team has been through every camera around the perimeter of the city. It's tedious but easy enough now that most of the population isn't present. She's not here." He sighs. "Or she knows about the cameras and has taken great pains to avoid them. But, Zeus, no one is perfect. She should have slipped up."

She doesn't have to be perfect when the Thirteen are a fucking mess. There are only a handful of us who have held the titles more than a year, and *none* have experience in anything resembling what we're dealing with now. We've been coddled, the people holding the thirteen titles playing at being modern-day gods, untouchable in the way only the rich and powerful can be. All those power games seem so petty now.

"Hermes doesn't slip up."

He curses softly. "There's no sign of *her*, either. I know she's in the city—she called Cassandra yesterday to tell her to stick close to me—but I've caught no evidence of her on tape."

If Hermes, that fucking traitor, can do it, then it's possible Circe can as well. We clearly have holes in our security, and have for quite some time. "Keep looking."

"I will." He hesitates. "Are we going to talk about the fact that you went against the Thirteen's vote and attacked Circe?"

I don't want to. The temporary coup worked to break the blockade but not to remove the greater threat. Hard not to see it as a costly failure. "It needed to be done."

"There are laws for a reason," he says quietly. "I've supported you since you became Zeus, but that support is not unconditional. If you keep breaking the laws, I'll be forced to stand against you."

His feelings are nothing more than I expected. There's a reason I only told my sister—Ares—and Athena about the coup. The fewer people who knew what I intended, the fewer people who could stop me. Apollo is a good man, and while that's benefited me to this point, it won't hold if I have to keep doing what's necessary to protect the city.

"I understand." I hang up and quicken my pace, but it's not fast enough to outrun the insidious voice tucked into the back of my brain. *Your father never would have let this get so out of hand. He would have killed Minos the moment he realized something was off about the man, without giving a fuck about the consequences. He was too damn charming to actually see consequences…another way you're failing.*

It would be a lot easier to banish that voice if it didn't speak truth. One of the first things I became aware of as a child was how I'd never be as good as my father. Though *good* is a strange word to use, considering the violence and destruction he subjected anyone under his control to. He killed three of his wives, including my mother.

Well, two of them. Circe was the shortest marriage of the three, only lasting a week after being forced to say, "I do." He saw her on the street and had to have her, a magical story of love at first sight, according to MuseWatch. The truth is significantly less romantic. My father was a conqueror; he couldn't stand the thought of something beautiful existing outside his control.

And Circe was beautiful. I don't remember her well—I was in my early twenties and wanted nothing to do with the prospective stepmother who was only a few years older than me—but I remember *that*. She was a lean white woman with dark hair and a spark in her green eyes that made me sick to my stomach. Because I knew exactly what my father would do to that spark, how he would crush it out of existence and leave her a shell of the person she'd once been. At least until he grew tired of her rebellion and she suffered an unfortunate *accident*.

But even I didn't expect him to come back from the honeymoon a widower.

Despite his monstrosity—or maybe because of it—Olympus ran smoothly under his rule as Zeus. I can hardly say the same, for all my determination to create a better world than the one he controlled. The longer I hold the title, the more I wonder if my father wasn't onto something with how he conducted himself.

He never had to deal with assassination attempts, an

unruly Thirteen who refused to vote to benefit the city, and a godsdamned siege.

My phone rings as I step through the doors of Dodona Tower. It's early enough that the receptionist behind the massive counter is still blinking blearily as they sip their coffee. Their eyes go wide when they see me, but I wave them off as I dig my ringing phone out of my pocket. "Yes?"

"We found where she made landing." None of the exhaustion weighing me down is evidenced in Athena's cool voice. She's been working herself to the bone, same as I have, but it never seems to touch her.

Another way you're proving yourself to be an inadequate Zeus.

I ignore the inner voice. "Tell me."

"They killed Poseidon's sentries and there are half a dozen boats cleverly hidden in a copse of trees a few miles north of the bay. It's inside where the barrier once stood, but only just. She could have just as easily cruised another half mile north to coastline we aren't able to cover with our numbers. She wanted us to find them, but not to find them fast. They weren't visible until we actually went into the trees."

Of course it's intentional. Everything that woman has done is intentional. Avoiding the search party entirely wouldn't send the message that she could have come ashore whenever she felt like it. It might actually allow us a moment of peace, which is obviously something Circe will never do.

She's been playing head games from the start. "Where did she go?"

"How the fuck should I know?" A sliver of frustration works into Athena's voice. "I'm not a tracker, Zeus. She could have cut into the city from here without issue, or skirted the city limits and headed west toward the country. I have no way of knowing."

"Send the information to Apollo. A camera has to have caught her."

"I will. Atalanta is taking a team west to see if there's any evidence they headed in that direction. I'll work with Apollo and Ares to create a grid for searching the city in this area."

I don't bother to point out that her grid search didn't work particularly well when Ariadne, Icarus, and the Minotaur were on the run. I wanted them alive, and instead, Ariadne and the Minotaur sailed off and now Icarus is under the protection of Poseidon, one of the few people I can't afford to piss off. As one of the three legacy titles—him, me, and Hades—we hold unprecedented power among the Thirteen. I thought bringing the three of us together in a temporary coup would turn the tide of this siege, but Circe was several steps ahead of us. "Do it."

I take the elevator up to my floor. My floor. The very idea is absurd. I might have scoured every bit of my father's love of gaudy gold from this place, but it still feels like I'm trespassing, as if I'll turn around to find him looming in the doorway, ready to cut me down to size with a few well-chosen words.

A year of holding this position, fighting to make it mine, and I'm no closer to making it happen. I'm going to be the first Zeus in the history of Olympus to see my city fall to invasion. I want to say the thought sits ill because of my concern for my people, but it's not entirely the truth. They're not *my* people. They don't love me, fear me, or even hate me. They wouldn't blink if I were to die and be replaced, and that apathy is what I can't stand. It feels too close to the way my father watched me when I tried and tried and fucking *tried* to shut my emotions down and smile through my fury and pain. Even when I finally accomplished going cold, it wasn't good enough because I can't make people like me. I only make them uncomfortable and hostile.

Fuck.

I have to stop thinking about this. I have Circe and six boats' worth of people to find. I have a crumbling city to set to rights. I have—

It takes two beats longer than it should for me to register that I'm not alone in my office. I move at the same time the intruder does, going for the gun in my shoulder holster. I don't normally carry—it would give the wrong impression to enemies and allies alike—but there's nothing normal about Olympus right now.

I barely manage to get my hand around the grip before

they grab my elbow and slam the gun back into the holster. Then they punch me in the stomach. My breath whooshes out, but I manage to keep from doubling over.

Then I get a good look at my attacker. The rage I've barely been able to keep contained flares white hot. "*Hermes*."

"In the flesh." She kicks out my knee, and this time, I can't keep my feet. I topple against my desk, and the bitch steals my gun. She ejects the clip and checks to make sure there's not a round in the chamber in a practiced move so smooth it's almost beautiful.

If she weren't a fucking traitor.

I shove back to my feet. "You have a lot of nerve coming here."

She tosses the gun away. "Sit down before you hurt yourself." She looks different than the woman I've come to know, at least superficially. Hermes is a short, petite Black woman with dark-brown skin and a penchant for glitter and bright colors. Today, she's wearing black jeans and a black T-shirt, her hair in box braids pulled away from her face. "We could sit here for days and argue which one of us is the true traitor to Olympus, but there's no time. Circe is in the city."

"I'm aware." My knee is a throbbing mass of agony, but I learned how to mask evidence of pain on my face a long time ago. "How do *you* know? You've missed every meeting

I've called, and you sure as fuck weren't putting your neck on the line last night out on the water."

"I wasn't invited last night," she says primly. "You were engaged in a law-breaking coup that at least half the Thirteen will be ready to riot over when they find out."

My face flames at the reminder of how I've likely made things worse instead of better. "You know what I mean."

"Yes, yes. To answer your question: I know Circe." She waves that away as if she didn't just drop a conversational bomb. "She's not one to get cornered, and she saw you coming a mile away." Hermes makes a cutting motion. "You're wasting time."

"I'm. Wasting. Time." I clench my fists, fury making my head feel like it's about to explode. I advance on her, ignoring the twinge in my knee. "*You* sponsored Minos. *You* sold him your house to host the party that started this all. You have betrayed the position of Hermes, betrayed the Thirteen, and betrayed Olympus. Tell me why I'm supposed to listen to you instead of arresting you right here and now for working with the enemy?"

"*I* betrayed Olympus? Please." She actually has the audacity to roll her eyes. "You're so busy worrying about me that you're not doing your fucking job."

If a person could die from anger, I would have done so years ago. My siblings found their own way to survive growing up in our father's house, but none of them held the dubious blessing and curse of being heir. Of being our father's primary focus when he was home. Of being the one he was determined to sculpt in his image.

So, yes, I learned to deal with my rage at an early age, to shove it down deep where it couldn't touch me, couldn't make me weak.

All of those learned behaviors have nothing on what I'm feeling right now. I move toward Hermes. "I have had enough of your antics. You will have your title removed, and—"

"Gods." She erupts in harsh laughter. "You think I care about the fucking *title*, Perseus?"

The shock of hearing my actual name slaps me out of this fury. Almost. "You fought for it, didn't you? All you had to do was steal one item, but you went so far beyond that you created a legend for yourself. Hermes, the untouchable. Hermes, the ghost. Of course you care about the title."

"The title was a means to an end," she snaps. "And that end is coming faster than anyone is ready for."

"Is that a threat?"

"No, you absolute dolt. It's the truth." For once, she isn't wearing her jester's smile. She glares at me as if *I've* disappointed *her*. "This system—the system that created your father, the last Poseidon, the last Ares, the last Apollo, the list goes on and on—is broken. It's *been* broken. It's never going to stop being broken because even the people who may have wanted change are chewed up and spit out into perfect little Olympian citizens. The Thirteen isn't the only rot in this fucking city, but it's the worst of it. We both know that."

I open my mouth to refute her but can't quite make the words come out. I know exactly what kind of monsters the Thirteen can be, and how little they face in the way of consequences when they hurt those who don't have the power and money to object. "I'm trying to protect this city."

"I know," she says softly. "But who is going to protect it from *you*?"

I can't stop myself from dropping my gaze, an instinctive avoidance of the point she's making. That I'm one of the monsters. That I've hurt this city and will hurt it more before my time as Zeus is done. When I look up, she's gone.

HERA

AFTER THE DISASTROUS NIGHT WITH MY HUSBAND, there's no escaping reality. This entire situation has spun out of control. I waited in the spare bedroom for him to leave for the day. A strategic retreat, or that's what I told myself as I listened to his footsteps pass mere feet from the door. Once he left, I took my time getting ready, hoping the familiar process would ground me. It didn't.

I pace about the penthouse, fielding texts from my sisters—Psyche reassuring me that she's fine, Persephone and Eurydice steadfastly refusing to consider evacuating to the countryside—and trying to *think*. Poseidon isn't returning my calls. Athena and Ares are very much Zeus's people. Hades will look to the lower city first, second, and last. He's only concerned with protecting his people there, and *his* barrier is still intact. The rest of Olympus can burn for all he cares.

As for the rest of the Thirteen? I can't trust them. If they get a chance to help themselves, they'll have no problem throwing me to the wolves to see it happen.

My opportunity to get ahead of Circe's rage is rapidly dwindling. In truth, it might already be gone, but that's a defeatist way of thinking. It's not over until it's over.

I don't know that Circe intends to sack the city, or if she's even capable of it with the people she has. If I were her, I wouldn't bother with civilians. History has shown that they're more than willing to be swayed by clever words and a pretty face. Circe has both. If she removes the Thirteen, then the path to the city is clear.

A decade ago, I would have stood by cheering while she rampaged. Even as a teenager I recognized the way the poison goes bone-deep in the legacy families—the same families responsible for most of the people who've claimed the titles since the founding of the city. But now? Now that my mother is one of the Thirteen? Now that Persephone is married to one of them and pregnant with his heir?

I'll rip out Circe's throat before I let her touch my family.

I hoped that killing Zeus would be enough to dissuade her from full-on invasion, but so far I've been unsuccessful. Time is running out to find a path forward that protects my mother and sisters.

My phone vibrates in my hand, a notification of a new MuseWatch article being posted. The site is a plague on this city, but it's useful at times. I open it mostly to distract myself than anything else...at least until I see the headline.

LEGACY TITLES ENGAGE IN COUP DESPITE LACK OF VOTES! CIRCE'S BLOCKADE BROKEN!

"What. The. Fuck." I quickly scan the article, my heartbeat racing in my ears. Zeus and the other two came together in the dead of night to attack Circe, despite the fact that we explicitly didn't vote for them to do so.

The article frames it as a positive thing, of course. They won. The blockade is broken. Trade can resume immediately. What it notably *doesn't* say is that Circe has been apprehended. And Zeus's poor mood last night suggests he, at least, considers the whole thing a failure. It all adds up to one conclusion.

She got away.

I pace another circle around the living room and grab my phone. I memorized Circe's number rather than risk keeping it in my contacts. It takes seconds to type it out, my heart beating too hard. This has all gotten so out of control. I recognized the risks when I agreed to marry Zeus and become Hera, but those risks feel like child's play compared to what I'm dealing with now.

The call rings and rings and rings before clicking over

to a recording saying the voicemail inbox is full. I curse and hang up. "After all the trouble you've caused, the least you can do is answer the fucking phone."

A text comes through a moment later from an unknown number. It's only a location—a bar in the theater district where I used to spend time with my sisters—and a time—thirty minutes from now. Barely long enough to get there.

I don't text back. The timing is too coincidental to actually *be* a coincidence. It's Circe, playing games just like she has been from the beginning. I shove my phone into my purse and yank on a pair of boots. My plans might be in shambles, but I knew I would be fighting an uphill battle from the moment I stood at the altar with Zeus and agreed to be his wife. I might not have anticipated Circe and all the trouble she brought with her, but I'm smart and can think on my feet. It would just be helpful if she spoke plainly about what she *wants*.

Ixion meets me in the parking garage the moment the elevator opens. Like everyone else on the small team I've gathered around me, he is an Olympian orphan who grew up in the orphanage that's every Hera's one responsibility in the city. When I took over, it was in a sorry state, barely getting by with a skeleton staff and far too many children. Children the city likes to pretend don't exist.

One of the first things I did upon marrying Zeus was divert all of the available funds associated with the Hera title to fixing the place up and hiring more people. A month later, Ixion approached me. In Olympus, when orphans reach eighteen, they're consigned to Ares, Poseidon, or Demeter—soldiers, fishermen, or farmers. Ixion and his crew had chosen the former, but they wanted to pledge themselves to *me*. Not my husband. Not my mother.

To a Hera who actually wanted to do their job.

As long as I continue to ensure the orphans of the city are taken care of and protected, they are loyal to me and me alone. It's an easy enough task. The Heras before me might have ignored their responsibility in favor of playing spouse to Zeus—willing or no—but power can be found in unexpected ways. Ixion and his team, trained and ruthless and perfectly loyal, prove that with some time and effort, Hera always had the potential to be just as powerful as the rest of Thirteen. I have every intention of reclaiming that power.

Ixion nods. "With how *he* stormed out of here this morning, I figured you wouldn't be far behind." His brown eyes search my face just as they do every time he sees me, looking for evidence that my husband has hurt me. Finding none, his shoulders relax a little. "Where to?"

Going to meet Circe with only my trio as backup is ill-advised. I know that. I should damn well turn around and go back to the privacy of my home until I can get my head on straight. Or I should call one of my sisters or my mother for more security. I don't. "Wine About It."

If he's surprised I'm asking to be taken to a little bar in the theater district at this hour of the morning, he gives no sign of it. But then, Ixion never reacts to anything I ask him to do or witness. If I were a better person, my heart would hurt at the fact that his loyalty has been purchased solely because I took care of *orphans*.

The drive takes no time at all. Normally, the streets would be clogged with cars and pedestrians, but the city is mostly a ghost town now.

It's not until Ixion pulls into the empty parking lot that I pause long enough to wonder if Wine About It will even be open. But when Ixion pulls at the door, Nephele and Imbros flanking me, it swings easily before his touch. Imbros touches my shoulder before I can follow Ixion inside. "Wait, please." Ze is always so damned polite. Ze is shorter than I am, with a thick body, dark-brown skin, and long locs pinned back from zir face.

On my other side, Nephele peers in the door and waits for Ixion's all clear. She's the same height as Imbros but built deceptively delicately—deceptive because I've seen her take a man twice her size to the ground when he came at me too quickly—with light-brown skin and shoulder-length black straight hair. She nods and motions me forward. "We're good."

I don't tell them that they're being too cautious. Even before Circe's siege, her machinations had Olympus in chaos.

She orchestrated the revelation of a little-known clause that allowed anyone who assassinated one of the Thirteen to take their position. The results were to be expected—seemingly endless attempts to murder the current Thirteen. I've dealt with less than the others, but some people *really* want to take my place in my husband's bed.

If they'd asked me, I'd tell them that they're more than welcome to him.

I ignore the twinge the thought brings and step through the door into the low light of the bar. I haven't been here in years, not since my sisters and I held season tickets and would stop by after every show. It was always loud and packed and filled to the brim with energy of people high off the excellent performances we just watched.

Now, it's as empty as the streets.

The bartender is the same old man it's always been, though I can't for the life of me remember his name. He smiles when he sees me but doesn't rush over. It's the first normal reaction I've had in a long time. I value it greatly.

I take one step toward the bar, but Imbros edges into my path. Ze nods to the curved booth in the corner. "Why don't you sit down and I'll grab…" Ze clears zir throat. "Drinks? Food?"

"Iced tea." I haven't been able to eat much in the last couple of weeks, due to… Gods, I can barely think it. My hand twitches, wanting to press to my stomach, but I muscle down the urge. I can count on one hand the people who know about the little parasite currently clinging to my uterine lining, fucking up my entire system. Nothing smells right. I no longer have access to my nightly wine or the joints I would smoke on the balcony to unwind. I hate it.

Except...I don't. Not entirely.

My throat burns and I blink rapidly, hurrying to the booth and the relative privacy the shadows there offer. Godsdamned fucking hormones. I've never lost control emotionally before, and I'll be damned before I do it now, embryo or no embryo.

Nephele slides in next to me, careful to keep a bit of distance between us, but Ixion just leans against the half wall next to the booth. Ready to leap into motion at the first sign of danger.

Nephele glances at me. "Do you want to talk about it?"

"Nothing to talk about." I learned a lot of lessons growing up as the eldest daughter of a mother like mine, and the first among those is that you can't trust anyone but family. Nephele's offer seems to be her genuinely wanting to make sure I'm okay, which is honestly nice. I still can't quite manage a smile. "But thank you."

Nephele *does* smile, and easily. "Anytime—and I do mean that, Hera. It's an open-ended offer to talk."

"I appreciate it." And I do, even if I'm more isolated now than I've ever been. I can't reach the lower city due to

Hades raising the barrier surrounding it. I refuse to abandon the city to my husband and his allies, so I can't follow my mother and Psyche into the countryside. I'm a wolf without her pack, and I'm still not sure if that makes me vulnerable... or more dangerous.

Imbros appears with the drinks—iced tea for me, water for the three of them—and then shifts away to take a seat at the table directly between my booth and the door. Another method of defense against an empty bar.

I manage one sip before my bladder makes a shrill demand. It's not the nausea and increasingly absurd side effects that irritate me the most. It's having to pee every fifteen minutes. I sigh and push to my feet, holding out a hand when all three shift to follow. "There's no one here and I have to use the bathroom. Just...give me a few seconds." It's past the thirty-minute deadline from the text, but there's no sign of Circe yet. I should have time to pee.

Nephele ignores me and slides out of the booth. "I'll watch the back door."

I know from experience that there will be no dissuading any of them. At least she doesn't follow me into the bathroom every time anymore. She just helps Ixion and Imbros cut off any access while I'm in there. *That* made me popular at restaurants before everyone evacuated.

I slip through the door and into a stall to take care of the persistent pressure in my bladder. I don't realize that I'm not in fact alone until I start washing my hands and the low sound of laughter raises the small hairs at the nape of my neck. "Oh gods, you really *are* pregnant, aren't you? You carry the next Zeus."

I spin around, drawing my switchblade and preparing to yell for help...but stop when I register the identity of the woman standing casually a few feet away. She's a slim white woman with short dark hair and a face that's pretty in a very changeable way. Right now, there's none of the cutting beauty I witnessed at our late night meeting on the water, only a roguish charm that is strangely forgettable, as though if I look away for a moment, I'll lose track of what she looks like.

Circe.

HERA

"EVERYONE IS LOOKING FOR YOU." IT'S SUCH A SILLY thing to say, but though I expected her to come here, I didn't expect her to pop out of a stall like a damn magician.

"I know." She's wearing a pair of fitted jeans, a tank top, and a leather jacket. Circe moves to the sink next to me and leans forward to swipe her thumb under one eye. "I told you that I'd reach out when I was ready. I'm ready."

It takes a single breath to get my head on straight—or as close to it as I can manage. She's here, which means I have an opportunity to twist this situation to ensure my family remains safe. She wouldn't seek me out if she didn't want something. "I'm listening."

"Good girl." Her lips twist. "I've been watching you for a while—a Hera who refuses to be broken by their Zeus. A warrior in your own right. Recruiting Poseidon was a clever move, even if it didn't quite work out the way you wanted."

My skin heats. She sounds admiring, but this is obviously a trap. Why else craft a compliment that stings so sharply? "You're saying a lot without saying much at all."

Circe laughs softly. "You're Hera. You know what this city does to those who can't fight back. Would you have married Zeus if the safety of your family wasn't in the mix?"

"No." There's no point in lying. I did what I had to.

"Only one of the Thirteen is voted on by the people. Historically, the rest are pulled primarily from the legacy families, each more rotten than the next. The best and the brightest are supposed to be the ones who lead the city, no matter what part of the city they come from, but that's not how the system actually works. All the Thirteen care about is their own power, not the responsibilities of a good leader." She speaks with a practiced air, as if this is something she's said many times before.

"A good leader," I echo. I almost laugh. "A good leader like *you*, I suppose."

She shrugs a single shoulder. "Why not? I'm intimately acquainted with how the majority of our citizens live, the ones who aren't invited to those glittering parties in Dodona Tower. The ones Olympus is built on the backs of. I was one of those people."

I was relatively young when Circe became Hera for

such a short time. I don't know what it was about her that had Zeus marrying her instead of adding her to the list of his more traditional victims. Olympus has always been willing to overlook the sins of the Thirteen, and Zeus especially.

The only person who dared challenge him was Hercules, his *other* son, after the horrible events with Leda. There was no justice for Leda. Hercules was run out of town and hasn't been seen since. I know he's still alive because there's a text thread in my husband's phone from a little less than a year ago. Zeus asked Hercules to come back now that their father is dead. Hercules asked if Zeus—Perseus, then—intended to take the title. When he affirmed that he did, none of the rest of his texts gained a reply.

I don't know what my face is doing, but apparently it's response enough for Circe. She drags her fingers through her short hair, ruffling it attractively. "The Thirteen are a holdover from a different time. We need to move into the future—a better future. Olympus should be ruled by a government that actually represents the people, under the guidance of, well, me."

"Strange how *you* don't need to be elected in this utopia you paint," I murmur.

Her smile disappears. "Did I say that?"

I brush that away. I'm not interested in arguing semantics with her. We've already been in here too long. It's only a matter of time before Nephele comes to ensure I'm okay. "You obviously want something from me. Tell me what it is."

"Direct. I like that." She turns to face me and props her hip on the sink. "Originally, I had intended to wipe Olympus clean of all evidence of the Thirteen and their bloodlines, but as information has come to light, it seems best to change course."

I motion for her to get to the point. "And?"

"I'm prepared to spare your family—as long as they are willing to renounce all claims to their respective titles and leave the city."

Renounce their claims. I burst out laughing. I can't help it. "Might as well wish for pigs to fly. It's about as likely to happen." My mother worked her entire life to become Demeter and she has no intention of giving up that power until her soul is yanked right out of her chest. Persephone carries the heir to the Hades title the same way I carry the heir to the Zeus title. Worse, she loves her husband with a ferocity I've rarely seen from her. She won't abandon him. And Hades would never abandon his people.

"Then they'll die." Circe says it simply, as if it's fact and not an obvious threat. "I respect you and what you have done to survive and protect those you care about, but I won't let you stand in my way." Her eyes flick down to my stomach. "I'm not interested in killing children—unborn or otherwise—if I have any other choice. Take your family and leave

Olympus. I won't chase you down, but if you ever return, your lives are forfeit."

Terminating my pregnancy was the first thought I had when I saw that plus sign on the test. The idea of perpetuating the monstrosity of Zeus nearly had me making the appointment. But this eventual child isn't just Zeus's heir, Zeus's child. They aren't even just a step toward securing power and protection for the people I love. They're *mine*. "I don't like it when people threaten my family, Circe. It doesn't tend to end well for them."

"Doesn't it? Zeus is still alive, after all." She smiles and turns away. "It's in your hands, *Hera*. Convince your mother to leave Olympus. Hades as well, since I'm feeling generous. If they stay, they *will* die. I cannot stress the severity of this reality."

The way she says it, it's as if a force of nature is coming for Olympus, instead of the machinations of a single vengeful woman and her followers. I glare. "You're outnumbered and outgunned, and yet you're talking as if your victory is a sure thing."

"It is." She adjusts her jacket.

"You've made a miscalculation. All I have to do is scream and my team will come rushing in to eliminate any threat against me. You won't be doing anything if you're dead."

"Cute." She pulls out her phone and types something on it. "Check your texts."

I almost bobble my phone getting it out of my pocket, and when I look at the screen, I wish I *had* dropped it. There's a video through the lens of what looks like a sniper scope, peering into a window and showing a woman...

Ice freezes my veins. Not just any woman. Persephone is pacing around the room, holding a phone to her ear with one hand and pressing the other to her blatantly rounded stomach. She's roughly fifteen weeks pregnant, but since she's having twins, she's showing as if farther along. "What the fuck?" I whisper.

"Next."

Another video pops up. It's similar, except it's Eurydice sitting on Charon's lap and laughing at something Orpheus is saying. She's wearing the same thing she was in the video call we had earlier today, a white T-shirt with a funky geometric graphic on the front.

"And to be thorough—one more."

I don't want to open the next text, but I have no choice. The third video is of my mother, her arms crossed over her chest and her face set in her best "I'm not mad, I'm disappointed" expression as she lectures Eros and Psyche. He sits on a chair and Psyche stands behind him, kneading his shoulders.

I tuck my phone carefully back into my pocket, feeling like I'm moving in slow motion. "You've made your point quite effectively."

"As they say, a picture is worth a thousand words. I'd say

a video is worth even more. I'll be in touch." Then the brazen bitch steps back and waves me at the door. "Get going now. It would be awkward to explain to your guards why you're having meetings with a mysterious woman in the bathroom. Someone might ask questions."

Part of me wants to charge her, to call my team to fulfill *my* threat. I don't. I stand there, my stomach roiling, until I have to rush back into the stall and lose what little I managed to eat today.

Circe *tsks*. "Darling, you're going to need a stronger stomach than that to get through what's coming."

"Fuck. You." I climb unsteadily to my feet and move to the sink to wash my mouth out as best I can, all while she watches with those sharp, green eyes. "It will never work, you know. You won't win."

"I already have." She shakes her head almost sadly. "Now, get going."

I stalk out of the bathroom. Nephele jumps at whatever she sees on my face, her eyes wide. "Is everything okay?"

"Peachy."

Circe is threatening my fucking *family*.

I knew they were in danger, but I should have realized Circe wouldn't risk bargaining without ensuring she'd come out on top. No doubt she'd arranged for those snipers to pull their respective triggers if she didn't walk away from this meeting. Going through all this effort might be a compliment, but it doesn't take away the fear rotting away my insides at the impossible task she's set before me.

Hades and Demeter, two of the titles least likely to abdicate and flee the city, ironically for similar reasons. My mother loves being loved and damn near worshipped. Hades couldn't care less about the perception of power, but he's content to use it to protect the people of the lower city. Both of them leverage their respective positions for the greater good.

My mother has expanded the food provided to the city almost exponentially in the last decade, purchasing land owned by various families and companies and bettering the systems and working conditions. She takes her job deathly seriously, and even her plots to set her daughters up with powerful people have been misguided attempts to both protect us and ensure her end goals are fulfilled. Yes, that benefits her first and the city a far second, but it *does* benefit the city.

Conversely, Hades spent most of his life embracing being the boogeyman of Olympus in order to ensure no one fucked with the lower city. Even now, he's willing to miss an opportunity to leverage his position to amplify his power because that would mean leaving his portion of the city unprotected.

I can't think of a single thing that would convince either of them to leave. They're both far more likely to laugh me out of the room and then try to kill Circe personally. If it could be done, they would have already accomplished it.

No, fuck that. I didn't marry godsdamned *Zeus*, didn't spend months in his bed, didn't conceive his future child, for it to end like this. Absolutely not.

I yank my phone out. "Give me a few."

"Um. Sure." Nephele falls back a few steps to give me the illusion of privacy.

It'll have to be enough. I should probably move away from the bathroom doors, but a small, petty part of me is happy to let Circe stew in there a little longer. I dial Persephone, punching through her Do Not Disturb without hesitation.

She answers, breathless. "Callisto? What's wrong?"

I have to close my eyes at the bittersweet sensation of hearing someone say *my* name. Not one Hera among many, but Callisto Dimitriou, singular and unique.

"Callisto?"

I wish I could avoid involving Persephone. Her situation is a perfect inversion to my misery. She loves her husband, her new role as queen of the lower city, loves the children she's currently pregnant with. She deserves all the best things, and I'm about to drop a bomb on her life. "I need to see you. It's important. An emergency."

She clears her throat, and when she speaks again, she sounds more like herself. "Are you safe?"

No. Not even a little bit. I haven't been for a very long time. "Please, Seph." The childhood nickname slips out despite my best efforts. "As soon as possible."

"I can't cross the barrier." She lowers her voice. "I want to see you—you have no idea how much I want to see you—but it's not just me I have to worry about anymore. It's Hades and our people and—"

"And the babies." I press my hand to my stomach, to the pawn within. A future child not created from love, but from necessity.

"Yeah. And the babies." She pauses. "I can't let you cross, either. I love you, Cal, but I also know you, and as much as I trust you, I understand that you're playing our mother's game now."

"Not on her behalf," I snap.

"No, not on her behalf." Persephone is silent for several beats. "I guess we needed the lessons she taught us after all, didn't we?"

"I guess we did." I close my eyes. I should have expected the conversation to go like this, but Circe rattled me more than I want to admit. I have no idea how a sniper—two—got into the lower city. They must have already been there when the barrier went up. "Can we meet on one of the bridges? I have to talk to you and it has to be in person." She'll have to hear me out that way, won't be able to sever the conversation by hanging up.

She hesitates long enough that I suspect she's going to reject the idea, but she finally says, "Tomorrow. I'll call you later with the plan once I've made the proper arrangements."

Another pause. "Unless Zeus did something and you need sanctuary?"

"No." The absurdity of it makes me laugh. No matter how much I hate my husband, he's never actually hurt me. In fact, he takes such care with me that it makes me want to scream. I'm not breakable—I never have been—and I certainly don't need to be protected by *him*.

But some things I can't admit aloud, not even to Persephone.

"Tomorrow, then. I'll wait for your call."

"Okay," she says. "Be safe."

Not a chance of that. "You too." I hang up and take what amounts to a steadying breath. Or at least I try. Nothing is going like it should. It was one thing to take personal risks with myself to murder my husband and establish myself as regent to the future Zeus of Olympus. The only one in danger if that plan went wrong was me, and my life is something I'm willing to risk. My family's lives, on the other hand? Absolutely not.

Circe made a mistake threatening them, but damned if I can see a route through this that doesn't end in blood and grief.

ZEUS

"DO YOU KNOW WHERE YOUR WIFE IS RIGHT NOW?"

I'm getting heartily tired of people asking me that question. I'm getting even more tired of the fact that my answer is usually *no*. Of course I don't know where Hera is. She doesn't talk to me. Not more than she absolutely has to. And every time I turn around, she's trying to slip a knife between my ribs.

Or cuddling up with that fucker Ixion.

I look up from the reports I'm wading through—more and more of absolutely fucking nothing—to find Atalanta standing in my doorway. "I thought you were supposed to be leading a team searching for Circe."

Atalanta is a handsome Black woman with medium-brown skin and scars across her face and hands. She wears her black curls back in a stylized mohawk. For as long as

I've known her, at least until this last year, she worked under Artemis. But after the events of Minos's party, she transferred to Athena.

I've always liked her. She would have made a stellar Ares. But I can't deny having my sister in the Ares position benefits the city as a whole, and me especially. I don't have to worry about Olympian forces turning against me when Helen—Ares—is in charge.

"I'm headed out again shortly." She leans against the doorway, apparently settling in for a conversation I very much don't want to have.

I sigh and motion Atalanta forward. "I assume you're here to give me a report, not just to engage in gossip."

"You know me, Zeus. I only gossip when I'm commanded to." She waves her phone at me. "I've sent you everything we have, as Athena ordered. All of the video feeds around the area where Circe came out of the water came back clean. There's no sign of her or her people anywhere. Which means that either she's a ghost—"

"Or she's in our system." I don't know enough about this shit to know whether or not that's easy to accomplish. Our camera network is one of those things that has always fallen under the jurisdiction of either Apollo or Hephaestus, depending on what the specific ask is. My father never concerned himself with the details, and he taught me not to as well. It's only now, when the wheels have come off the bus and everything is on fire, that I wish I knew more about the specific ways Olympus runs in the nitty-gritty detail. It'd make it a lot harder for people to put one over on me.

"Or she has found her way into our system," Atalanta confirms. She grimaces. "I'd almost admire her if she wasn't set on death and destruction and all that bullshit."

"She certainly is capable," I say neutrally. I was raised to look at everyone around me, except family, as a potential enemy. Atalanta has always had proximity to the Thirteen, and she failed to acquire a title of her own. Surely her ambitions haven't quieted? "Why haven't you taken advantage of the assassination clause? *You're* certainly capable enough and Artemis repaid your loyalty with pain."

She laughs, the sound deep and pleasing. "And inherit the mess y'all have made? Absolutely fucking not. I'd rather burn the place to the ground."

That's a troubling response, but I keep my expression locked down. She's not the only one who thinks about burning Olympus to the ground. The sentiment seems to be more and more popular as time goes on. Each day that passes brings new challenges and new ways to fuck everyone over. "I'd prefer to salvage it."

"Of course you would. If you weren't Zeus, who would you be?"

She starts to turn toward the door and I realize she never

gave me the information that I hadn't asked for but that she obviously possesses. "Atalanta."

She pauses and glances over her shoulder, her deep brown eyes glinting in amusement. "Yeah?"

"Where is my wife?" The words feel dragged out of me. I hate admitting any kind of weakness, let alone admitting it to a potential enemy. Considering I can count people who are not potential enemies on one hand and still have fingers left over, it means I rarely admit weakness at all. But if Hera hasn't been dissuaded from her antics, then I need to know. I'm already looking over my shoulder for half a dozen enemies. I don't need to be doing it for my wife as well.

At least not any longer. Not after her last attempt failed.

Atalanta grins. "She's down at Wine About It, day drinking with that handsome fellow who's always following her around. Seems like a great place for a romantic encounter." She strides out of my office before I have a chance to respond.

All theater productions have been postponed until the dust settles. I'm surprised any of those businesses are open at all, let alone that Hera was aware of it.

Even as I tell myself to make the call, to have someone else keep an eye on her, I'm already in motion. I grab my jacket and pull it on, heading out the door. I have access to my email and all of the data systems through my phone. I can look at the information Atalanta gathered on the way. Not that there's anything to look at. Just empty video feeds.

Circe has to be in this city. Where else would she go? All the Thirteen, excepting Demeter, are in the city proper. Hades is somewhat protected by the secondary barrier still surrounding the lower city, but Circe has proven she can get through Olympus's barriers. I have no doubt she made contingency plans for this very thing happening. I'd be a fool to assume otherwise, and so would Hades. He won't be taking any chances, not with his people and not with his pregnant wife.

Persephone, at least, seems willing to listen to her husband and avoid taking unnecessary risks. Unlike her sister, my wife.

I almost call a driver, but I don't think I can handle yet more people looking at me out of the corner of their eyes, aware of how my wife continues to make a fool of me. Maybe she's not planning another assassination attempt. Maybe she actually *is* having an affair with Ixion. He's handsome enough. Why not make a fool of me in that way, too? She certainly gives *me* no softness.

She didn't want this marriage. It was an act of political expediency. It's the same reason I married her, needing to get Demeter and all her various alliances on my side instead of working against me. There's no reason to resent my wife for not caring about me. There's no reason to care about her at all.

But then, I've been a fool in a number of ways. What's one more?

I don't call a car. I take one of my own, sliding behind the wheel for the first time in... I honestly can't remember. Even as a teenager and young adult, I always had a driver who doubled as a bodyguard. Can't be too careful with the heir to Zeus. If there was an added bonus that he reported my every move to my father, then so much the better.

It feels strange to grip the wheel, to back out of the space, to leave the parking garage and turn out onto the mostly empty road. Strange...but not bad.

I make it to the theater district in record time. The location Atalanta gave me is tucked off the main thoroughfare. I park a few blocks away and walk. It would probably be wiser to stake the building out and see exactly who Hera is meeting, but each step has my barely buried anger rising higher. We don't have time for this shit. We don't have time for infighting and backstabbing and political machinations. We have a literal enemy in our midst and my wife is fucking around.

I shove through the doors hard enough that Imbros bolts up from where ze leans against a table and has zir gun halfway drawn before ze registers who I am. Even then, ze doesn't immediately release the butt of zir gun. Ze eyes me with suspicion.

My wife couldn't have asked for a better set of protectors...or are they her lovers, too? Why stop at one?

I hate this. I've had lovers in the past and I've never felt this kind of possessive jealousy. It feels like there's a monster inside me clawing to get out. Even though this is an arranged marriage of convenience, at least for the first couple of months, I *tried*. I was kind to her, as much as I'm able to be. I brought her flowers. I found out what kind of food she likes and had it cooked for us. I spent every moment in our bed ensuring that she was experiencing as much pleasure as I was. More, even.

And all my efforts were rewarded with her derision. She hates me. There's nothing I can do to change that. There's absolutely no reason for that knowledge to sit like a hot coal in my gut.

I tried to be as good of a husband as I could be for her, and she would have none of it. Instead, she plotted to kill me. And now, when our city is at its most vulnerable, she's meeting up with Ixion, Imbros, and Nephele to pursue her selfish interests.

I barely register the fact that Hera looks particularly lovely today. She always looks lovely. Though *lovely* is too tame a word for my wife. Her beauty is violent and cutting, all angles and viciousness. Her long dark hair is pulled back into a high ponytail, and though the color is high in her angled cheeks, she looks…tired. Surely not. Surely I'm seeing things. Hera would never allow for something as mundane as exhaustion to affect her.

She stares at me as I cross the bar to get to the booth that she sits in next to Ixion. Too close. Always too damn close. "What are you doing here?"

"I could ask you the same thing. I was under the impression you'd be spending the day at your orphanage." The orphanage has been the heritage of every Hera since the founding of Olympus. My father found it to be a silly little hobby, but I'm aware of the good *my* Hera has done with that so-called hobby. I worry that Olympus will see more orphans before this is done.

"I am. I was." She looks away. "I just needed a moment."

Something is off. Hera usually meets me with derision and malice, and I can't remember a single time where she stumbled over her words.

I look at her again, closer this time. I note the faint smudges of darkness under her eyes, the smattering of what almost looks like freckles on her cheekbones and the way her hand shakes as she lifts her drink to her lips. Something's wrong. Actually wrong. Even Ixion, the bastard, can tell. He hovers over her even more than he normally does. "I need to speak with my wife," I finally say. "Alone."

He glares at me. "I don't take commands from you."

"Stop trying to order my team around," Hera snaps, sounding almost like her normal self. Almost. "And stop staring at me like that."

"Like what?" I ask it absently, still focusing on the clear evidence that something is wrong with her. Her color is off, too. A little too pale, almost green. "Are you sick?"

"Would you care if I was?" She sits back in the booth and

crosses her arms over her chest. It's infuriating how beautiful my wife is. Hera waves a hand in a move that's almost careless—if not for the tension in her shoulders. "Run along, Husband. You've done your due diligence and checked up on your poor little wife. As you can see, I'm alive and kicking and hardly up to no good."

"You're always up to no good."

Her lips curve the slightest amount before she seems to catch herself and stills the motion. "Don't you have a war criminal to chase down? Or can you even call Circe that when all she's done is poke at the cracks that already existed?"

Her words don't echo Hermes's, but they're close enough that I narrow my eyes. "Have you been talking to Hermes?"

"What? She's back in town?" Her surprise seems genuine enough, but I've learned that Hera is a superb actor when motivated. If she's working with Hermes to do... I don't even know what the fuck Hermes is doing. I barely had time to process the barrier being down, let alone contemplate all the things Hermes mentioned in her brief visit.

"Do you know something about why she left?"

Hera shakes her head slowly. "You'd be better off asking someone like Cassandra or maybe Dionysus. Hermes and I tolerate each other, but we're hardly friends."

Her words match what I've seen, but that doesn't make them the truth. I turn away, barely catching myself before I drag my fingers through my hair in frustration. Hera and I aren't alone. Her trio watch us with wary expressions, and there's a bartender lurking in the shadows.

So many walls that she insists on throwing up between us. If we had been a true partnership in the way I originally wanted, maybe we could have gotten the rest of the Thirteen to vote to take on Circe properly. Maybe we could have united to stop the threat against the city before the conflict reached this point. It's not fair to blame Hera solely for that, but I can't help blaming her in part. She may have agreed to this marriage, but she never wanted it.

She never wanted me.

Before I realize what I intend to do, I'm already speaking. "Everybody out!"

HERA

I AM STILL REELING WITH SHOCK THAT MY HUSband is *here* of all places, let alone commanding my people—and the godsdamned owner of the building—out. "What are you doing?" I mean for the question to come out sharp and serrating. Instead, the words waver around the edges. Almost as if I'm afraid.

The strange thing is…I'm not.

My recent conversation with Circe has shown me what true fear is. It's my sisters' and mother's faces in the sights of a sniper rifle. What are my husband's cold temper tantrums compared to that?

It's because of Circe that I'm still so shaken, because of this damned baby in my stomach that I'm feeling strangely weak and sick to my stomach. Not because of *him*. Even when my husband loses his temper and actually finds the capacity to be more than a human-shaped icicle, he still draws the line at abuse in any form. Smart of him, because even in my diminished capacity, I would cut off his hand rather than let him hurt me. I am my mother's daughter, after all.

And it's been a long time since I actually properly stabbed someone.

While I'm sitting there, wrapped up in my own thoughts, Ixion is looking at me for direction. Of course he is. He doesn't answer to my husband; he answers to me alone. I nod. It seems Zeus and I will be having this fight one way or another, and I'd rather not do it in front of an audience. The bar owner would likely take to MuseWatch and report every bitter detail. My team might very well shoot my husband.

Why don't I let them?

I shove that thought away before it can take root. I won't let them for the same reason I don't stab him in his sleep, for the same reason I haven't given in to my mother's less and less subtle recommendations to poison him. When Zeus dies—and he will—it can't be linked to me. It can't affect my future child's reign as leader of Olympus. I will allow no scandal to touch them before they've even drawn breath.

"Go on, Ixion. It's okay." I sit there and I watch my people file out of the room, each looking more unhappy than the next. They don't go far. I can see the outlines of the trio and the bartender through the glass of the door next to the street.

I turn my attention back to my husband. "Well?" He's still standing on the other side of the table, looming over me. Still staring at me with a strange expression in his pale blue eyes. It looks almost human. I snap my fingers, more to jar myself out of the strange feeling twisting in my chest than to gain his attention. "Zeus. Speak. You threw a hissy fit to get me alone, and now you're just sitting there staring at me. Let's get this over with."

He plants his hands on the table slowly, in a way that makes me think he wants to rip it right off the floor and throw it to the side. "Are you here on a date with Ixion?"

The question is so shocking that I forget to mask my response. My jaw drops and I stare at him. "What?"

"Ixion. Your lover, Wife. That's the only thing it could be, right? Because not even you would be foolish enough to continue with your plans to murder me while the city burns around us." He speaks softly, practically biting out each word. "You may be safe from me, but *he* is not. Cease your plotting, or I'll kill him myself."

A shiver goes through me, and I can't even pretend that it's fear. This is the most honest I've seen him. It proves that, for all his icy exterior and attempt at civilization, my husband is a monster right down to his core. He's just as twisted and broken as I always suspected.

Just as twisted and broken as I am.

I hate the feeling inside me, the sensation of a bell ringing in perfect tune with his. I hate recognizing something in him that I understand on an intrinsic level. I hate…

"You'd kill him for the sin of fucking me and pretend it's because of some greater plot against you." The words slip free despite my best efforts. I'm on a roller coaster and the brakes are gone, hurtling me forward. It's terrifying. It's exhilarating. I can't decide if I want it to stop or to continue to the inevitable conclusion.

Zeus tenses his hands on the table, but he surprises me. He's always had more control than I know what to do with. He doesn't manage to tuck his rage away, but instead of the expected burst of physical violence against the table or an unsuspecting chair, he slides into the booth next to me. And keeps sliding until we're pressed together tightly and he has to loop his arm around my shoulders.

Even as I tell myself not to, I can't help leaning against him, just a little. He's so incredibly warm in a way that makes me wonder why I didn't realize I was cold before. More than that, he smells good. *Intoxicating*. At a time when even the most comforting smells now turn my stomach, my husband alone is so tempting that I have to constantly remind myself I cannot press my nose to the hollow of his throat and inhale deeply every time we're within touching distance.

"Hera."

I know that tone. Even as I tell myself to straighten my

spine and put some distance between us, I press my thighs together in anticipation. "Don't."

"Say yes." He reaches over and winds my ponytail around one fist, so gently that my head is guided back one slow inch at a time. Until my throat is completely bared to him. It's always like this. A seduction with no subtlety to speak of.

Except it's never like this, with no veil of darkness to shield the truth of ourselves from each other.

My husband never takes. That would be too easy, too simple. Instead he makes me a willing partner, sharing equal blame in every illicit thing we do together. This marriage wasn't supposed to include sex, at least not until the allotted grace period is over. Zeus needs an heir, after all. He *has* one; he just doesn't know it yet. All I have to do is tell him that I'm pregnant and any excuse to be intimate disappears like smoke.

But I don't tell him this time. Just like I haven't told him every night since the pregnancy test came back positive.

"We're in a bar in the middle of the day. Anyone could walk in. What would your precious MuseWatch think of a story like this?" Just like that, I remember what else MuseWatch has been reporting on. I narrow my eyes. "Or are you too busy prioritizing a fucking *coup*?"

"There and gone," he murmurs. "It's over."

"Over…" I'm having a difficult time focusing with him so close, looking at me so intensely. "What do you mean, 'over'?"

"It was only intended for a single night to aid our efforts to remove Circe." He narrows his eyes. "But you're not really worried about a coup, are you? There's no one here, Hera. No one to see." He cups my jaw in a way that's both comforting and threatening. Threatening because all he has to do is squeeze and I'm done for. That pressure makes me come undone in a way I don't understand. I refuse to examine the fact he's the only one who holds the particular skill set to make me react in such a way.

I'm falling. Maybe I've already fallen. Desire weaves its spell around me and I want to blame everyone but myself, except I know it's not the truth. From the moment I learned his taste, Zeus has been a drug I want to kick…but never seem able to.

In desperation, I grind out, "You assume I came here on a date with Ixion. Surely you aren't so jealous as to fuck me when he's *right there*."

"I don't know why you came here, Hera." He says it almost absently, his gaze intense on my mouth. "But if it was for Ixion, he's going to get an unsubtle reminder of whose wife you are. Regardless of where you spend your charms."

His words are rough and possessive, and they have no business making my pussy pulse. I don't belong to him. Not any more than he belongs to me. "And what of *your* lovers, Husband?" I've seen the way people fawn over him. They're not subtle in their aims. He's Zeus, after all. No one expects him to be faithful.

Something hot and feral alights in his eyes. "Feeling possessive, Wife? If you want to stake your claim, just say so. I have no problem with that." He leans down, so close that I imagine I can feel the barest movement of his lips against mine. I know I don't, though. He never kisses me without permission, never touches me until I say yes, never fucks me until I beg for it. I still don't know if it's all a game to him or if he genuinely wants to ensure I'm completely consenting. Most of the time I assume it's the former, but in moments like this, I'm not so sure.

"I'm... I'm not." What am I saying? I have no idea.

"Of course not. You don't even like me."

This is wrong. It's not following our established pattern. Of me resisting, of him waiting me out. He sounds like he wants to claim me, and fool that I am, my body suddenly wants to be claimed. I have shit I'm supposed to do, circles I'm supposed to frantically spiral through. I'm so godsdamned afraid, I can barely breathe. And yet, in the circle of his arms, a small, weak part of me is suddenly sure everything will be all right. A lie, and not even a comforting one. Not when it's at the hands of Zeus.

My resistance snaps, and I snap with it. "Stop gloating and do it, then."

"So angry," he murmurs. He's still close enough for me

to feel the movement his lips make in the miniscule distance between us. "I used to think you're angry at me, but that's not the truth, is it? You wouldn't fight this so hard if you truly hated me."

I tense. "I *do* hate you."

"I know. Now close your eyes and tell me what you want."

My face burns. He's right. I have to close my eyes because it's one insult too many to be this vulnerable without the comfort of darkness. He's never approached me like this—in public, where we might be witnessed. We've never even had sex in daylight hours. The only time we fuck is in our bed at the end of long, exhausting days. Not that exhaustion ever seems to touch Zeus. When he has me beneath him, or over him, or in front of him, he's tireless and downright relentless in the pursuit of my pleasure.

Something's changed and I don't know what it is. That should scare me, but I can't think past the need for him to touch me more. To offer me a sliver of escape before I have to fix my world. "Kiss me. Touch me. Make me come."

I practically feel his self-satisfied smile. "That was hardly enough detail, but I suppose I'll make it work."

And then there's no more space for words because his mouth is on mine. I don't wait for him to coax my lips to part before I'm devouring him right back. I have no intention of moving, but my hands are in his hair and it's everything I can do not to climb on top of him. All from a kiss.

Except it's not just a kiss, is it? It's the promise of more. This man knows my body better than any of my past partners, and he uses that knowledge with ruthless efficiency. He's playing chess while I'm coming undone. It's an insult that only makes me despise him more, but I can't shake my addiction to how he makes me feel in those moments when my body takes over.

More. All I want is *more*. Even if it burns me in the end.

ZEUS

MY WIFE IS UP TO NO GOOD. I SHOULD DRAG HER back to our penthouse and lock her up until this conflict is over. For her safety, yes, but also to keep her from meddling while I get shit figured out. *If* I can get this shit figured out. At this point, I don't even know if it's possible.

It's hard to think about all the problems threatening to break me with Hera going soft and sweet against me. She's only sweet when my tongue is in her mouth. Her hands fist the front of my shirt, a silent demand for more.

I shouldn't. Fuck, I shouldn't have come here at all. The idea of my wife with Ixion makes me lose all sense of decorum. Even her attempting to murder me matters less than the idea of her with someone else, with *him*.

But she's not with Ixion right now; she's here, with me, kissing me as if she's a spark that I've poured gasoline on.

My wife is sweetest when she's coming, and I'll be damned if I allow even a sliver of distance between us before then. I skate my hand down her chest, over her stomach, to the band of her pants. She makes a sound and parts her thighs. A clear invitation, but not clear enough for my purposes.

My father forced himself on people. Regularly. He used his power and influence to ensure no one said no, and even if they did... I may have had no choice in taking his name, in stepping into the title left open by his unexpected death, but I'd rather die than carry on *that* legacy.

Breaking the kiss almost hurts, even though I don't create any additional distance between us. The intimacy of being this close with her pointedly closed eyes is too much. I have to close mine, too, to retreat to familiar darkness.

I drag my mouth along her jaw to her ear. "Tell me what you want, Wife."

"You know what I want." She grabs my forearm, her sharp nails pricking me through my shirt. "Don't you dare stop. I say yes, Zeus. Just...*yes*." The last as I undo her pants and slip a hand inside.

She's so wet she's soaked her panties. If I were a different person, if she were, I would rub the proof of how much she wants the husband she claims to hate in her face. I know better. To do that is to lose her. My Hera is a prideful, vicious creature and she'd rather never touch me again than allow me even a sliver of perceived power over her.

She might run cold and furious, but she melts for me the moment I press two fingers into her molten heat. Her gasp sears me right down to my soul. If she'd allow it, I would merely watch her expression as I pick her apart at the seams, would drink in every little sound, every shift, *everything*.

Since that truly is one intimacy too many, I claim her mouth again. In the months we've shared a bed, I've learned what Hera likes, how she claws me hard enough to bleed when I hook my fingers deep inside her, how she whimpers at the feel of the heel of my hand against her clit.

In all that time, though, we've never done *this* outside of the bedroom. I know there's no risk of someone walking through the door, not with that bastard Ixion guarding it, and that knowledge alights something new inside me. He's protecting us from observation while I fuck my wife, the woman he wants as his own.

I nip her bottom lip and move back to murmur in her ear. "What will your lover think of me claiming you like this where anyone could see?"

"Zeus…" Her whole body clenches as I coax her closer and closer to orgasm. "Please… *Please*."

She hates it when I affect her enough to make her beg. I'll be punished for this pleasure later, but in this moment I can't bring myself to give a fuck. For the first time in days, I'm only thinking of *her* and not everything that continues to go wrong. "I'll give you anything you ask for." I wish it wasn't the truth. I lower my voice. "Come for me, Wife. You're almost there."

She clenches around me, her pussy fluttering in a way that makes me growl. My cock is so hard, I'm distantly concerned I might be doing permanent damage with it trapped in my slacks. As if sensing the direction of my thoughts, Hera drops her hands from my arm to scramble at my pants. "Take them off. Take them off right now."

I open my eyes and look around. The windows in this place are too damn large. Even if no one can come inside, there's little to shield us from onlookers. I'm not sure I care. Not when I'm finally *feeling* instead of thinking. I allow her to undo my pants and pull my cock out.

Hera lightly drags her nails down my length, *her* eyes still closed. "Stop thinking so hard."

"I'm not thinking of anything but you, Wife." I pull her onto my lap with her back against my chest—a tight fit with the table—and shove her clothing down around her thighs. Just enough that she can lift herself and I can guide her back onto my cock. Even as close to coming as she was, she still has to squirm her way down my length, taking me one slow inch at a time.

It's intoxicating to watch, even more so to feel. We never have sex in the day, saving our *duty* for the late night, the lights all doused. I never get to see her. It's a power play, but it's an effective one. Too effective.

Right now, witnessing her sliding down my cock, it's everything I can do not to come before she gets a chance to take me completely. I grab her hips and yank her down onto me, earning a breathy moan in the process.

I can't afford to lose control, to forget the truth of this situation. She may be my wife, but she's the enemy nonetheless. I slide a hand around her to press between her thighs, right against her clit, and catch her chin with my other hand, turning her face toward me. Her eyes are still closed. "Does your lover fuck you like this, Wife?"

She parts her lips slowly, as if coming out of a dream. I stroke her clit, undermining her ability to answer. Hera licks her lips, and I realize too late that I never should have given her this weapon to use against me. Jealousy has always cut both ways. "Yes," she murmurs. "Ixion fucks me until I lose track of how many times I come."

I don't make a decision to move. One moment I'm staring into her achingly gorgeous face and the next I'm rising, shoving the table forward and bending her over it. And then I'm inside her again.

She cries out and arches back, giving me a better angle to take her from. It's not enough. It will never be enough, because no matter how good I make her feel in this moment, the moment always ends. She'll go right back to hating me just like she always does. And maybe that shit is mutual. Maybe I hate her, too. At least I hate how good she feels, how she opens herself to me when I'm buried inside her, and how quickly those doors slam in my face the moment the sex is finished.

Well, I'm nowhere near finished. Not with rage fueling me.

I pull out of her, ignoring her cry of protest, and spin her around to lift her onto the table. She stubbornly keeps her eyes shut, but she's so damn soft, the woman I married nowhere in evidence, replaced by the one I only find in the midst of fucking.

I jerk her pants to her ankles, but they won't make it past her boots and I'm too fucking impatient to attempt to remove them right now. Instead I tip her back and duck down to kneel between her spread thighs. "Does Ixion lick your pussy until your thighs are shaking and you're begging for him to let you orgasm?"

She laces her fingers through my hair, already lifting her hips toward my mouth. "Of course," she gasps. "He goes for hours."

I can't tell if she's lying. It makes me wild with rage, with need, with the possessive yearning to mark her as *mine*. My Hera, my wife, the future mother of my children. I drag my tongue through her folds before I can think too hard on how that future may never come.

Hera pulls on my hair, and I allow her to guide me up to her clit, using the opportunity to press two fingers into her again and hook them just the way she likes. The moment I do, her head falls back and her thighs start to shake. "I hate you," she whispers.

No, you don't.

I don't speak the words aloud, but I convey my disbelief in the way I roll my tongue against her clit. She tastes so fucking good that it threatens to overwhelm me. Ixion can go for hours? So will I if she'd just give me the chance.

Telling her as much will give her another weapon to use against me. I have to hold myself removed... Have to...

Hera comes, her thighs clamping around my head, her throat a long line as she moans her way through her orgasm. She's still fluid and limp as I rise and pull her to the edge of the table. "Say yes."

"Yes." She wraps a fist around my cock and guides it to her entrance. This time, it's easier to slide into her. I'm not fool enough to believe she actually welcomes me, but it feels too good to worry about it.

I pull her close, grinding into her as I cup the back of her neck and kiss her. She moans. Gods, she sounds like a different person when I'm inside her. Like someone who might actually care about *me*.

Not Zeus. Not the leader of Olympus. Not a member of a legacy family that can sketch their lineage back to the founding of this city. *Me*. Perseus. The one who will never sit easy on the throne. The one who is far too aware of all the ways he fails. But not in this. I might be king of a crumbling city, but my wife is still gripping my hips, urging me to fuck her harder, needing the pleasure I'm giving her, even if she tells me she hates me all the while.

I want this to last forever.

It won't. It never does. One of the first things I learned in life is that good things always leave too soon. This time is no different. Hera orgasms, her pussy pulsing around my cock. There's no hope of holding out, not when it feels so damned perfect. I grind into her, kissing her hard as I fill her.

I want to stay like this forever. To live in this peaceful moment where no one is asking anything of me and there are no impossible hurdles in my immediate future. A moment where my wife isn't shoving away from me as if my very touch is burning her.

That desire has me shifting closer instead of away, pressing my forehead lightly to hers as our ragged exhales mingle. My nose bumps hers. It's such a small touch, a near-innocent one, a sign I desperately want to take for intimacy even though I know better. We may have sex, but we don't share intimacy, not in any way that matters. If there's the shortest pause after we orgasm, a time of peace measured in heartbeats, neither of us have ever commented on it. We sure as fuck haven't sought to extend it the way I'm doing now. "Hera…"

I know I've made a mistake the moment she tenses in response to my voice. Hera plants her hands on my chest.

With her pants tangled around her ankles, there's no smooth retreat. I have to duck under her legs, which is a fucking problem because it puts her pussy at face level, perfect and flushed with desire...and leaking my come.

My cock twitches, but a quick check of her face tells me she might pull her cute little switchblade if I keep touching her. It's always like this with Hera: cold until I think I might die from it, but as soon as the lights go out, she burns me right up.

I reach out to help her off the table, but she knocks my hand away, her head ducked to avoid meeting my gaze. Alarm blares through me. This is wrong. She's often furious after she comes, but never like this. Never brittle. I shove my cock back into my pants and give her some space. "Hera—"

"You've proven your point, Zeus." She snaps my name hard enough that I flinch. "No matter what I do, I'll never escape you."

Her words hurt even more than the way she hurriedly pulls up her pants. I'm the worst kind of delusional to wish for a relationship that isn't a constant fucking war. To wish for a spouse who wants me without restriction. To wish for...a lot of things. But this isn't a normal part of our ongoing series of battles. She's not attacking. She's *fleeing*. And it scares the shit out of me. "You said yes."

"I *always* say yes to you." She finishes righting her clothing and wipes at her smudged lipstick. I can actually see her putting herself together, piece by piece. "Get that look off your face, Zeus. You didn't force anything. I wanted it. I always want it, even if I loathe you all the more by the end."

I hate that she sees right through me. I hate even more how I exhale in slow relief. "Then what's wrong?"

"What's wrong?" She scoffs. "Someday, you'll get tired of humiliating me like this. Do you know how much I hate that I want you?"

"About as much as *I* hate wanting *you*." Fuck, I didn't mean to say that. It doesn't matter how much I tell myself to keep control. She snipes at me, and I rise to the bait. Every. Single. Time.

All my stress and anger and, yeah, fear comes rushing back, eliminating the short escape we just fled to. I slide out from behind the booth and straighten my clothes. I can see the outline of Ixion's broad shoulders through the window in the door, and it just pisses me off all the more. Is he her only lover? Or are all three of her precious guardians taking turns giving my wife the pleasure that she only reluctantly accepts from me?

I spin to face her. "Be home for dinner tonight."

"But—"

"No fucking excuses." I start for the door. I'm done playing her games and wondering what my wife is up to. "If you're not there, then I'm going to hunt you down and I'll fuck you wherever I find you—no matter who's there to witness it."

HERA

WHAT AM I *DOING*? ZEUS'S WORDS RING THROUGH me like the clearest bell. Not just his words. His touch. His taste. The feel of him inside me. I should have said no the moment I realized where our argument was heading, but with fear riding me so hard, I let myself be selfish, let myself sink into the pleasure I find at his hands.

Even if he's the enemy. Even if I have active plans to see him dead.

Instead, I just rode his cock in the middle of the damned bar. I just fucked my husband while my sisters' and mother's lives are in danger. I stand there, feeling more lost than I've ever felt, and watch him walk away from me. I should be grateful for the reprieve, but instead it's one blow too many.

"I can't do this." I am calm, collected, and occasionally violent, but I have *never* let fear get the best of me. There's always a way out. I just need to *think*, except I can't even do that right. I'm barely showing other symptoms of my pregnancy, but it increasingly feels like my thoughts are wrapped in cotton.

My husband stops and looks at me, his strong brows pulling together. "Hera?"

"I can't do this," I say again, sharper. "What the fuck am I doing?" My voice gains a shrill edge, but I can't stop it. *Fuck, fuck, fuck.*

Zeus crosses the distance between us in three large steps and catches my elbows. "Look at me."

I don't want to, but I'm helpless to do anything but open to the deep, soothing command in his voice. His blue eyes contain so much, and I can't read any of it. I choke out an exhale. "I hate you."

"I know. Now, breathe for me. Slowly in and out through your nose." He mirrors my breathing, guiding me through it until my thoughts start to settle. "That's it, Hera."

My hard-won calm slips through my fingers. I jerk my elbows out of his grasp. "My name is *Callisto*."

Instead of snarling at me, Zeus's expression goes contemplative. He searches my expression. "Callisto," he says slowly, as if savoring it on his tongue. The same way he savored *me* just a short time ago.

It roots me in place. I can't tell if I'm breathing. I can't do anything but stare at Zeus…at… "Perseus."

He closes his eyes and shivers—actually *shivers*. I don't know if I take a step forward or if he does. All I know is that the new distance between us disappears as if it'd never been there to begin with. My husband reaches up slowly as if to cup my cheek.

His phone rings before he can make contact.

Something like regret blooms in his pale eyes. "I have to take that."

"Okay." I don't move, though. I just whisper, "I have to go. I have things to do."

"I know." He takes one slow step back, and then another, and digs his phone out of his pocket.

The moment is over. Maybe it was never there to begin with. Psyche and Eurydice were always so careful about who they slept with, claiming that sex made them fall for someone so much faster. It's never been a problem I've had, but I've also never slept with the same person for more than a couple months—and I've *never* lived with a partner.

People view us as stepping stones to power. We are Demeter's daughters, after all. Even our mother looks at us that way, though I suppose she's also concerned with *our* having power, not just consolidating it for her. As my mother has gotten fond of saying in the last month or so, she's not going to be around forever; at least she can die knowing her girls are taken care of. As if she's not in her midfifties and thriving, war or no.

I watch my husband walk out the door, his phone to his ear, and call myself seven different kinds of fool for the small sliver of loss that cuts through me when he disappears from view.

He is not my ally. He can *never* be my ally.

I smooth my shirt with shaking hands. My body aches from what we just did, but there's no time to think too hard about how much *better* the sex was today. How he wasn't cold and removed, how he was right there with me, our fury spiking desire higher. How good it felt for him to hold me, just for a moment, after. I shiver a little at the thought of next time.

No, damn it. That's not the correct priority to be focusing on right now. I scrub my hands over my face. I have to get out of here. I push forward to shove out the doors…and almost trample Ixion in the process.

He catches my shoulders, his expression murderous. "Are you okay?"

"I'm fine." I don't bother to smile. That won't reassure him at all. "Let's go. We have a long drive and I have to be back by dinnertime."

To his credit, he takes me at my word, even though he doesn't look happy about it. Ixion and the others are incredibly protective of me. They also hate my husband, and why not? Historically, the number one threat to Hera is Zeus.

It will take several hours to drive into the country to

where my mother and Psyche are currently overseeing Olympian civilians, but I can't trust this conversation to a phone call. It's going to be a hard enough sell as it is. Step down and abandon the city... As if that's not the opposite of what my mother has spent her life doing. Circe set me an impossible task, but the consequences of failing are too damned high. I *have* to make them see reason.

If I can get Psyche on my side, that will help immensely. She always knows the right thing to say, the right approach to take.

Ixion and Nephele wait with me while Imbros pulls the car around. The displeasure of all three is apparent, but none of them challenge me about being fine. They're right to worry, but it's not my husband who's to blame.

It's Circe.

Nephele climbs into the back seat with me. "It's okay if you're not fine, you know." She waits for me to fasten my seat belt before doing the same. "He's a monster."

No, he's not.

I bite down the words, not sure where they even came from. Of course my husband is a monster: he's Zeus. Except he's not entirely Zeus, is he? He's also Perseus. That's one thing I've never bothered to consider, that the man I married wasn't always the cold and fearsome leader of the Thirteen and Olympus. At some point in the past, he was a baby, a kid, a teenager, growing up in the household of the last Zeus. *He* was a true monster, and if Persephone had married him the way she was supposed to, not even our mother's machinations would have saved her from harm—or possibly even death.

Surely *that* man didn't save his violence and viciousness only for his spouses. Surely his children were subject to it as well.

My chest pings at the thought. My mother may be hard to deal with at times, and her plotting is often at her daughters' expense, but we grew up knowing we were safe. Out in the countryside, the suffocating rules of the city proper are nowhere in evidence. No one cared if we were perfectly put together at all times. No one was trying to use us as pawns to get to or hurt our mother. We were just children, wild and beloved.

Even without knowing the details of my husband's childhood, I know it wasn't like that for him. No one creates such a perfect icy persona unless they have to in order to survive. His sisters went a different route—Helen with her golden perfection and Eris with her fury. And Hercules left the city, though the story is still muddy on whether that was his choice or not.

So, no, I don't think Perseus had a safe childhood. Certainly not a happy one. It shouldn't matter. Bad things happen to all sorts of people, and while it's tragic, it doesn't excuse their perpetuating abuse onto others.

Perseus just...hasn't done that. Yet. But he will, won't

he? Because he's not just Perseus, someone who might have had a chance to leave the generational trauma behind the way Hercules apparently did.

He's *Zeus*.

The changing scenery drags me from the death spiral of my thoughts. The city falls in increments, tall buildings giving away to shorter ones which in turn give way to rolling hills and fields. Although I have every intention of keeping my emotions locked down, my heart beats faster and my lungs feel like they expand to twice their size, as if I can taste the country air even through the windows.

Home.

It's not, though. It hasn't been home for nearly half my life at this point. Mother wanted us to have a clean break, so the interludes to the country became less and less common as we got older—as she became entrenched in the city's intrigue.

"It's beautiful," Imbros breathes.

That's right. Ze has never seen the Olympian territory outside of the city proper. I clear my throat. "It is."

At least until it's not.

It happens so fucking fast. One moment, we're surrounded by the fields in late stages of harvest, and the next it's a tent city. Ixion has to slow down as he turns onto a dirt road that leads into a converted field. The ground is a long way from frozen, so it's a muddy mess.

All around us, the displaced citizens of the city move

about in some semblance of a rhythm. People in every season of life, from a toddler barely able to walk to an elderly couple hunched with age. Kids run between the gaps in what I belatedly realize is a line of adults waiting for…something.

Ixion carefully navigates us through it all, slowly enough that it would probably be faster to walk. I don't suggest it. I'm too busy picking up signs of my mother's influence. We reach the head of the line, discovering it's actually two lines—one for food and one for job allocation. It takes a lot of work to keep a displaced community running, and while my mother has an extensive staff, I imagine they'll need help.

Not to mention, it's not a good idea to have so many people in crisis without giving them something productive to focus on. We've displaced so many people in an effort to protect them; I suspect it's not all for nothing.

We park in front of a large tent, which surprises me a little. My mother loves her luxuries, and while this is spacious and looks expensive, it's hardly a house. Ixion leads the way, holding open the fold that functions as a door. I meet his gaze. "Please wait outside."

He nods. Ironic that he and the others are less worried about me with my family than they are with my husband. Not that my mother would ever overtly hurt me. However, if a few eggs get cracked in the making of her grand design, she counts it as a worthy sacrifice. Even if those cracked eggs are her daughters.

I see Psyche first. Even here, in the midst of the worst crisis the city has seen in our lifetimes—maybe ever—my sister is every inch an influencer. She's wearing fitted pink trousers that hug her generous hips and a cute knit black sweater over a polka-dot button-up shirt with a Peter Pan collar. Her hair is perfect, the long brown strands curled and pinned back from her pretty, round face.

She lights up when she sees me. "Callisto!" Psyche crosses the distance between us and enfolds me in a hug that instantly lowers my blood pressure. She's so fucking *good* at that. "I didn't know you were coming."

"I'm not here for long." I hug her hard. "Fuck, I missed your face."

She laughs a little and waits for me to loosen my grip before she steps back. "I missed you, too." She swipes her forehead with the back of her hand. "Mother is out surveying some problem with the western fields, but she should be back soon."

I glance back at the entrance to the tent. "How did she manage to put this together so quickly? We're miles away from her property."

"This area was privately owned by some corporation or other who wasn't utilizing it. She bought it for a song." Psyche shrugs at my bewildered expression. "You know how Mother is when she gets her mind set on something."

Yeah, I guess I do. "Smart of her to bring the people to

this space instead of overrunning the farmland necessary to the city's survival."

"It was. Speaking of... Have you eaten?"

It's tempting to lie, but she'll see right through me. "No."

"I think we have the makings for turkey sandwiches around here." She starts to turn away.

My stomach lurches at the very thought. "No!" I take a breath and try to temper my tone. "No, that's okay. I'm not hungry. I'm not feeling particularly well these days."

"You should eat. Or maybe drink?" She says it slowly, watching me closely. "I could use a glass of wine. I'll pour two."

Psyche is arguably the smartest of my sisters, the one who sees the most. I already know what I'm giving away when I shake my head slowly. "No," I whisper. "No alcohol."

My sister studies me intently. I can actually see her cataloging the circles beneath my eyes, the broken blood vessels in my cheeks from throwing up earlier, the tense way I hold myself, ready to protect my stomach. Her hazel eyes go wide. "Callisto..." She shifts closer and takes my hand. "Honey, are you pregnant?"

I've been muscling through this mess on my own for months, doing what I needed to in order to protect the ones I love. Asking for help just brings the risk of endangerment, so I haven't dared. Instead, I've pushed through with alliances with Poseidon and Dionysus, two people I don't trust as far as I can throw them, in order to remove my husband and ensure I was in a position to protect my mother and sisters.

And for what? Circe still came, and if she's offering me an out—one Hera to another—it's such a long shot as to be a death sentence. I've never been clever with my words like Psyche or quick to use a sunshine mask to manipulate like Persephone or *good* like Eurydice. I don't see a way through.

Here, with my sister's sympathy wrapping around me, I buckle. My knees give out and I would have hit the ground if Psyche hadn't caught me around the waist and half carried me to a nearby chair despite our height differences.

She urges me down and disappears for a few seconds, returning with a bottle of water. "How far along?"

The pregnancy is the least of my problems, but it's easier to focus on that than everything else in play. At least for a little while. "Seventeen weeks, I think." I accept the bottle, but don't open it. "I haven't gone to a doctor yet. I can't risk everyone in Olympus knowing."

She drags over a second chair, close enough that our knees touch. "How long have *you* known?"

Admitting the truth will hurt her, but lying will hurt her more. "Four months."

Psyche nods slowly, a line forming between her brows. "Callisto..." Every time she says my name, it's a balm to my very soul. "I've kept quiet because you made a choice that saved my life, perhaps literally. I've let you keep your own counsel, even though I know you're making moves that put you in danger." I start to speak, but she holds up her hand. "But you're *not* alone. You have us, and you've always had us. If you can't talk to anyone else, talk to me."

Months of keeping my own confidence have my mind screaming that I need to stay quiet and not involve her, but it's too late. Psyche's in as much danger as the rest of us, and I'm the only one who can save her. I just need to cooperate with Circe, to backflip through the hoops that bitch has set out, to talk my mother and Hades into leaving Olympus.

I...can't do it alone.

The thought makes me dizzy. I reach out, my vision blurry, and Psyche catches my hand and clasps it between hers. "Please, Callisto."

I crumble. "Do you have ginger tea in here by chance? This might take a little while to lay out."

"I think so." She squeezes my hand and then heads toward the back of the tent where there's an honest-to-gods kitchen. Because of course there is. Our mother wouldn't know the concept of roughing it if it slapped her in the face.

I stand on shaking legs and follow Psyche to where she's filling a kettle with water. "It started on my wedding night…"

ZEUS

THE CALL FROM ATHENA TOOK ME ON A WILD-goose chase. A woman who might be Circe was spotted in the university district, which led to two hours of combing every street and business with nothing to show for it. I'm practically weaving on my feet when I stumble through the doors of Dodona Tower. I need some food and possibly a catnap before I figure out the next steps.

The only warning I get for what's coming is the receptionist looking a little guilty. When the doors open to my floor, my sisters are waiting for me.

Eris waltzes over, wearing a long dress that ghosts over the floor, and presses a glass of scotch into my hand. "Sit down before you fall down."

I stare at the drink and then at her. "What the fuck is this?"

"An intervention," she snaps. "Now, do what I say or I'm going to take you out at the knees, and you're too old to bounce back from that as easily as you did when we were kids."

I blink. Eris has always been the sharpest of my siblings, but usually she keeps that part carefully concealed. Apparently her husband is rubbing off on her. Ares steps in front of Eris and motions to the chair in my office—but not the one behind my desk. "Sit down, Perseus. It's time we talked."

Even *she* looks a little different than normal. MuseWatch once coined Ares—Helen, then—as the most beautiful woman in Olympus. It's still there, but she's gained an edge that she never possessed before. With her hair slicked back and her clothes nondescript and dark, she almost seems like a different person. Until I catch her eyes and see the familiar stubbornness there.

I could storm out, but I'm so damn tired that sitting down with a drink sounds really fucking nice right now, even if it comes with a conversation I don't want to have with my sisters. With anyone. Maybe Hercules had the right idea. He left Olympus years ago and hasn't looked back. Not even for us.

I drop into the chair and motion for them to get it over with. "Commence with the intervention."

My sisters exchange a glance. They don't look overly

similar—Ares with a warm summer beauty that literally stops traffic on occasion and Eris with the same cold glamour our mother possessed. Ares's red highlights show in the lamp behind her and Eris has hair dark as the darkest night. And yet they are undeniably related. It's there in the careful way they hold themselves, our father's training running strong despite our best efforts.

Ares is the one who begins. She perches on the edge of my desk and crosses her arms over her chest. "The coup was a risk and I agreed to help because I saw the benefit of dealing with Circe once and for all." She sighs. "Also, you didn't give me much choice, seeing as how you'd already started the damn thing before talking to me."

I sigh. "But?"

"But you failed," Eris snaps. "The rest of the Thirteen would have forgiven damn near anything if you were successful, but you went around them, undermined their power, and Circe still escaped."

"The blockade is gone. That's a success."

"Tell that to MuseWatch."

I frown. "I did. MuseWatch ran with my narrative this morning."

My sisters exchange a look. Again, Ares speaks first. "That was the original story, but there have been two in the last hour debating whether you're abusing power and what recourse the citizens of Olympus have if you are."

I curse. Of course. I should have known it wouldn't be as simple as leaking a single story. I *did* know, but I've been a little too busy to set up the promised follow-up interview with Clio Mousa. "I'll deal with it."

"That's not all." Ares shifts nervously. "You're behaving erratically. It's starting to worry our allies."

What few allies we have left. I take a too-big drink of my scotch, relishing the way it burns down my throat and warms my stomach. "We're hardly in a normal scenario right now. Never in the history of Olympus have we existed without the barrier. There are enemies within the city, and surely our *allies* can see that we need to move decisively."

"Perseus."

Every time they say my name, it snaps me back to earlier today, to my wife's lips forming it, to the softness in her tone that I've never heard before. I scrub my free hand over my face. "*What?*"

Another of those shared glances. Eris clears her throat, not quite meeting my gaze. "Look, I know I walked away from the Aphrodite title when you needed me there, and doing so hurt your position. I realize I don't have much of a leg to stand on, but you've been seen all over Olympus acting out of character. And I'm not just talking about the coup."

They're not wrong about my unraveling at the edges, but I'm not in the mood to cooperate. If they want to do an *intervention,* they can spell out exactly what I'm doing that's so worrisome. "If you're not talking about the coup, what *are* you talking about?"

Eris hesitates, actual worry flickering over her expression. "Today—in the middle of the day—you were recorded fucking your wife in a godsdamned bar in the theater district."

I'm out of my chair before my brain fully processes her words. I snatch the phone out of her hand, horror and fury rising with each racing beat of my heart. "Who the fuck *dared* record us?" I can count on one hand who knew we were there in the first place.

If I thought for a second that Ixion was responsible, I'd be happy for an excuse to kill him with my bare hands. But as soon as I see the video, I know it couldn't have been him. The short recording is grainy in a way that suggests it was an interior security camera. That means there's only one possible culprit. "The bar owner sold this to MuseWatch."

"That's not really the point," Ares cuts in. "The rest of the Thirteen already didn't have much confidence in you, but you're actively undermining it. You look like a fool. Everyone believes Hera and Circe are leading you around by your nose in turn."

I'm barely paying attention. Upon closer inspection, I'm only moderately relieved to note that the footage is too low quality to see the details of our nudity. Not that it matters; the motions themselves are clear. The video stops when we do, cutting off well before that moment where she said my name, the moment that might have been a turning point for us.

It won't be now.

Olympus has made sure of that.

This fucking city. It takes and takes and takes, and the trade-off might be power, but what the fuck is the point of power when I can't protect my sisters, can't even shield *my wife* from a godsdamned sex tape?

"*Perseus.*" Eris snaps her fingers in front of my face. When I look up, she snatches the phone from my grasp. I fully expect her to lay into me, to be like Ares and belabor the point that my relationship with my wife should be the least of my concerns right now. She doesn't. She glances at the phone and sighs. "I'm sorry."

Ares pushes off the desk and flops into the chair next to mine. She pulls off the band holding her hair back and drags her fingers through the newly freed strands. "This is such a clusterfuck. We evacuated everyone to save them from the invasion, and now there's no invasion and no blockade. We look like fools. We're losing the confidence of the civilian population, disrupting their lives for no damned reason."

"There *is* an invasion," I snap. "It just looks different than we expected." Except I'm not certain of that, am I? Even after all the time I wasted today, I'm still not sure the woman spotted in the video was actually Circe. If it was, she *allowed* herself to be seen. Like she wanted me to play the fool, searching for her when she's nowhere to be found.

Like she wanted me distracted.

"Maybe she's not in the city at all. At least not anymore." I sit upright. "Are we tracking people leaving for the country?"

"With what manpower?" Ares throws up her hands and slumps back into her chair. "Everyone is either on perimeter, searching for Circe, or managing the civilians who waited to evacuate. There's no one left to monitor those on the road, and why would there be? They're allowed free movement."

Eris moves around to take the spot that Ares vacated against the desk. "Perseus." She waits for me to give her my full attention. "You're grasping at straws. We might not know if Circe is actually in the city, but what we *do* know is that the Thirteen are fracturing and the city will pay the price of that fracture. *That's* the problem that needs to be your focus. We have all the resources available searching for Circe. We need *you* to stabilize the public's perception of what's going on in Olympus. You need to convince the rest of the Thirteen that you're not a power-mad dictator in waiting."

I don't care about Olympus or the Thirteen.

I don't say it. I can't admit that finally holding the Zeus title, the one thing I spent my entire life working toward, has only made it clear that this isn't what I want. It's never mattered what I desired, though. It's about duty. "If you feel so strongly about the stability of Olympus, you never should have stepped down as Aphrodite."

Ares curses, but Eris doesn't flinch. She meets my gaze steadily. "Walking away from the title doesn't mean I stop being able to observe, to think. You need to take your own advice, Perseus. Stop reacting and *think*. Sele isn't me, but they're doing a fine job as Aphrodite. More than that, there isn't another alternative."

Alternative. To power, to the titles, to... Why does this keep coming up? I narrow my eyes. "Have you been talking to Hermes?"

She blinks. "I haven't seen Hermes in...months? I don't know. A long time."

"She's around," I mutter. I didn't take her comments earlier seriously, but now I wonder. If bringing down the Thirteen has truly been her goal all along, then she was a traitor from the start. "She popped by my office to tell me that we should dismantle our system of government and set up...something."

"How does she plan on doing *that*?" Ares shakes her head. "The Thirteen have always existed. It's a fundamental part of what Olympus is."

"So was the barrier, but look at it now." Eris shrugs when we both glare at her. "I'm not saying we should rush to topple what's left of our government. Just pointing out that things are changing—have been changing for some time."

If nothing else is true, that is. "We don't need change. We need stability." The words feel dragged out of me. I'm so fucking tired, but there's no one else. There's never been anyone else. Trying to find Hera before the video does so I can be the one to break the news to her is a fool's errand. This is Olympus; gossip travels faster than the speed of light. "And we can't have true stability until Circe is removed as a threat."

Eris shrugs. "You're not wrong, but there's a lot of damage that can be repaired in the meantime. The coup with Poseidon and Hades can be spun to prove that the three legacy titles are in an alliance for the first time in generations. That's powerful. We just have to use it."

"It won't be enough to bring Artemis around." Ares laces her fingers behind her head. "She hates our entire family and your stepping down as Aphrodite hasn't changed that. You're right that Sele was a good choice for Aphrodite, but they're going to play things safe to protect themselves. Same with Hephaestus. Xe will look after xir people, because that's where xir loyalty lies. Their respective votes about the attack on Circe's blockade prove that. If either of them makes alliances, it won't be until the dust settles."

"Dionysus isn't cooperating, either." Eris examines her nails. "It seems he's in your wife's corner now."

I truly wish I could say that her corner and mine are one and the same. They aren't. "Demeter is mercenary, but she knows where her best interests lie. She's worked too damn hard to marry one of her daughters to me to undermine that now."

"Maybe," Ares says almost reluctantly.

My sisters exchange another one of those speaking glances. I hate it when they do that. "What?" I snap.

"Demeter's loyalty only lasts as long as your power does." Ares stretches and shoves to her feet. "So let's do what we have to in order to ensure your power doesn't falter."

I look from her to Eris and back again. "Athena is in my corner. You are." I nod to Ares. "Apollo is." I reach for another name, but come up short. *Fuck*. Four out of thirteen is shit odds. "I'll talk to Poseidon and see what I can do. Hades, too, for that matter. We worked together well during the attack on the ships. We can come together again to defend the city."

"I hope so." Eris plucks the bottle of scotch from my desk and takes a long drink. "Because I'm pretty sure you only have one chance to get this train back on the tracks. If you fail…"

Failure is not an option. My father's voice haunts me, a nasty little reminder that Zeus has *never* failed, and if I do, I'll be the first. That was the metaphorical whip he used against me countless times over the years. Don't fail the title, the family, *him*. I clear my throat. "If I fail?"

She meets my gaze. "Don't fail, Perseus. For all our sakes."

HERA

"AND THAT'S WHEN I FOUND OUT I WAS PREGNANT."

Even when laying so much of myself bare, I don't tell Psyche about my intentionally reaching out to Circe. I hesitate, considering the best way to approach this. Psyche has a much stronger moral compass than I do and she cares about people almost as deeply as Eurydice does. She had a chance to leave Olympus behind and chose to stay. I need to pick my words carefully to get her on my side, to ensure we can come together and figure out how to convince our mother, Hades, and our sisters to escape while we can.

"Psyche!"

I startle so badly I almost fall out of my chair, but Psyche doesn't so much as flinch. She glances to the door as her husband, Eros, shoves into the tent. "Psyche, we have a problem. There's something—" He stops short when he catches sight of me. For someone who used to be a fixer for his mother, the woman who was Aphrodite two title changes ago, he looks far more rattled than I've ever seen him. This is a man with more than a few bodies to his name. What could possibly be on the phone that he's clutching so tightly to cause *that* look on his face?

"Oh. Callisto. You're here."

I'm not one to jump to conclusions, but it's hardly half a step to get to the realization that this concerns me. I hold out my hand. "Give it here."

Naturally, he ignores me and moves to my sister. The look he gives me is almost sympathetic as he hands the phone to her. "It was posted on MuseWatch a few minutes ago."

Watching the color drain from my sister's pretty face is an experience I would like to extract myself from. "What is it?" I demand.

Psyche takes a deep breath. "Were you with your husband before you came out here?"

Heat flares beneath my skin, quickly followed by a dread so deep it threatens to swallow me whole. I lunge across the space between us and snatch the phone out of her hands.

A video of me...and Zeus. "Fuck."

Even without sound, I know the beats of our breathing by heart, the soft, sharp words exchanged that drove us both into a frenzy and made us forget ourselves. It's horrible seeing the shared intimacy now, even after I intentionally closed my eyes to recreate the familiar darkness in the moment, retreating from the vulnerability my husband draws forth from me every time he touches me, kisses me.

And now that vulnerability is out in the open for all of Olympus to see.

My thoughts drain out, replaced by furious static. Who did this? Was it a trap that Zeus set up? But no, that doesn't make any sense. He didn't know where I was going, and this video undermines him as well; not as much as me, but he can't afford *any* scandal or weakness in our current climate. The only person who knew where I was, who would be willing to undermine me so cruelly…is Circe.

That bitch. I'm going to fucking kill her.

I don't realize I've said the words aloud until Psyche and Eros exchange a look. My sister clears her throat. "There's not much recourse for this, but—"

"I'll take care of it." Even as I tell myself not to, I scroll down to the bottom of the so-called article and read the first few comments. They're exactly as lurid and tasteless as one would expect. Strangers, seeing me in a moment of vulnerability that I would never show to the world. What little respect I have garnered as Hera is gone now. This video makes sure of that. Now I'm just another spouse of Zeus to be objectified.

I can't let this distract me, but how am I supposed to do anything else? I'm not particularly prudish, but there's a wild difference between consensually engaging in acts in front of an audience the way Persephone and Hades do and *this*. It paints what was already a charged interaction in an even uglier light.

Did I really tell my husband to call me by my actual name? What the fuck was I thinking? The only small grace in this entire clusterfuck is the video being without sound. At least all of Olympus can't hear how pathetically I mewl for him to fuck me. Small mercies, because they can *see* how pathetic I look when I'm coming on Zeus's cock.

I haven't had a chance to talk to my mother, to present my still-forming plan that will save our family, but I can barely reason past the racing thoughts. I'm in no shape to go round and round with her and lay out an argument that she can't reject. I don't even *have* an argument she can't reject. All I have is fear and rage.

I toss the phone to Eros and stand. "I'm trying to meet with Persephone tomorrow, but I'll be back the next day. Keep my sister and mother safe until then. Do you understand me? Because if you don't, I'm going to skin you alive."

Eros raises his brows. "You already know that I'd die before I'd let anyone touch Psyche. Your mother is a different beast altogether. If you want Demeter to consent to protection, take it up with her."

I can't face her right now. If Eros has seen the video, then it's only a matter of time before she does, too. My mother, who never sets a foot out of place as far as the public is concerned. My mother, who's almost universally beloved by the civilians in Olympus. She's going to be so fucking disappointed in me.

She may have had her dalliances here and there, but she's always been the very picture of discretion. No one even knows that she and Poseidon had a prolonged affair up until relatively recently. For me to misstep like this, to allow this video to be taken, let alone distributed, is a failure. She won't see it as anything else, no matter what sympathies she might feel for my plight. She'll want to know how I plan on combating the dip in public perception. She'll want me to have a scheme already in place, and I can barely concentrate enough to put one foot in front of the other.

If I tell her I couldn't give a shit about public perception as long as my family is safe from Circe's coming purge, she'll see it as a weakness. She'll think I don't believe we can win. And she'll be right. We *can't* win. We have yet to be victorious in a single fucking battle against Circe and her people.

But nobody wants to talk about that.

"Callisto, don't go back to the city tonight." Psyche starts to move toward me but stops when I shake my head sharply. She looks so worried that my heart aches, but I don't have the words to comfort her right now. She glances again at Eros. "We have plenty of beds. Just stay here until you can calm down. I can't begin to imagine what you're feeling right now, so I won't patronize you and say I do. If Eros knew you were here, he wouldn't have allowed you to find out like this."

I glance at my brother-in-law, at his carefully blank expression. "I know." He might be a murderer, but he would never do something to upset his wife—and upsetting me upsets Psyche.

She presses her lips together and lifts her hands before letting them fall back to her sides. "It's not a good idea to drive when you're so out of sorts. It's not safe."

"You should know better. I don't drive anywhere." I force my expression into an irreverent smile. "I'll be fine. I have my team with me."

Instead of looking relieved, she only seems more concerned. "I know they mean a lot to you, but you've only had them such a short time. They aren't your family."

"I know." And, frankly, that's part of the attraction. I don't wish any ill on my team, but the fact remains that they can take care of themselves. If it were a choice between them and my sisters, it would be no choice at all. That makes me a monster, no question, but I'm willing to live with it. "Stay here. Stay with him." I jerk my chin at Eros. "Stay safe. Please."

"I will, but we have to talk about—"

"Later," I cut in before she can speak the truth of my current predicament aloud. "And until we do, I don't want anything we discussed to be shared. Promise me, Psyche."

I've never seen my sister look so conflicted. She worries her bottom lip and finally nods. "Okay. I promise to keep your confidence, but only until the day after tomorrow. Then all bets are off. So don't be late when you come out to us again."

As threats go, it's efficient. If my mother finds out I'm pregnant from anyone but me, especially in such a tumultuous time, she's liable to go on a rampage. No one wants that. "I'll be here. I promise that, too." I turn around and walk away before either of us can say something we'll regret. I know Psyche doesn't like this, but I don't, either.

A fucking sex tape.

Even as I tell myself not to, I pull my phone out and look. Texts from Ares, from Persephone, from Eurydice. Not from my husband. If those three and Eros have already seen the video, then it's all but guaranteed he has as well. There's no reason for it to hurt that he hasn't reached out to make sure I'm okay. Of course I'm okay. It's a fucking video... showing me in an incredibly intimate moment I never would have shared publicly if I had any choice in the matter. But it's sex, and no matter how vulnerable I was in the moment, Olympus has seen its fair share of sex tapes. Surely this won't hold water when held up against the threat of Circe and the evacuation to the countryside. Surely our people have better things to worry about than me fucking my husband in a semi-public place.

Surely…

But I know better, don't I? It's written there on Ixion's, Nephele's, and Imbros's faces when I approach the car. They've all seen it, and even though they stood outside the building while it was happening, it still clearly affects the way they view me. It's going to affect the way *the entire city* views me.

Nephele opens her mouth, but I hold up a hand before she can get a single word out. "I don't want to talk about it. I would like to go home."

Home. The very idea is laughable. That penthouse I share with my husband is no home to me. It's a prison to be endured until this sham of a marriage is at its end, preferably with his death. And yet the closer we drive to the city, the more my heart rate can't decide whether it wants to ease or pick up. The more the memories of what happened earlier today—and now writ large in grainy video for all the city to see—echo through my body.

It's disastrous to still want him after everything. It's horrific to crave his lips forming my true name, even when I hate him with every fiber of my being. It's absolutely unforgivable to want his cold steadiness to calm the inferno inside me.

No doubt he'll come to me with accusations instead of comfort. And what use do I have for comfort? If that's what I craved, I should have stayed in the gentle embrace of my sister and mother. Or at least Psyche. My mother may play gentle for the public, but there are thorns beneath the facade. There always have been.

"Fuck," Ixion breathes. "We have a problem."

That's absolutely not what I want to hear right now. I lean forward and press my fingers to my temples, hard. "What problem?"

I see what he means the moment I ask the question. The road ahead of us was empty, but now there is a single nondescript black SUV blocking the way. Circe? But why would she bother to move so publicly when her threats are best made in the shadows?

I get my answer as we coast to a stop a short distance from the blockade. A familiar Black woman steps out of the SUV and stretches, her warrior's form on full display. Atalanta. What the fuck is she doing here?

She strolls to my window as if completely unaware of the fact that every single person in this car, barring me, is reaching for their gun. I motion for Nephele to roll down the window and barely manage to get my expression locked down before she obeys. "Is there a problem?"

Atalanta smiles tightly. "You could say that. Athena would like a word."

I make a show of looking around, of motioning to the empty fields on either side of the road. "She's in the city, and I'm heading to the city. Why bother with all the theatrics?"

"Cute." She jerks her thumb to indicate the car. "We

can do this the easy way, or we can do this the hard way. It's your choice, Hera." It's hard to tell because she's so naturally charming, but I swear there's a hint of derision in the way she says my title.

I glance at my team, each doing their damnedest to convey the fact that they are willing to fight their way out of this. But what's the point? Fight our way out of this and…go back to the city where we're still surrounded by enemies? Not to mention that Athena's people are all, to a person, trained assassins. Atalanta may have started with Artemis, but that makes her no less fearsome.

There's only a single car, but…Athena is not to be underestimated. If she's determined to talk to me *here*, out in the middle of nowhere, then she's not going to let me go without having that conversation. It will mean a fight, which might end in my people being hurt.

I must care more than I previously thought, because the possibility leaves me cold. "Fine. Let's have this conversation." I glance at Ixion. "If they move, follow them, and we'll reconvene back in the city."

No one looks happy with this—at least no one except Atalanta. I step out of the car and walk side by side with her across the short distance to the SUV. Even as I tell myself not to show weakness, I can't help but sneer. "What? No cute little quip about my newfound fame?"

She rolls her eyes. "No matter what you might think

of me, I'm not a fucking monster. So no, I'm not going to ridicule you about a video that was obviously taken without your permission. Shove off with that nonsense." We reach the SUV and she holds open the door, waiting for me to slide in the back seat.

There's no going back after this. Athena could shoot me in the head and dump my body in the middle of the countryside, and no matter how hard my team fights, they'll end up joining me in some unmarked grave. With all the chaos, it might be ages before someone finds our remains. I wonder if my husband would feel relief at being rid of me.

No. That's defeatist thinking. If Athena wanted to kill me, she'd do it in the dead of night when it couldn't possibly be traced back to her. This is a conversation, plain and simple. I will *not* show weakness. That doesn't stop me from palming my switchblade as I slide into the back seat.

Except it's not Athena waiting for me. It's Hermes.

HERA

"YOU!" I LUNGE ACROSS THE SEAT, ONLY TO BE brought up short when Atalanta grabs a fistful of the back of my jacket. Before I can shrug out of it, she hooks an arm around my waist and yanks me against her stronger body. Pinning me.

"That's about enough of that." She gives me a little shake. "We're here to talk, not fight, so calm down."

It takes a beat for her words to register past the roaring in my ears. *We.* Not *I*. Sure as fuck not *her*. "So you're a traitor, too."

"Tomato-tomahto."

Hermes shakes her head slowly, her expression uncharacteristically serious. "This game is bigger than traitors and treachery. Put your big girl pants on and have a conversation. This is your only chance."

I almost tell her where to shove her conversation. I don't give a fuck what Hermes is playing at, not when the stakes are so damned high. This all started because of Circe, yes, but Hermes has been at the heart of the mess, too.

She's the one who invited Minos to the city. *She's* the one who gave him her fucking house for his little murder party. And *she's* the one who I'm nearly certain brought down the barrier, once and for all.

But she's still on the playing field, so I can't afford to ignore her. I elbow Atalanta. "Let me go. I'll behave."

"You'd better." She releases me, but only after giving me a shove into the back seat of the car and slamming the door behind me. Within seconds, she's around the front and in the driver seat. Even as I tell myself not to react or give them any reason to suspect I'm afraid, I can't stop myself from trying the door handle. Locked.

"Come now, Hera. My company is hardly unfortunate enough that you have to throw yourself from a moving vehicle." The worst part is that Hermes sounds much the same way she always has, bright and irreverent. She's changed up her hair from her usual natural curls, styling it in box braids that reach the middle of her back. I feel like I've been run through the wringer, but her dark-brown skin glistens with vitality. She looks fucking good, and it pisses me off.

"You have me where you want me." I slump back against the seat and cross my arms over my chest. It's petulant but

I'm so fucking tired. This has been the longest day, and if there's one person who never plays by the rules, it's Hermes. She never seemed to do anything *useful* with that rebellion, but that just proves she's better at the game than most. She's been playing us all along. "Hats off to you, I guess. No point in indulging in this game of pretend anymore."

Hermes shrugs, her smile dimming. "It wasn't all pretend. I've held this title for damn near a decade, and not even I'm that good."

"Forgive me if I don't believe you after the way you've acted for the last year or so."

She bursts out a bright, bitter laugh. "You know that saying about glass houses and stones? You should try looking in a mirror. Everyone in this city is a liar. I'm hardly the worst of them."

"That's up for debate."

True to form, she doesn't make me wait long for a reaction. She rolls her eyes and flicks her braids over her shoulder. "Everyone is so damned serious these days. It's a real bummer."

"Hermes." Atalanta meets her gaze in the rearview mirror. "Stop fucking around."

"Yes, yes." She waves it away and focuses entirely on me. "You have to talk to your husband."

Of all the things I expected her to say, those words didn't even make the list. It surprises me so much that I burst out laughing. "I thought you were the one with all the information. Obviously not. Otherwise you would know that I can't tell my husband shit. If you want to deliver a message he'll actually listen to, you should have gone to Ares or Eris."

"You're deeply underestimating your effect on him. I'm not going to be lewd and point out that in all my years of knowing him, he's never once stepped out of line enough to allow a video of his…extracurricular activities…to make the rounds on MuseWatch. Not a video, not a photo, not an audio recording. Nothing. He forgot himself with you, which means there's still hope."

I blink. I don't know which part of her words to process first. I've never followed MuseWatch as closely as my sisters did; the prattling on about the illicit lives of the Thirteen and the legacy families bored me to death. They're human. They fight, they fuck, and then they die.

Maybe I should have been paying closer attention.

No, that's not something to get sidetracked by. If my husband got carried away enough to get distracted—I pointedly ignore the little flicker of warmth as I contemplate that—it just means I'm not safe with him. That's nothing new; I've never been safe with him. "Get to the point."

Hermes's expression morphs back into something uncharacteristically serious. "I tried to talk to him, but his father's shit is too heavy. He's indoctrinated."

I raise my brows. "'Indoctrinated' is a strong word."

"Would you prefer 'traumatized'? PTSD? It all fits." She shakes her head. "Regardless, you've never believed the hype around the Thirteen. Surely you can recognize the system doesn't work. It *never* worked—not for the people who needed it the most. You should know that better than anyone, Hera." The emphasis she puts on my title prickles my skin.

I want to argue, but I would just be doing it for the sake of arguing. "Say I agree with you, which I don't know if I do... What do you expect me to do?"

"It's time for a new order of things. A different structure of government. The Thirteen can no longer rule Olympus."

This time, when I lunge at her, Atalanta's not close enough to stop me. It's not until I have my switchblade to Hermes's throat that I realize she let me get close...and that she has her own knife pressed to my stomach. She's still and relaxed as she smiles. "Fast, but not quite fast enough."

I am so damned tired of everyone in the room thinking they are the smartest motherfucker to exist. I glare down at her. "You're working with Circe."

"I'm not."

Lies, lies, and more lies. My hand's shaking so hard I have to choose between moving back or cutting her. I move back. Barely. "You want the same thing she wants. You're working to bring down the Thirteen, just like she is. Stop fucking lying to me."

"I'm not lying." She speaks slowly and calmly, inching her knife away from my stomach. "Wanting the Thirteen to no longer be in power isn't the same as wanting to annihilate them, no matter how much some of them deserve it."

None of this makes any sense. I shove away from her. We all know I'm not going to stab her now, and continuing to posture like this only makes me look weak. Weaker. Fuck. This whole situation is fucked. "You're arguing semantics. I don't have time for this."

My family's lives hang in the balance. Maybe Hermes doesn't want them dead the way Circe does, but her plan will end with the same result. "You have to know there isn't a single member of the Thirteen who will step down unless they're forced to. If you're not working with Circe and you're not willing to kill them, then you're going to fail. You've *already* failed if you're still trying to *reason* with Zeus."

In the front seat, Atalanta snorts, but it's Hermes who answers. "You'd be surprised what people will agree to if they're desperate enough. But you're right, I have no desire to murder my way through the Thirteen and the legacy families in order to raze this power structure. It would take a lot of time and effort, and you never really get blood out from beneath your cuticles." She makes a show of examining her nails, painted a bright neon yellow. "Which is where *you* come in. If you can convince Zeus to step down and ensure that none of his siblings move up to take his place, that will send a message the others will heed. This city is full of sheep who think they're wolves. They just need one to take the plunge first, and it *has* to be a legacy title."

The laugh that bursts from my lips contains an edge of hysteria. No matter how different Hermes claims she is, she and Circe are obviously moving along the same wavelength. "From the moment he gained sentience, my husband was trained by an abusive monster to take the title Zeus. He won't hand it over until he's dead. There's nothing that I—or anyone else—can say to change that truth."

"Then he'll die." Hermes doesn't say it like it brings her joy, more like it's an unfortunate side effect of a problem outside of her control. "You've seen how the Thirteen abuse their power, even if you've been relatively protected by virtue of your *mother's* power. How many times have you looked around at the legacy families and felt nothing but loathing? For all that you're part of them, you're separate enough to see how toxic their excess is. Your mother is aware of it. She might be one of the most excessive of them all, but at least she cares about the greater population. The same cannot be said for the rest of them."

"*You* are part of the Thirteen. Don't act like you're better. You've been enjoying those excesses for a very long time, Hermes."

"I have my reasons. I always have. We can argue about that, or you can acknowledge that you're against the wall and you don't have a choice. Because you're one of the Thirteen too, Hera." She flicks her wrist, pointing her knife at my stomach again. "And you don't get to extract yourself with divorce or your husband's death, either. Not when you carry the next Zeus."

It takes everything I have not to press my hand to my stomach, as if that would protect my little parasite from danger. I lift my chin. "Conjecture. I'll talk to Zeus for my own reasons, but I'm telling you now, it won't work."

"We'll see." She nods at Atalanta. "This is far enough."

As the car rolls to a stop, my frustration blooms hot and sticky on my tongue. I want to scream, but if I start screaming now, I can't guarantee I'll stop. "Ares considers you a friend, or at least she did. Dionysus, too. Even Hades. I don't understand why you're doing this."

Hermes doesn't look at me. "Sometimes friends have to hurt in order to help. They might have been my friends once I became Hermes, but there's a whole life I lived before I claimed the title. A whole identity. The Thirteen took something—someone—from me, and I vowed I would live to see their downfall. You know how to play the long game, so I'm sure you'll appreciate the patience I've demonstrated."

None of this makes any sense. If she was going to orchestrate the downfall of the Thirteen, why wait until now to do it? She could have started at any point during the last...

Realization dawns. "Every time someone said, 'Hermes has her reasons,' they had no idea, did they?"

"A lady never tells." The words are right, accurate to the Hermes I thought I had come to know. The tone, however, belongs to a stranger. Hard and tight and filled with the kind of rage that has no end. A rage she's been hiding since she became Hermes. Maybe even before that.

"If you do something to threaten my baby again, I don't give a shit how fast you are, I'll slit your throat." I issue the threat calmly, enunciating each word carefully.

Atalanta snorts, but Hermes smiles slowly. "I always said you Dimitriou women are interesting. Don't stop being interesting now, Callisto."

The car stops, and the locks disengage. I waste no time getting the fuck out of there. My head is spinning, but for all that drama of her staging this conversation, I don't really have much new information. Zeus has labeled Hermes a traitor for some time now. I don't think anyone quite realized the depth of it—or her ultimate goal—but not that much has changed.

I stumble back to where my car waits, and Nephele opens the door for me. It's only when I'm back inside the dim interior that I start to shiver. All three of them look at me with worried expressions, but I shake my head. "Not now." Maybe not ever.

As much as I trust them to watch my back and protect

me, can I trust them with this? There's a reason I held back telling them what Circe plans. Their loyalty begins and ends with me as Hera. If I lose my title, I lose my trio. I can't trust them. Not fully.

The city rises before us in all its glittering glory. It's a little dimmer than it used to be, but no less beautiful. Strange how, despite my best efforts, it really does feel like home. I don't want to see it razed to the ground.

Ixion finally clears his throat. "What did Athena want?"

I almost forget myself and ask him what the fuck he's talking about, before it belatedly registers that I was supposed to be meeting with Athena, not Hermes. The implications of *that* are even more complicated than everything else. Atalanta is working with Hermes? How did those two even cross paths in a way that would orchestrate any kind of relationship? It's not important in this moment to know the answer to that question, but the not knowing threatens to eat away at me. I believed I was getting a handle on all of the petty politics and backstabbing, and every time I turn around, it's proven to me again and again that I have no idea what the fuck I'm doing.

I don't bother to smile. "The same old, same old. Threats, threats, and more threats."

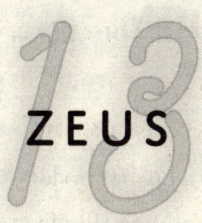

ZEUS

IT'S FAR TOO EARLY TO GO HOME AND I HAVE FAR too much to do. I'm so fucking tired. When I was younger, there were whole days and weeks when my father wanted to ensure I had the endurance to be Zeus. I learned to go for a very long time without sleep—and to mask the symptoms that come as a result. Among other things. I don't like to think about those times. I especially don't like to admit that he might have been right, at least in this.

I make my way from the center city and out to the shipping docks. After the attack on Circe, I allowed Poseidon's bleeding heart to convince me to have the Aeaean sailors escorted to a safe space instead of tried as enemy soldiers. It was a calculated decision on my part. I owe no loyalty to Aeaea. But after seeing them, Icarus's claim that they are just people trying to provide for their families struck truer than was comfortable. Those defeated sailors kneeling on the deck weren't warriors. Half of them seemed confused about why they were even there in the first place.

I know what my father would have done in that situation. It doesn't matter why an enemy is an enemy; there's only one way to deal with them. You destroy them. But I'm not my father and, for better or worse, I never will be. Recent events have more than driven that truth home.

My only hope of coming out on top of this conflict with Circe is to keep Poseidon and Hades on my side. It's not worth burning those bridges for the sake of vengeance and frustration. So, when Poseidon asked this of me, I didn't even try to fight him.

He should be back in Olympus by now, having completed his self-appointed task. Sure enough, when I finally track down his second-in-command Orion, they point me back to the house where the title of Poseidon has traditionally lived. I know for a fact that *this* Poseidon, a surprise inheritor of the title after his uncle and cousins died unexpectedly from a strange illness, chooses to live in the guesthouse behind the manor proper.

I understand that. His uncle left a toxic shadow, the kind that almost makes me believe ghosts are real. It's the same reason why I haven't set foot in the penthouse owned by my father since his death. No one knows that, though. As far as my sisters are concerned, I took the burden of dealing with our former family home upon myself so they wouldn't have to. It's a testament to how terrible our father was that neither of them questioned it after the initial conversation.

The truth is that...I tried. A new Zeus can only ascend once the previous Zeus has been put to rest, and though there's a headstone in the legacy family's graveyard with my father's title and birth name on it, nothing about that man has been put to rest. Going into his residence—into my childhood home—is...

There's no use thinking about it now. Maybe once I've removed the threat of Circe once and for all, it will finally feel like a manageable task to go through his things and dispose of everything. To clean out that place I will never again call home and to sell it to some bloodthirsty hopeful who believes living in the same residence as a past Zeus will result in his power rubbing off on them.

Except...Poseidon isn't at the house. Or the guesthouse. Or on the grounds. My frustration blooms with each failure to track him down. This was supposed to be a relatively quick errand, and it's turning into a grand waste of time.

Just like the search for Circe.

Going off a lingering suspicion that I've been played, I finally find Poseidon back at the shipyard in a meeting with Orion and Pallas. It seems to be winding down, which just confirms that Orion sent me on a wild-goose chase to get me out of the way. I give Poseidon's second-in-command a long look, and though they can't quite meet my eyes, they don't shrink into themselves at my displeasure. It makes me respect them more, for all that they wasted time I don't have in abundance.

Poseidon, naturally, doesn't seem pleased to see me. He never is. If ever there was a man uncomfortable with the cloak of power that comes with a legacy title, it's this one. He doesn't play the games Olympus is known for, doesn't engage in any kind of drama, doesn't leave his shipyard more than he absolutely has to. It's convenient. He's never causing problems…or at least he never used to.

One day soon he and I are going to have to have a very frank conversation about the fact that he worked with my wife in the attempt to assassinate me. But not today. I have bigger fish to fry.

Poseidon is a massive white man with deep-red hair and beard, and the kind of body that looks like he tosses around kegs of beer for fun. His skin is a little paler than normal, no doubt from stress, making his freckles stand out in stark contrast. He's still wearing the same clothes he had on last night, all black, and his hair is wild from him obviously running his fingers through it. "Zeus. What are you doing here?"

I look from one of them to the other, finally settling on Pallas. "I think the more important question is what is *she* doing here." Pallas is the daughter of the late Triton, the oldest of seven. The youngest, Zuriel, slipped through the barrier some time ago and ran off to Carver City. That fucking city seems to be a magnet for wayward Olympians. Like my brother.

There's no use thinking about Hercules now. Focus on the task before you.

Pallas is a couple of years younger than me and beautiful in the way that all her sisters are. Triton had more wives than my father—which is saying something—and as a result, all seven of them look remarkably different. Honestly, it's a blessing they favor their mothers. Triton wasn't much to look at—or to be around—but he was useful, at least until he betrayed this city and lost his life as a result.

Pallas is short and petite, her long straight black hair pulled back from her delicate face. Her light-brown skin is smooth and perfect, no doubt with the help of both genetics and a horrendously expensive skincare routine. I've seen what my sisters consider reasonable when it comes to that sort of thing, but my wife doesn't seem to share the same fascination.

No. I'm not thinking about Hera right now.

Poseidon shifts, attempting to draw my attention away from Pallas. "No point in wasting time beating around the bush. After this conflict with Circe has seen its end, I'm stepping down and Pallas will ascend as the next Poseidon."

I blink. "What?" Surely I just heard him wrong. He may not have wanted it, but once people have titles, they don't give them up without a fight.

Except Eris did. She only held Aphrodite for a few months. Bearing the burden of Zeus was easier with her sharing the load. It's different with Helen as Ares. She wanted to become Ares to prove that she's more than a pretty face. She's done a damn good job of seeing her responsibilities fulfilled.

With Eris, we both understood the burden that comes with holding this kind of power. We both were trained from the time we were children to be able to bear that power. But, while Eris was willing to marry for the benefit of Olympus, she actually had the audacity to fall in love with her husband. She almost died in the wake of that mess, and the only thing she asked me while lying there in the hospital was to release her. It's not something she technically needed my permission for, but I gave it all the same.

I know what my father would say. That I'm a sentimental fool. Eris is a sharp tool and was willing to be used ruthlessly in the pursuit of stability for the city. If I'd pushed, she would have folded. It's what we were trained to do.

I couldn't do it. She never asked anything of me but this, and watching her find such unexpected happiness in her little polycule has been bittersweet in the extreme.

As a legacy title, I don't have that option. We don't step down. We cling to our power until death takes us. Except Poseidon isn't following the rules.

He doesn't shift nervously as I contemplate him. He's not even tapping his thigh in the way that he always does when stressed. He simply meets my gaze steadily. "I'm stepping down," he says almost gently. "I'm starting Pallas's training now to ensure a seamless transfer. She's more than capable of holding the title."

If there's even a title to hold at that point. I haven't forgotten about Hermes's little visit, or the way she seems to want the downfall of Olympus just as much as Circe does, admittedly in a slightly less murderous fashion. "But why?"

Poseidon glances at Pallas and Orion. "Could you give us a minute?"

They don't quite bolt out of the room, but they move with great efficiency. And then it's just Poseidon and me. I don't like what I see on his face. He's always been shit at masking his expressions, and right now, he's looking at me with something akin to pity.

I turn away. "No Icarus tagging along? Did he finally wise up and run?"

"I asked him to stay." Poseidon hands over that piece of information with a frankness that sets my teeth on edge. The man hasn't learned to lie in all the time I've known him, and the secondhand embarrassment is almost too much to bear. I would never expose myself like that to someone who might as well be an enemy. I don't wish him harm, but he should know there's no guarantee I won't use any and all information against him. He should act as if I'm a threat in order to protect himself.

I make myself turn back to face him. If he can be brave enough to hold a frank conversation, then I suppose I can meet him halfway. "Why? It was clear that he loved you, and you him."

"Yes," Poseidon says simply. "But neither of us are our own people right now. I have responsibilities to Olympus, to my people, and Icarus has responsibilities to his. When this is over, I'll go to him."

As simple as that. Something strange and insidious takes root in my chest. What would it be like to love someone that much? To be willing to walk away from the things we've been taught to want more than anything? People lie, cheat, steal, and murder to claim one of the Thirteen titles of Olympus.

Poseidon is going to set his down for the sake of love? I'm…jealous.

Apparently my silence speaks for itself, because he continues. "Triton might have kept his daughters sheltered to a criminal degree, but Pallas is smart—and kind and fair. It will take her a little bit of time to understand exactly what she needs to do to be Poseidon, but I'll be there with her until she's steady on her feet."

In the end, there's not really much say, is there? This isn't my choice, no matter how little I like it. It's his. "Okay."

"Okay?" He repeats it almost as a question but then gives himself a shake. "I've received the bare-bones update from Athena and Ares, but is there any additional news?"

I'm pathetically grateful to be back on solid ground once more, even if that solid ground is currently a shit show. "Circe has us on a wild-goose chase. There have been half a dozen sightings of her around town, but every time we rush out to apprehend her, it's either a mistaken identity or she disappears like a ghost. We're wasting time and resources, which is no doubt exactly what she wants, but I don't know what the fuck else to do." I hate admitting inadequacy, but there's no one here to witness it except Poseidon himself.

He scratches at his beard. "I told Demeter to keep an eye on the mountains bordering the countryside."

My head jerks up so fast that my neck twinges. "What did you say?"

"It's all patterns, isn't it?" He motions vaguely with his big hand. "Every step of the way, Circe is showing us something over here"—he wiggles his fingers—"while she's doing something over here that furthers her goals." His other hand comes from behind his back, where it has been hidden previously. "She did it with Minos and his party and the assassination clause, sowing discord in the city."

The pieces click together faster and faster. "And in the lower city, with Hades. She had him chasing his tail while she was filtering people into the city and setting up the blockade."

"The blockade was a distraction, too."

Maybe, maybe not. There's no way she could have

known about Icarus's blackmail, or that it would work. She was betting on the Thirteen not being able to unify to vote and attack her—a bet she would have won if not for the temporary coup. *We* weren't sure until we were on the water that Icarus's former patrons would obey his order to abandon Circe, sending four of the five ships back to Aeaea. There's no way *Circe* could have known. If we hadn't acted, I suspect those ships would have actually taken action at some point.

But Poseidon is right. Circe has hedged her bets from the beginning. She did it with the ships, too. Otherwise she would have been aboard when we attacked. Or the ships would have used their weapons on the city the moment they had a chance. Instead, they sat out in the water, igniting terror and confusion and cutting off our trade. Even so...the mountain pass? "There's no way through the mountains."

"Isn't there?" Poseidon shrugs. "Maybe that's the truth. Or maybe we just assumed it was the truth because the barrier made us complacent. All our maps of those mountains predate the founding of the city and the formation of the barrier. There might be passes that have changed in the intervening time. That kind of thing wouldn't necessarily be visible by satellite. We'd never know."

Circe shouldn't know, either, but there's no space for *shouldn't* when it comes to that woman. I nod slowly. "I'll talk to Ares and have her divert some of her people to scour the foothills that make up the perimeter around the civilian encampment. There's no guarantee that we'll find a pass even if it exists, but at least we won't be caught flat-footed if there's an attack from that position." Even as I say it, it feels *right*.

Of course Circe would attack from where we least expect it. Of course she would have me chasing my tail in the city proper while she sinks her claws into the civilians in the countryside—where we evacuated them. Again. "Fuck." I rub my hands over my face. "Do we bring them back to the city?"

"I don't know." Poseidon looks just as agonized as I do. "There don't seem to be any good choices."

"Truer words, Poseidon, truer fucking words."

ZEUS

MY WIFE DOESN'T MAKE IT HOME IN TIME FOR dinner. I should have expected that. Not just because of how tumultuous our relationship is, but because of everything that happened today. My losing control in the bar. The fucking video being released not an hour later. Everything.

I should be more understanding. If I were a better man, I would be. But as the minutes tick by into hours, all I can hear is Atalanta's voice in my ear.

Do you know where your wife is?

Foolish of me to think she would come to *me* for comfort. She hates me. She's told me so often enough to have it inscribed on my bones. The only time she lets down her mask is when she's orgasming, and even then it's done in the dark. If she's looking for comfort, she'll have gone to her mother, her sisters, or…her lover?

That thought of her in the arms of another drives me out of my fucking mind. Not enough to lose control, though. The only time she actually manages to get under my skin so effectively is when she's in the room with me. So I don't dump the entire dinner that I ordered catered—her favorite—in the trash. I meticulously pack it away and store it in the fridge. Even as I go through the motions, I can hear my father's mocking laughter in the back of my mind. Telling me I'm a fool, a cuckold, a little bitch. Why bother with this small act of kindness when she's in someone else's bed?

I don't have an answer now. I don't think I ever will. This marriage is nothing more than a sham, no matter what high hopes I harbored in my deepest, darkest heart. Shattered now. And I have no one to blame but myself.

I'm so focused on my mental spiraling that I almost miss the sound of the door opening. My body acts before my brain has a chance to decide what avenue of approach I should take. There's no space for strategy with my emotions riding me so hard.

The sensation only gets worse when I stride through the doorway and find my wife shrugging out of her coat, looking deliciously rumpled. Even as I tell myself not to, I search for signs of someone else's touch. I am not sure if I don't find any because there's none to find, or because there's still evidence of my hands on her, my mouth against her skin.

She doesn't jump when she sees me, but there's resignation

in the slump of her shoulders that hits me right in my fucking heart. "Oh. You're home."

"I told you to be here for dinner. That was hours ago."

I don't know what the fuck I'm doing. Why am I accusing her when I should be asking her how she's doing? My mouth opens, and more poison spills out despite how tumultuous I feel. "Or did you really go to your lover?"

Her brows slam down and there she is, my vicious, furious wife. I shouldn't crave this side of her the way I do, but it's familiar territory. If I'm shit at comfort, at least I know how to draw her into a fight.

"You are unbelievable." She stalks toward me, tossing her coat to the side. "Here's a hint, Husband. If you actually want information, maybe start with questions instead of accusations."

"Fine." Gods, I can't stop myself even as a small part of me is yelling to slam on the brakes. It's too late. It was too late from the moment she accepted my proposal. "Did you go straight from coming all over my cock to fucking Ixion?"

Hera is magnificent in her fury. She glares up at me, her hazel eyes sparking the way I'm addicted to. Even her sneer is perfection. "I don't know why you're so surprised. After that little show we put on, all of Olympus knows I'm not satisfied."

She's so close that one harsh breath could bring us chest to chest. I grab her hips and eliminate the distance between us, wishing I could eliminate the emotional distance as well. It will never happen, but at least I have the physical. "Lie to yourself if you must, but don't fucking lie to me. I know what you look like when you come."

"Do you?" She tilts her head and slides her hands up my chest, leaning close enough to speak directly into my ear. "Or am I just very, very good at faking it?"

One moment I'm standing here, trying to process the audacity of her lie, and the next I have her pressed against the wall. Damn it, no. It's not supposed to be like this. I start to pull away, but she hooks the back of my neck, holding me close.

I shake my head, hard. "Hera—Callisto—hold on. Wait. This isn't how I wanted this to go."

Her sad smile strikes right to the very heart of me. "We don't know how to be anything else but this." Her nails prick my skin. "Take it out on me—and I'll do the same to you."

I dig my fingers into her hips, as if that contact would be enough to ground me instead of tossing me right off the edge of reason. "The video. I had no idea—"

"I know." That simple statement goes so far and yet nowhere near far enough.

I drop my head to press my forehead to hers. "Are you okay?"

"No. Not by a long shot." She slides her free hand back down my chest to hook in the band of my pants. "But having an uncomfortable, awkward conversation isn't going to make me feel better. I can't bear to think anymore. I might lose what's left of my mind."

I don't know if she means to hurt me with that statement, but it *does* hurt. How can it not when it highlights my inadequacy? I will never have the right words to make the people I care about feel better. Not my sisters, sure as fuck not my wife. No doubt the video spun her out as much as it did me, and instead of allowing me to talk it through with her, all she wants is a good fuck.

So be it.

But first, there's one thing I have to know. I hate myself for the vulnerability exposed by my even putting my worry into words. "Hera. Callisto. Wife." I close my eyes and inhale deeply. "Is there a lover? Is it Ixion?"

"Do you have a lover? Maybe several? I see the way Ganymede watches you. Not to mention all the little Hera hopefuls, wishing you'll follow in your father's footsteps and shove me down a flight of stairs so they can step over my still-warm body to accept your ring."

Something in my chest flutters in a truly worrisome way. I lean back just enough to catch her gaze. "Are you jealous?"

"How could I possibly be jealous?" She almost pulls off a flat tone, but there's a thread of something else in her words. Something I resonate with. "I don't even like you."

"Right. How could I forget?" I focus on gentling my grip and sliding my hands down to cup her round ass. "Answer my question. Then I'll answer yours."

The moment stretches out between us, poised with the possibility of changing everything. I've never lied to her, but that doesn't mean I've been perfectly honest, either. I haven't touched anyone from the moment I accepted her deal—and I won't as long as I wear her ring on my finger—but I understand the reputation that goes hand in hand with my title. Philanderer. Murderer. Monster. Why wouldn't she assume the worst? It's not as if we've had a single honest conversation in the duration of our marriage.

I see the exact moment she decides to cut the fragile peace between us. Her smile goes sly even as her gaze goes distant. "Why stop at one lover, Husband? It takes so many to keep me fulfilled."

The most fucked-up thing? I don't know for sure if she's lying. I want to believe she is, that she just wants to get under my skin and strike to the very heart of me. But I'm not certain. And because I'm not certain, the monstrous part of me that I fight so hard to keep under wraps rises to the surface with a roar shaking me to my bones.

I release her hip to grip her jaw in a way designed to make her knees buckle. Because no matter what the fuck she's doing when she's not with me—or *who* she's doing—she can't deny the moments we share in the dark are real.

"I know the feeling. I'm insatiable. How could one person possibly fulfill *my* needs?"

"I hate you," she whispers.

"We are in perfect agreement there," I lie. Things would be so much easier if I actually loathed her, if I didn't crave an intimacy we've never managed to share. Not that we've tried.

She slides her other hand down to the band of my pants and undoes my belt in a quick, practiced move. "You're lucky I don't shove you out a fucking window."

Suddenly, I'm so sick of this shit. I release her and step back. She stumbles a little, and it takes everything I have not to reach out to catch her. Hera rights herself before I have a chance to, which is perfectly on brand. She doesn't need me. She never has. Maybe it's not fair to want to be needed by her, but I'm not feeling particularly fucking fair right now.

I stalk to our living room, leaving her to reluctantly shadow my steps. None of the massive windows that overlook the city open, but the door out to the balcony does. I shove it wide and step out. It's a little after mid-October, but the wind reeks of winter, harsh and cutting and so cold that it makes my face prickle.

I turn around as Hera steps through the door and hold my arms out wide. "Here you go. One good shove and your Zeus problem is no more. That's what you want, isn't it? That's why you've gone through the trouble to coerce Poseidon into treachery, to work with Ariadne and the Minotaur to bring down Dodona Tower, no matter what other people might have been hurt in the process."

"No one else was going to be hurt," she snaps. The wind whips her hair around her face, almost as if its embodying her anger. "I made sure of that, even if the plan didn't end up working out."

It's fucked that her finally admitting her treachery is a strange sort of comfort. I take a step back until the railing digs into my ass. "Well, now you can be *truly* sure of it. It's late. No one will be walking down the sidewalk. If you want me dead, then have the fucking decency to do it yourself." To topple me from the height of the tower I'm supposed to rule…just like my father.

For the first time in our marriage, my wife actually looks lost. She blinks those big eyes at me, her beauty so sharp it takes my breath away. It's unforgivable that, even now, I want her so desperately I can barely think past it.

"Zeus…"

"No, you don't get to call me by that title. You don't get to pretend Zeus is all I am. Say my name, Wife. Don't be a coward now."

Instead of rising to the gauntlet I've thrown, her lower lip quivers. It's the tiniest movement, quickly quelled, but I see it—and she knows I see it. "I should do it." She crosses to me and fists the front of my shirt. "There are so many people in this fucked-up city who want you dead, me first among them. You're a fool to give me this opportunity."

I am. I can't pretend otherwise. And yet I don't move, waiting to see what she'll do. Even as her grip tightens on me, the pressure of her knuckles against my chest growing, I'm not entirely certain if I'm going to let her shove me over the railing or not.

But she doesn't do it. She stares up into my face and shakes her head slowly. "I hate you."

"I know." The two words come out almost as an apology. They certainly feel like one.

Even so, I don't expect her to go onto her toes and slam her mouth to mine. The wind screams around us, but I stop feeling the cold the moment her tongue slides into my mouth. This means something, though I can't think clearly enough to figure out what. A reprieve, possibly. It's certainly not proof that Callisto doesn't have the audacity to commit murder. We both know she has audacity in abundance.

I break the kiss with a low gasp. "Say yes, Wife."

For once, she doesn't fuck around. She's already backing up, tugging me with her. "Yes. Now. Hurry."

I sweep her into my arms and carry her into the relative warmth and safety of our home.

HERA

TODAY IT FEELS LIKE THE WORLD HAS SPUN AROUND me, faster and faster, until there's no safe space. Not my sisters, not my mother, not the city I've only recently claimed as mine. Not until I stepped through the door of *this* penthouse and found *this* man waiting for me. Poison words, each harsher than the next, and yet it's familiar and…yes, *safe*.

The day I stop lying to my husband is the day I lose this safe space.

Even knowing that, I allow my head to rest on his shoulder as he carries me through the living room and down the hall to the bedroom we share. His pulse beats steadily despite the dramatics on the balcony.

I almost pushed him.

There was a split second there, a moment of pure desperation, when I actually started to move forward, to shove him over the railing. A perfect ending to mirror his father's death: a sad accident, or maybe a desperate personal choice. Except I couldn't do it. All these months of plotting, of lining up events to kill him...for nothing.

Zeus steps into our bedroom and kicks the door shut behind him. "Callisto."

I never should have exposed this particular weakness. The only people who still call me Callisto are my sisters. Not even my mother does, too pleased with my ascension to Hera. Giving this intimacy to *him*? Unthinkable.

I want him to say my name again. Again and again and again.

I wriggle until he sets me on my feet and then plant my hands on his chest, walking him back toward the bed. If he's kind to me now, I don't know if I'll ever reclaim the coldness I need to get through this greater conflict. There needs to be ice in my veins to protect my family. "Take off your clothes."

For a moment, I think he might argue, might try to claim control again, but some decision is made in my favor behind those heated blue eyes. He holds my gaze as he unbuttons his shirt and shrugs it off. His belt whisks through the loops with a sound that makes my thighs shake. His pants are next, sliding down muscular thighs and then kicked away. I realize my mistake too late.

The lights are still on.

We've only had sex like this twice—once on our wedding

night and once earlier today—and both affected me too deeply, even with my eyes closed. Worse now, because there are no nerves to distract me from the sheer beauty of his naked body.

Or from the scars.

I cross to him and press my hand to the line of nearly perfect circles running from his stomach up to the center of his chest. Cigarette burns. I've seen the like in the orphanage, though these are so old, they're nearly clear and shiny, barely raised at all. I lift my gaze to Zeus's—except he's not Zeus in this moment, is he?

He's Perseus.

There's no need to ask who did this. Only one person would dare touch one of the Kasios family, let alone the heir. The king of monsters, the one who harmed Circe and so many others, the one who sent my sister running into the arms of Hades, the one who imprinted his violence and ambition into the blood and bones of every single one of his children.

If I trusted Perseus enough to open the door to my heart even a sliver, I would ask him about his childhood. I would confess that there's no lover in my bed, secret or otherwise, and there hasn't been since I agreed to marry him. I would tell him all the fucked-up shit that happened today. Even if he isn't one to comfort, I have no doubt he'd destroy both Hermes and Circe…if he could find them.

It's too late. There's no hope for us. If I can't bring myself to shove him off a building, I'm still not going to step between him and the bullet coming for him, regardless of who holds the gun. Hermes or Circe, the end result is the same.

I don't ask him about the scars. I pretend not to notice the raw look on his face. Instead, I walk to the light switch and flick it off.

Guilt threatens to rise in the new blanket of shadows covering us, in the way he exhales so carefully. I cross back to him and press my hands to his chest again, this time to push him down onto the bed. The moonlight coming through the window is too bright, showing the long lines of his body as he props himself on his elbows to watch me undress.

There's no telling how much detail he can see, but I make quick work of my clothing and straddle his hips. "I want it hard and fast." No point in pretending I don't need this. Truth be told, there hasn't been a reason to pretend I'm going through the motions for a long time, but I'll die before I admit it.

"No."

The simple word is the only warning I get before he rolls us, pinning me easily in my shock. Zeus never tells me no. Not when it comes to sex. "What?"

"It's a simple word, Callisto." Gone is the sharp bite of his words, replaced by something deep and sensual. It scares me. Not because I'm afraid of what he might do to me, but because it's never been like this. We've always been two bodies meeting in pleasure, colliding in orgasms, wrestling for dominance. It's harsh and demanding and so much pleasure that, at times, I feel like I might die of it. Even earlier today in the bar, there was no softness, only carefully honed cruelty.

I don't know what to do with soft. It threatens to buckle things inside me that I need to stay strong. I say the only thing I can, the only thing that I *know* hurts him. "I hate you."

"I know." He catches my hands and presses them on either side of my head. "You might need hard and fast, but *I* need to feel you come apart on my tongue."

I open my mouth to argue…I think…but nothing comes out except, "Okay."

Perseus—because, damn it, this is *Perseus*, not Zeus—kisses me and releases my hands. I barely have time to register the freedom before he drags his mouth down my sternum and over my stomach. He pauses and I have a moment of pure panic wondering if he notices the faint curve that wasn't there a few weeks ago. It's not enough to scream *pregnant*, but my clothes aren't fitting properly anymore, and Perseus is the only one who's ever this close to me.

But he doesn't sit up and accuse me of hiding a pregnancy from him. He keeps descending to push my thighs wide, baring me completely. There's no space for shyness, not that he gives me the opportunity to even consider experiencing it. Not when his mouth immediately covers me, his tongue parting my folds to roll against my clit. We fucked earlier today and I came multiple times. I shouldn't be hovering on the edge because of a single lick.

Then he does it again.

"Fuck," I breathe. I dig my hands into his hair, not trying to guide him, just holding on and letting him take care of me. Because even as I tell myself I'm imagining things, that's what this feels like. It's not cold, it's not frenzy. It's…care?

That doesn't make any sense, but there's no space to think. He presses one finger and then two into me, a slow finger fuck as if he intends to go all night. Every curl drags his touch over my G-spot, coiling my pleasure tighter.

I love this moment during fucking. Every touch is perfect. My need is so large that my skin may split from it. Time ceases to have meaning. When I feel like this, it's almost as if we could keep going forever. It feels like *magic*.

I've only ever experienced it with him.

Which isn't to say I've never had good sex before. My first girlfriend after moving to the city was all frenzy in the bedroom and we could go for hours before exhaustion finally set in. That's not what *this* is. From the very beginning, Perseus has set out with a terrifying intent to know my body. There's no wasted movement, no fumbling around in enthusiasm. There's only perfection.

He presses his thumb and ring finger to either side of my

folds, creating pressure with each stroke, pressure he matches with his tongue. "Oh fuck." I'm so close, I'm shaking, my body feeling like it belongs to someone else...like it belongs to *him*. "Perseus, *please*."

He freezes. "Say it again." The words are hot against my flesh. "Now."

Three strokes and there's nothing left of my resistance. My back bows, my orgasm cresting hard enough to hurt in the best way possible. "*Perseus*."

"That's right, Wife." He doesn't pick up his pace, but his tone has gone ragged in a way I've never heard before. "You come so perfectly."

A second orgasm draws a scream from my lips. Or maybe it's a continuation of the first. I don't know. I can't *think*. It's glorious.

This time, when he moves up my body to settle between my thighs, there's no breath left to tell him I hate him. I have no words at all—except one. "Perseus." I wrap my legs around his hips, pulling him closer. "*Perseus*."

His exhale is a fragile, trembling thing, but there's no hesitation as he guides his cock into me. He's never anything other than perfectly possessed. Tonight is no different. He moves into me slowly, thoroughly, using every bit of his knowledge with the clear intent to drive me to new peaks.

He fucks every thought out of my head, every worry, every fear. It will all be there in the morning, waiting to pounce the moment I open my eyes. But right now, in the dark, tasting myself on his lips, there's nothing but *us*.

"There you go, Callisto." He kisses my neck, wedges his arms beneath my body to hold me to him as if even the miniscule space between us is too much. I know better than to believe this to mean anything at all, but I'm too scattered by pleasure to remember why. I shatter into a million pieces again and again, and every time, he's right there to gather each one and hold them safe in my moment of perfect weakness. "I've got you, Wife. I..." His strokes lose their steady rhythm.

Even this is somehow perfect, too. I hold him closer as he follows me over the edge, as he grinds into me, as he fills me. His heart pounds against his chest—against *my* chest where it presses to him—in the exact frantic rhythm as mine. I can't think properly, but I make no effort to try as I cling to my husband. I've been adrift, will be adrift again, but in this moment, he's the only solid thing that exists.

As if he's in agreement, he holds me closer instead of moving away and presses a gentle kiss to my temple. "Whatever it is, it can wait until morning."

What can wait until morning? I'm barely able to think. I don't remember closing my eyes, but they feel fused shut. I nod slowly. "Okay. Until morning."

He eases to the side, but only enough to settle on the mattress next to me. I refuse to feel grateful that he doesn't go far…but I am. Especially when he pulls me into the cradle of his body and wraps his strong arms around me. My muscles and bones weigh a thousand pounds. Even if I wanted to, I can't dredge up the effort to climb out of our bed and leave him.

I…don't want to.

He kisses the nape of my neck. "Sleep, Wife. I'm here. You're safe."

Fool that I am, I actually believe him.

16

ZEUS

MY WIFE FALLS INTO A RESTLESS SLEEP WITHIN MINutes. Unconsciousness eludes me, though. It often does these days. Sleep is a vital part of maintenance to ensure your brain works properly to anticipate your enemies and see the knives threatening before they have a chance to slide between your ribs. A contradiction to my father's training to go without sleep, but my father was a study in contradictions. Once he was satisfied that I could function without sleep for the approved amount of time, he moved on. I didn't. Insomnia became a fact of life, something to endure like I endured so many other little torments.

I managed to hide my late-night wanderings and inability to sleep from my sisters, but Hercules caught me on more than one occasion. He never said anything—that's not how he operates—but we would share a moment of perfect understanding before we'd go on our separate ways. Fuck, I miss him. I hate him, too. Our father's love, if you want to call it that, is a burden we four were meant to share in equal parts, but Hercules didn't play the game. He walked away and never looked back. I'm so jealous I can barely see straight.

I roll onto my side and prop my head in my hand. Hera—Callisto—lies on her back, one arm thrown carelessly wide and the other resting lightly on her stomach. Her stomach that feels different than it has previously.

I reach out with a shaking hand and hover it a bare inch above the gently rounded curve. It's not much; I wouldn't have noticed it at all if we didn't share a bed so regularly, but there's no denying its presence. In the light of the full moon, I finally allow myself to study the other changes I've been too distracted to notice. Those marks on her cheekbones—broken blood vessels. I would've registered them earlier if I was paying closer attention instead of letting my anger guide me. She wears makeup to cover the marks during the day, but I've caught sight of them and wondered. Her breasts are larger, too, her nipples several shades darker.

She's...pregnant.

I don't make a conscious decision to move, but I find myself outside the bedroom and stalking down the hall before my brain fully catches up to my body. Surely I'm wrong. She would've said something if she was actually pregnant.

Except, this is Callisto. Of course she wouldn't have said anything. She wants me dead, and if she's carrying the next Zeus, she can remove me with little consequence. Suddenly it all makes sense. Why she decided to move now instead of months ago.

I've been such a fucking fool.

I still am, because I can't stop the bright kernel of something light and hopeful taking up residence in the base of my throat…but it only lasts a moment before sheer terror snuffs the feeling out. I never intended to let my wife murder me, but if she doesn't, if I live, if we annihilate Circe?

She'll have the baby.

I'll become a father.

I don't know how to *be* a father. Or at least not a good one. I can barely handle being Zeus, and one could argue I'm failing at that spectacularly. But to take on a new role, one where the stakes are so much higher…

I lose time again. One moment I'm standing in the hallway, feeling like an abyss has opened up beneath my feet, ready to send me hurtling into an eternal darkness. The next, I'm out on the balcony again, my phone in my hands.

I dial the memorized number by rote, but even as I lift my phone to my ear, I don't actually expect him to answer. He hasn't in a very long time. Whether that's because I don't call often or because he got tired of arguing with me about whether he should come back to Olympus now that our father's dead... Well, I know the answer to that, don't I? And it's late. Any respectable person will be tucked into their bed with their two lovers, not answering their phone.

When the ringing clicks over to voicemail, I don't think. I just dial him again. I don't know what the fuck I'm doing, but I need my brother right now. He's the only one who will understand.

He picks up the third time I call. "Damn it, Perseus, I told you I want nothing to do with your war or whatever the fuck you have going on right now." He never calls me Zeus. I love him all the more for his rejection of anything related to the title. "I'm busy and—"

"My wife is pregnant." My wife is *pregnant*. My knees buckle and I sink onto the metal chair on the balcony. This is real. This is happening.

The words hang between us. Of anyone, Hercules understands what I'm feeling right now. He never wanted children. Eris doesn't, either. I think Helen does, but she's always been the healthiest of the four of us, the one who refused to bend or break under our father's abuse. She'll be a particularly vicious mother, but only to those who threaten her children. But me? The heir, the one molded in our father's image? How can I be anything other than the monster *he* created?

My brother exhales slowly. "Congratulations?"

"You don't really mean that."

"Yeah, Perseus, I do. I know you want kids—and not

just because you are a good, obedient Zeus who needs to breed heirs." He pauses, and when he speaks again, his voice has lost some of the venom. "Why are you calling to tell *me* about this?"

That's the question, isn't it? "I don't know. She hasn't told me. I don't know if she's ever going to, at least until she can't hide it any longer. It's not like we have a happy fucking marriage." Children were always going to be part of it, though. It was in the contract we both signed before getting married. Zeus needs heirs, and Demeter intends for her daughter to be the mother of those heirs. The better to link her bloodline with the rulers of Olympus. But that's Demeter's goal, not necessarily Callisto's. "I..."

Hercules, damn him, doesn't cut in and offer me a reprieve. He simply waits, allowing me to fight my way through the fear thickening my throat until I can barely breathe past it. "Our father was a monster."

"Yes."

Each word feels like it's dragged from somewhere deep, bloodying me in the process. "He...abused us."

"Yes," he says simply.

That simple acceptance is like a dam breaking inside me. Words pour forth, with only the night and my brother's disembodied voice to witness. "I don't know how to do this. The only fucking role model we had was an abusive, narcissistic monster. Mother died. We barely met Circe before she was gone, and Lamia didn't last much longer. How the fuck am I supposed to be a father? I don't know what to do." I slump back in my chair, my bones feeling brittle and in danger of shattering. "And she's no better. Her mother loves her and her sisters, but Demeter's a goddamn monster, too. She didn't hesitate to barter her daughters for more power. I'm nearly certain she's killed as many of her husbands as our father killed wives. What kind of parents will we be?"

Hercules is silent for several long beats. Finally, he says, "The kind of parents you want to be."

A rough sound escapes me. It's not quite a laugh, far too bitter and broken. "It's not that simple."

"I think it is." There's the faint echoing sound of footsteps. My brother is pacing as he talks to me. "I never had much desire for children, at least not of my own, but there are a lot of parents around here. Our situation may have been somewhat unique because of the way Olympus is structured, but the sad fact is that abusive parents are a dime a dozen. We don't have the market cornered on that experience. And you know what? It doesn't matter. The people I know might have some shit to unpack, same as we do, but they're putting in the work to ensure their children have a better life than they did. A safe life. A healthy life with loving parents who protect instead of harm. You can do the same."

He makes it sound so easy, but it's not fair to be mad. I just dumped a whole boatload of trauma onto his shoulders, and he's handling it admirably. Now is the time to hang up, to release him from this awkward conversation, but I can't quite make myself do it. "I don't even know where to start."

"This might be shocking, but I suggest you start by talking to your wife." Hercules chuckles a little. "She could surprise you."

"Maybe I'll do that." I don't tell him that a mere hour ago I was on this very balcony, not entirely certain if my wife was going to push me off it or not. My brother wouldn't understand, for all that he has a nontraditional relationship with the man who used to be called Hades and his consort, Megaera. Instead, I take a deep breath and force some brittle charm into my tone. "How are things with you?"

For a moment, I think he won't allow me to change the subject, but finally he sighs again. "They're good. Really good." He goes on to talk about the various changes they're making to the kink club he works in, gossiping easily about the various parents in question he mentioned earlier. They're just names to me, and yet I allow my brother's voice to soothe some of the ragged edges the night has exposed. I know he's doing it on purpose, just like he's always done.

Roughly thirty minutes later, Hercules's voice trails off. "Go back to bed, Perseus. Things will be simpler in the morning."

I'm not so certain, but I understand that this conversation is over. "Thank you. For picking up. For everything."

"You're going to be okay. The only person who expects perfection is you. Try to loosen up."

The problem is that if I loosen up, people die. More people. That's not my little brother's problem. He's got his own life to live and he's made his boundary incredibly clear. He's never coming back to Olympus, and so Olympian problems and politics and bullshit are no longer his business. Again, jealousy pricks me, hard enough to draw blood. What would it be like to walk away from all this? The very idea is inconceivable.

Who am I if I'm not Zeus?

I don't have an answer to that question. I'm terrified of what it would mean to set aside the title I've spent my entire life preparing for. I would be *no one*. No goals, no power, no fucking personality. And no wife.

Callisto only married me because of the influence my title holds—and my promise to use that influence to protect her family. She never wanted *me*, Perseus, the man. And I barely knew her, her reputation speaking more than the woman herself. I think we'd had maybe one conversation in all the time she's lived in the city proper.

Without my title, I'm nothing. I've experienced what *nothing* feels like at my father's hands, and I will never allow it to happen again. No matter what plans Circe or

Hermes or any of the others attempt to play out, one thing remains true.

When all the dust is settled and the bodies are buried, I will be Zeus.

Or I'll be dead.

HERA

I WAKE ALONE. I SHOULD HAVE EXPECTED IT. I *DID* expect it. Zeus and I may share our nights, but we work on vastly different schedules. My husband is an early riser; he's usually gone well before I roll out of bed in the morning. Especially in the last couple months. Yesterday was a pointed exception—in so many ways. I stretch slowly, registering all the little aches and pains in my body.

I am absolutely not bothered by his absence. Not in the least. I'm the one who shut off the light last night, who turned away from the intimacy he offered. It makes no sense to crave his presence like a comfortable blanket I want to wrap around myself. Fighting with him is normal enough to ease my stress, that's all. Or maybe the pregnancy hormones are fucking with my head.

I look at the time and curse. It's later than I expected—much later. I'm supposed to be meeting Persephone in less than an hour, and she's not one to wait if she thinks I'm fucking around. The fact that I got her to agree to this meeting at all is a testament of how much she cares for me.

And I'm going to use that care to manipulate her.

I launch out of bed and hurry to the closet, where I pull on three different pairs of pants before cursing and tossing them in the corner. None of them fit. There's no time for this shit. I finally land on a slightly loose sheath dress that my stomach still presses against too prominently, but once I throw a sweater over the top, it's not too bad. It's hardly the visual perfection I've been aiming for since taking over Hera, but desperate times call for desperate measures. There's been no opportunity to expand my closet.

No, that's not actually true. All I'd have to do is request some clothing from one of the many assistants I keep pretending I don't have. The problem is that making the request opens the door to commentary on my body, to speculation—and *that* I cannot have. Not until I'm ready. I could go shopping myself, of course, but I've been hesitant to do so. It's almost as if buying new clothing means admitting to myself that I actually *am* pregnant.

There's no accounting for how confused I am about my feelings on this entire situation.

Boots are next, my favorites paired with thick socks. I yank my hair back into a slick ponytail and pause to look at myself in the mirror. I'm a fucking mess. The hollows beneath my eyes seem larger than they were yesterday despite getting a full night's sleep for once. The broken blood vessels in my cheeks are so prominent they make me uncomfortable. But there's no fucking time to go through the necessary process to cover them with makeup.

I grab my purse and phone as I head out the door. It's only when I reach the parking garage that I realize I didn't tell Ixion about this particular excursion. I almost pause to call him, but that means losing more time than I can afford. Instead, I snag the keys from the bottom of my purse and click the unlock button until I can figure out which of the seemingly countless nondescript black SUVs filling the parking spots is mine. The third from the end beeps in response, answering that question.

I haven't driven in a very long time. It feels strange to climb into the driver's seat. Strange…and kind of freeing at the same time. I grip the wheel and take several deep breaths that do nothing to soothe me. "Okay, one minute to think about it. That's all I get. Then I have to get my game face on."

Another long, slow breath. "Last night was a shit show." Saying it aloud into the stillness of the car makes everything so much more real.

I don't know how to feel about the jagged ways Perseus and I cut each other. It should mean we're perfectly incompatible, but the worst part is that I think we could be a solid match if we got out of our own way. I hate even considering that, because it means that…maybe I don't hate him at all. Something changed yesterday. If I were more courageous, more fearless, I would have embraced that change instead of running from it.

But I did run from it. I take another deep breath. It's a little silly to sit here talking to myself, but with my words settling into the space around me, I can almost imagine I'm talking to one of my sisters. "I deal in facts, not fantasies and not dreams. I can't know if something changed for him, so I have to continue to operate as if it hasn't." That's the easy part. The bit that's not easy, that I can't even bring myself to voice… Things *did* change for me.

Not knowing where his head is at…it wasn't the wrong call to flip off the lights and turn away from the intimacy we might have been able to achieve. Cowardly, yes, but we've made our beds. It's too late to try to change his mind now.

My husband is going to die. Circe may be willing to let my family—and even Hades—walk away from Olympus, but there's no possibility she'll extend the same offer to Zeus. He's not the man who hurt her, but he's part of the institution responsible for the harm she experienced. Zeus has to fall for Olympus to fall, and she's too smart not to know that.

My stomach lurches, and I barely scramble out of the car in time to dry heave onto the dirty pavement. I don't care if he dies. I *can't* care if he dies. I already have the lives of my sisters and mother—and their fucking partners—sitting on my shoulders. One more person will break me. I can't save him, and even if I could, I wouldn't. I can't weigh my husband's life against my family's. There's no scenario where that comes out in his favor.

No, the path is permanent and set beneath my feet. There's no space for regrets or dreams. I have to keep moving.

I drag myself back into the driver's seat and muscle through my nausea to back out of the parking spot and leave the garage. The spot where Persephone and I are supposed to meet is a little rocky spot just south of Juniper Bridge. I'm not even certain it can be called a beach. It looks more like a broken-up slab of concrete. It's nothing like the beach on the lake in the foothills where we spent so much time in our youth. Perfect sand, perfect temperature, perfect childhood.

The wind is cutting enough to make me wish I grabbed one of my longer coats, but it's too late to worry about being cold now. Even in the late morning, the fog swirls heavily along the surface of the river and up onto the banks, creating a gloomy and eerie atmosphere. It's thick enough for anyone to be hiding just out of sight, watching. My skin prickles and I wrap my arms tight around myself.

Persephone, when she arrives, does so with all the dramatics of the queen of the lower city. It makes me smile despite myself to watch the small boat cut through the fog, my sister standing at its prow, straight and confident. She appears massively pregnant, for all that I'm technically further along than she is. Twins will do that. She's also not alone, which is about what I expected. I'm not certain how she convinced her husband not to attend, but she's flanked by Medusa and…Orpheus.

The boat crunches up against what passes for the beach, but I'm already moving. I grab Orpheus by the front of his shirt and drag him splashing into the shallows. I barely feel the icy river cutting through my boots and dress as I punch him in the face. "You motherfucker."

"Callisto!"

I punch him again, sending him staggering back into the water. It's satisfying to see a bruise already blossoming on his perfect fucking face. His brother, Apollo, is handsome, but Orpheus got all of the pretty genes of their Korean mother. She was a model once upon a time, and used that fame to leverage a place for herself in one of the legacy families. He got all of his petty bullshit from her, too. He broke my sister's heart, and even if Eurydice chose to forgive him, I have not.

Strong arms wrap around me, pinning my hands to my chest and hauling me out of the river. Medusa. She's a tall, muscular white woman with short blond hair and the kind of good nature that makes everyone around her smile. She's also one of Athena's former assassins, which means she's not to be fucked with. She carries me a few steps farther and sets me back on my feet. "That's enough of that, Hera."

Orpheus stumbles out of the water, his clothes plastered to his lean form. He's already shivering. A vicious burst of glee goes through me at knowing how he'll suffer the entire trip back to the lower city. It's not enough, it will never be enough, but at least it's a start.

Persephone props her hands on her hips and glares. "That wasn't necessary."

"I think you'll find that it was." Despite everything, I grin. "Don't lie and tell me you didn't want to do it, too."

Her lips twitch, but she stills the expression before it can take hold. "Orpheus is now a member of the lower city and, as such, I cannot allow you to continue to assault him. You got two punches in. Be satisfied with that."

Eurydice was distraught for *months* after the attack orchestrated by Zeus, I won't be satisfied until he's suffered just as much as my sister, but I recognize a losing battle when I see one. Persephone is just as stubborn as our mother, and just as unwilling to bend when she sets her sights on something. I'm still not entirely certain what Orpheus did to earn a stay of execution from *her*. It might have something to do with Eurydice taking him back and forming a triad with him and Charon.

I hold up my hands. "I'm satisfied. Are you, Orpheus?"

"Sure. Satisfied." His teeth chatter from the strength of his shivering.

"Oh, for fuck's sake." Persephone shrugs off her massive

cloak and holds it out. "Take off your shirt and put this on before you freeze to death and I have to explain to Eurydice how I got one of her boyfriends killed."

He looks like he wants to argue but finally shakes his head and does as she commands. My sister only has to elicit a single shiver and Medusa releases me and moves to drape her coat over Persephone. This is fucking ridiculous.

I give Medusa a long look. "Do you need my sweater to complete the circle?"

She smiles, so fucking handsome that if I weren't Hera and she wasn't in a long-term relationship with Calypso, I might set out to seduce her. But even I know better than to cross Calypso.

Medusa shrugs. "The cold doesn't bother me much." She glances at Persephone. "As entertaining as this has been, clock is ticking."

"Right." My sister crosses to me and takes my hands.

It's Psyche all over again. There was a time, not long ago, when we all shared a house and a life. I never realize how much I miss those simpler days until I'm in the presence of one of my sisters again. It makes me shudder. It makes me *weak*. All I want is to go back to that safety, and it's not going to happen unless I can pull this off.

Persephone squeezes my hands. "What's going on? What was so important that we had to talk in person?"

I might have told Psyche about the parasite, but

Persephone is essentially queen of the lower city. If any of my sisters understand the stakes of what we're up against, it's her. And so, for the first fucking time in so long, I tell the truth. "Circe is in the city."

"I know. Hades said they weren't able to reach the ship before she escaped, and she made landing on the coast."

"No, Persephone. Circe is *in the fucking city*. She sought me out. She told me what's coming. I need you to listen to me right fucking now because our very lives depend on it."

Persephone goes still. "What do you mean?"

"I don't know if she gives a shit about the civilians, but she's gunning for the Thirteen. She wants to dismantle our entire power structure and she can't do that as long as the titles exist." There's no point in mentioning Hermes technically wants the same thing. Hermes isn't the one threatening my sisters and mother. "She's going to kill anyone who doesn't step down. That means Hades. That means them." I press my hand to my sister's stomach. "Unless we leave. If we walk now, she'll give everyone in the family a stay of execution."

Persephone searches my face with hazel eyes nearly identical to mine. It doesn't take her more than a moment to run through scenarios. My beautiful, cunning sister lifts her chin and I know I'm in trouble. "My husband has seen more sorrow than one person should ever bear. He will never step down, will never betray his people's trust—*our* people's trust.

I understand Circe was hurt by the establishment and by the last Zeus, but that doesn't give her license to pass that hurt onto the people I care about."

"Persephone—"

She shakes her head, cutting me off. "I know you hate Olympus. I know you hate the Thirteen and the legacy families and everything else about our lives since we came to the city proper. I understand, Callisto. I promise I do. But this is *my fucking family* we're talking about." She releases my hands and takes a step back. In this moment, I know that I've lost her. "Tell Circe that if she crosses the borders into the lower city, I'll cut her throat myself."

No. No, no, no. This can't be happening. I stumble after her, suddenly losing all grace and poise. "Persephone, you have to listen to me. She already has people in the lower city. They have you in their sights—literally. If you don't do what she wants—"

She shakes her head again. "*Think*, Callisto. It doesn't matter if Hades steps down, because he's a legacy title. Even if the Thirteen are gone, the people of the lower city will follow him, no matter what his name is, no matter *where* he is. Circe can't let him live. And she can't let me—us—live, either."

"But she promised…" Even as I say the words, I recognize what Persephone is saying as truth. But desperation keeps me going. "If he left the city, if you left the city, she wouldn't try to hurt us."

"No. That's my answer, Callisto." She starts to turn back toward the boat. "I'm here for you, and I love you. If you want to seek refuge in the lower city, I will fight to make it happen. But I will *not* ask my husband to give the lower city and his title. Circe doesn't have the market cornered on suffering, and it would do her well to remember that."

I open my mouth to keep arguing, but I never get a chance to. A boom sounds, so loud that it makes my ears ring, and pain blossoms in my shoulder. I blink and press my hand there, my brain not wanting to process what the red against my skin means.

I've…just been shot.

HERMES

HERA IS MORE RESOURCEFUL THAN I REALIZED. SHE also doesn't listen worth a damn. It would make me like her more under different circumstances, but we aren't in different circumstances. Hera, Persephone, Orpheus, Medusa, all standing out in the open without the slightest bit of concern about a sniper. I don't know what they're thinking.

"We're in a *war*, people," I murmur under my breath. I exhale slowly and pull the trigger at the same time. It would be the easiest thing in the world to riddle them with bullets and put an end to this once and for all. Hades would crumble without his beloved Persephone. Zeus wouldn't, but it would still fuck with his head something fierce to lose his Hera. Following in Daddy's footsteps and all that. Even killing Orpheus would serve me, because it would send Eurydice and Charon into a death spiral, which would further destabilize

Hades, Zeus, and Demeter in the process. A neat solution. There's only one problem.

I *like* them.

Well, maybe not Demeter, even if I appreciate her cunning. But the others? When Hades disposed of the last Zeus, finally realized his potential, and fell madly in love with his new bride? I cheered just as loudly as the rest of Olympus. He's what passes for a unicorn in this city—a genuinely good man.

But, no matter my personal feelings on the matter, I can't allow them to have this meeting and go their merry ways to fuck up my plans.

I shut down the frenzy of my thoughts and focus on my targets. Hera's got a wicked graze in her upper arm. I should have known such a small injury wouldn't be enough to take *her* down.

Persephone gets a careful bullet graze across her back. Thankfully, Medusa is pinning her in place so I don't have to worry about her jerking and endangering herself. Next is Orpheus, throwing himself forward to protect Hera. She's so furious, I can practically feel the energy of it from here, high up on an abandoned building's roof.

"You silly noble fool, *stay down*." I pull the trigger again, but I misjudge Orpheus's trajectory and take him in the upper chest instead of the arm. Shit. I think I broke his collarbone, but with surgery and a nice extended recovery, he should be fine. Probably. Most importantly, he's down, Persephone is down, and Hera is down. I fire off one last shot to skim Medusa's leg so she doesn't feel too guilty when the adrenaline wears off. She's a good bodyguard; she's just no match for *me*.

I pack up my rifle in automatic movements, dismantling it and strapping it into the case, which then slides into my bag. I'll clean it when I get to safety. In the meantime...

I trot down the stairs and through the dusty building, plastic sheets still covering the windows from where the company ran out of funding and, in a rare instance of nepotism failure, the owner's family didn't swoop in to pay for the construction to be completed. I dig out my phone and call the paramedics.

The operator answers immediately. "Hello, what is your emergency?"

"There was a shootout!" I pitch my voice to match the man I heard on the street earlier, yelling at his wife about... something. "Four people are down." I rattle off the address and then hang up. Most of the first responders are in the country with the rest of the city's population, but some of them chose to stay behind. By my calculations, there should be an ambulance scooping up my hapless victims inside of five minutes.

I slip out the door, pull my hood up, and whistle a cheery tune as I walk away from the scene. After two blocks, it's clear no one is around to pay the least bit of attention to me. But then, I'm good at blending in when I feel like it. Everyone expects Hermes to be loud and boisterous and sparkly. A walking disco ball, even. It's so much part of my branding that when I *don't* dress and act like that, even people I know have a tendency to overlook me.

It's a very simple trick, but simple tricks are often the most reliable. Classics are classics for a reason.

My temporary destination is another half-renovated building a few blocks away. There's a lot of that in the upper city right now. Dozens of big projects were put on hold when the news of the assassination clause broke—an irritatingly clever move on Circe's part.

Circe.

I'm going to have to face her eventually. I want to say with all confidence that I know how I'll react when we finally end up in the same room, but even I'm not that much of a liar.

On an impulse, I pull out my phone again and dial Cassandra. We haven't talked since our last spat a few days ago when I told her to stick close to Apollo, and I wouldn't be surprised if she sent me straight to voicemail. But Cassandra is a softy, even with all her thorns. She answers. "You have some nerve calling me right now."

"I'm made up of nothing but nerve, darling. You know that." I can't help putting on the charming facade. After so many years as Hermes, court jester, the lines between *her* and *me* have blurred to the point where I don't always make the conscious choice to don the mask.

"I'm sure you have a reason for calling," she snaps.

In this moment, I can almost wish things between me and the snarling redhead *did* work out. She's the only relationship I've had since Circe died—or didn't die, as the case may be—where I could almost see a future with her. Cassandra was hurt by Olympus just as much as I was, and even when this damned city kept kicking her while she was down, she never let it break her. I loved her as much as I'm capable of these days. I guess I love her still, which is why I keep trying to convince her to leave town. "I gave you a warning all those months ago, and you didn't take it."

"The warning where you told me to go home so you could stand by and let Minos *kill* people."

I'm not above getting my hands bloody, but… I sigh. "I doubt you'll believe this, but I was only there for information and to keep an eye on his ambition. I didn't realize what he intended until it was too late."

Cassandra's silent for a beat. "You warned me I was in danger."

"Of course I did! You were there with Olympus's *spymaster*. Apollo has always stuck his nose where it doesn't belong, and I didn't want you to get killed in the process."

"Hermes, I swear…" She gives a sigh of her own. "You know I can't take your word at face value. You were there. The murder happened. You didn't even try to stop it."

I hate to have it reduced to that, but I can't argue. "Yes.

I was there. Theseus murdered Hephaestus. I didn't stop it." Because, for better or worse, it *did* serve my intent to destabilize Olympus further. I still didn't wish ill on that Hephaestus, for all that he was a raging dickhead. I just didn't try that hard to do anything about Theseus's intent once I figured out what Minos was about.

"Why are you calling? It's not to clear your conscience."

"Darling, my conscience is hardly up for debate. No, I'm calling with another warning, and I *need* you to heed this one. For both your and Apollo's sake." I might not like the man overmuch, but she does. He treats her like she's the most precious gem in all the world, which I approve of. Cassandra deserves to be worshipped and coddled; Apollo shows every sign of doing both. "Circe made it into the city, and it wasn't desperately fleeing Zeus and the other two. She planned it. She fully intends to kill every one of the Thirteen and abolish Olympus's entire governing system."

Cassandra's most lovely and awful trait is that she sees too much. Worse, she's smart enough to connect inconvenient dots. "You also want the Thirteen gone. That's what this is about, right? All the shit you've been pulling in the last year, it's all to change things."

My life would have been simpler if I could have loved her the way she deserved. Having her as a potential adversary sucks. The cheer drops from my voice. I need her to take me seriously, to fucking *listen*. "Not like this, Cassandra. If I wanted them dead, they would have been dead years ago. There isn't a locked door in this city that can keep me out."

"So you're calling to tell me to…get Apollo out of Olympus?"

The tone of the question means she's still not taking this seriously. "Yes. Right now, Circe will be focusing on Zeus, Poseidon, and Hades, but it's only a matter of time before she decides to work her way through the rest."

"Including you."

I stop short. I might be Hermes, might play the part of the member of the Thirteen who delivers messages and secrets and knowledge, but I've always been aware that I'm different from the rest of them—and not only because I want to see the whole structure of their power shatter. The vast majority of the Thirteen—both now and stretching back through Olympus's history—come from the legacy families. Whether families *become* legacy because they've had members tapped to become one of the Thirteen or the Thirteen only pull from certain families that already entertain an absurd amount of money and privilege is up for debate. Chicken, egg, and all that.

"I'm not like the others," I say finally. I can't quite inject my usual irreverent cheer into the words. Sometimes truth cuts deep. "I never have been."

Cassandra is quiet for a long time. Finally, she says, "I hear you and I acknowledge your warning. You know I'm no fan of the Thirteen and the legacy families. I always wanted to get out of this city. But, Hermes, Apollo's roots run deep. Orpheus is still here, and so are their parents."

I refuse to acknowledge the little twinge of guilt from the fact I just shot Apollo's little brother. He's fine. Mostly. "None of them will be safe if Circe realizes her goals."

"Yeah, I got that." She sighs. "Look, I'll talk to him. I can't make any promises beyond that."

It's more than I expected. I don't tell her to leave him in the dust and take off. We both know she won't. She loves him as much as he loves her, and I'd be significantly happier for them if I wasn't worried Circe planned to rip out his heart and break Cassandra's in the process. "There's not much time. Talk fast." I hang up before she can completely diminish my hope of a future where she'll be okay.

When I became Hermes and took the first step toward toppling the power structure that took the person I loved most in the world, I never thought I'd be in a position to care about the very people whose downfall I'm orchestrating.

I stare at my phone as sirens scream past the building I'm in. Six minutes. They really are stretched thin, aren't they?

I scroll through my contacts and pause over Dionysus's name. We haven't spoken since Minos's party. He carries a lot of guilt over Pan getting hurt, and he blames me as much as he blames himself. Maybe that's fair, maybe it's not. Ultimately it means he won't take my call even if I try.

I don't try.

Instead, I pull up my neat little app, courtesy of Atalanta, and cycle through the video feeds in the city. There aren't any in the encampment out in the country, which sets me on edge. If I were up to no good, that's where I'd be.

I'm still not sure if it's a stroke of genius or completely foolish that I sold that property to Demeter. She's not aware she bought it from *me*, of course. I don't telegraph my origin story; besides, owning that piece of land was horribly nostalgic. It's where I used to live, after all, so many years ago. It's the *only* piece of land I've ever owned and selling it to Demeter to set up a camp for the refugees from the city feels like a strange sort of cosmic balance. I won't be needing it in the future, after all. The Thirteen will fall, and that includes me.

There's a life waiting for me outside of Olympus. I don't know where yet, and I'm just superstitious enough to not think about with *who* too closely...though Atalanta's face hovers in my mind's eye.

I almost call her just to hear her voice, but I manage to resist. She's been my steadfast friend through this entire process. If I tell her I warned Cassandra again, she's going to rip me a new one. She's probably got a point, but it's nice to be reminded I have a heart under all the hurt. Cassandra and I fell apart because we were never going to be the love of each other's lives. Atalanta didn't like her much, and if

I know the reason why, there's no space to address it until we've accomplished our goals. The possibility of *after* is too nebulous to contemplate.

Unfortunately, I can't gallivant off to the country to chase down my concerns because there are too many cats still left to herd in the city itself. "Time to get to work."

ZEUS

"THERE ARE REPORTS OF GUNSHOTS ON THE RIVER Styx."

I look up from the bag I'm currently throwing things into in preparation for a quick trip out to the countryside. Poseidon's warning from yesterday still rings true in my head. He's right about Circe being three steps ahead of us this whole time, which means he might be right about her doing something in the mountains. I intend to go out there with my sister and see for myself.

It takes several long moments before Ares's words penetrate. "What did you say?"

"Gunshots." She looks a little too freaked out for it to be a generic shooting. She keeps glancing at her phone, which beeps with a spattering of incoming text messages. "Oh, fuck. Perseus…"

I go cold. "Tell me."

Ares looks up, her hazel eyes too wide. "There are four people injured and being rushed to the hospital." I actually take a step toward her as she sputters. "Two are Hades's people. Persephone is there, too."

What the fuck was Persephone doing on our side of the river? I'm already heading for the door. "I'm going to call Hades on the way to the hospital. We can't have him rampaging through the upper city. We'll stand guard over her until he arrives and I'll do my best to minimize the chance of this spiraling."

"Perseus."

I glance over my shoulder to find my sister ghost pale. "What?"

"There were *four* victims." She clears her throat. "The fourth person is Hera."

My thoughts fall to perfect silence. Hera has been shot. *Callisto* has been shot. *My fucking wife has been shot.*

"I want Patroclus and Achilles on this personally," I say softly. Calm. I'm too fucking calm. It feels like there's a barrier between me and the rest of the world, but it's just as well because I can barely control the hurricane of emotions threatening to split through my skin. "Tell them to find whoever did this and bring me their head. You and I are going to the hospital now."

To Ares's credit, she doesn't even try to argue that we had

different plans for the day or that Circe is likely behind this attack and using it to distract me and Hades. She simply follows me to the parking garage. When I head for the driver's side, she plucks the keys out of my hands. "I'll drive while you make your calls."

The first person I call is Hades. I barely let him answer the phone before I cut in. "There was an incident on the banks of the River Styx involving both of our wives and two of your people. I don't have the full details of what happened, but they are alive and being rushed to the hospital. I'm heading there with Ares right now to provide personal security. I highly suggest you make your way there as well. I'll let the hospital staff know to let you through."

His shocked inhale is the only external reaction he allows. "I'll be there as soon as possible." Hades hangs up before I can say anything else, which is just as well. I have nothing else to say. This happened on my side of the river; therefore it's my responsibility. I'm not certain why Persephone was here in the first place, let alone what my wife was planning that brought her here, but that matters less than the reality. They were here. They were shot on my watch.

Helen dials her phone and puts it on speaker. A small courtesy I would appreciate if I could appreciate anything in this moment. Achilles's charming voice answers. "Hey, princess. I thought you were headed out to the country with—"

"We have reports of shots fired and four victims. No

deaths to my knowledge, but Hera and Persephone were both among those injured."

Instantly, all flirtation is gone from his tone. "Why am I just hearing about this now?"

"Because of the people involved, the reporting security force called me instead of going up the proper chain of command. It was the right thing to do." She glances at me and then returns her attention to the road, flying through a yellow light in the process of turning red. "I need you and Patroclus to go over the site with a fine-tooth comb to figure out what the fuck happened. I want the gunman, Achilles."

There's movement on his side of the line: he's obviously already in the process of obeying her orders. "We'll get the information, princess. And then we'll bring you their head on a platter."

"Thank you." She swallows hard. "Be careful and keep me updated."

"Always do."

She hangs up and shoves the phone into the pocket of her jacket. "We're almost there. Just hold on for a few more minutes."

I am holding on. I think. There is a yawning emptiness inside me, deep and dark and ready to devour. This fucking city. It demands its price in blood again and again, never satisfied. And for fucking what? The thankless task of ruling?

I won't pretend every member of the Thirteen stretching

back to the history of the founding of Olympus have been good people or even good rulers. But there needs to be *someone* in charge. No matter what perceived benefit we get from it, the cost is always higher than anyone should be expected to pay.

They shot my fucking wife.

Helen veers into the hospital parking lot and, without asking, pulls up to the front of the emergency entrance. "Figure out what's going on. I'll park and find you."

I'm already out the car and charging through the doors. The person behind the desk sees me coming and their pale face turns sickly green. They half shove to their feet, get tangled with their chair, and crash back down into it. "Zeus! Zeus, you're here. I have a report, uh, right here."

I hold up a hand. The barrier of ice around me is so thick I'm able to speak perfectly normally. "Where is my wife?"

"She's in a room. I could take you to her. Or, actually, John can." They motion frantically to the nurse standing in the doorway behind them.

I need to go to her, but there's Hades to consider. I fucking *hate* that I have to consider anything other than getting to my wife's side as quickly as possible. I clear my throat. "And the other three victims?"

"Um..." The receptionist rifles through the papers in front of them. "Persephone is getting stitched up right now. Orpheus is in surgery for his broken collarbone, but the doctor expects him to make a full recovery. Medusa is with Persephone; she won't leave her side."

All alive. That's all I need to know. "Hades will be here shortly. Have someone ready to take him to his wife as soon as he arrives."

"Yes, sir." They motion frantically at John again, and he steps forward to lead me down the hall past a set of locked doors. It's miniscule security—only the doors themselves and no actual people to ensure someone doesn't slip in. I make a mental note to tell my sister to ramp it up for as long as such high-profile patients are within these walls.

I shove past John into a small room with a hospital bed and a machine beeping steadily beside it. Callisto sits in the bed, her expression a mask of displeasure. She has a thick bandage on her upper left arm and several scratches on her face, but seems otherwise okay. That doesn't stop me from rushing to her side. I reach out but stop short of touching her. "Tell me what happened."

She blinks up at me, pure shock on her gorgeous face. "What are you doing here?"

"Someone. Shot. You." I bite out each word. I can't stand to be this close and not touch her, not reassure myself that she truly is alive and okay. Almost tentatively, I cup her cheek. I fully expect her to push me away or deliver some kind of sharp comment, but she just closes her eyes and leans into my touch, ever so slightly. "Tell me what happened," I repeat.

"I needed to talk to my sister. She wouldn't come fully into the upper city or allow me into the lower city, so this was the best compromise we could come up with. I don't know how the shooter knew we would be there, but they started firing so fast that they had to have been watching the river. I was hit first. Medusa shoved Persephone to the ground, but Orpheus had to be a hero and tackle me, which was when he got shot. I had to hold the fucker together until the paramedics arrived."

I'm all too aware of my wife's feelings on Orpheus. My father used him to hurt Eurydice in an effort to draw Persephone out of the lower city, and though reports say Eurydice has taken him back, Callisto is not one to forgive or forget. The fact that she didn't let him die is a testament to something, but I'm not entirely certain what.

"You were shot first."

She opens her eyes and leans back just enough to break the contact of my fingertips against her skin. "It's just a graze, albeit a deep one. I needed stitches. Persephone seemed mostly okay, but I know she was hurt. What were her injuries?"

"Similar to yours. Orpheus is the one in surgery. Your sister's fine, according to the nurse. Her husband will be here shortly."

"Fuck," Callisto breathes. "This was already a shit show, but I've just made it worse, haven't I?"

Yes, but I'm not about to tell her that. Not when she's

looking so frail in that hospital bed. Not when someone *put* her in that fucking hospital bed. Achilles and Patroclus are some of the best, trained by Athena herself. If anyone can find out who the shooter is and where they went, it's them. And when they do, I'm not going to be satisfied with simply a head on a platter. I want the gunman to *suffer*.

"Where is your team?" It's the first time I've seen her out of the penthouse without the trio since she acquired them.

A faint flush takes up residence in my wife's too-pale cheeks. "I slept late and didn't inform them of my plans. I didn't think it would be a problem to go by myself…" She shudders. "Apparently I was wrong."

I open my mouth to ask her about the baby, but click my jaw shut before the words emerge. Foolish sap that I am, I want her to tell me about the pregnancy in her own time. I clear my throat. "I'm going to go find the doctor and get some more information on the others. Stay here."

"I want to check on my sister." She must see me getting ready to argue, because she reaches out and tentatively touches my hand. "Please, Perseus. It's my fault she got hurt. I need to see her."

"Give me a few minutes, and then I'll escort you there myself." I don't know how the fuck I'm supposed to let her out of my sight now. I step out of the room and close the door softly behind me.

Only then do I slump against the wall as all the adrenaline

and fear and fury race through me, my heart beating so hard it's a wonder I can't feel it rattling against my rib cage. My thoughts swirl and spiral and finally fade entirely.

She was fucking shot—she could have *died*—and I wasn't there. She didn't tell me where she was going so I could send someone to look out for her. Why would she? She doesn't trust me. She never has. I'm starting to wonder if she ever will.

I reach out and grab the arm of a doctor walking past. Their badge says that their name is Rex. "My wife is in that room behind me. She's pregnant and she was shot. I need you to check her thoroughly to make sure she's okay. And…the baby, too. Do you understand me?"

"I… But I'm a…" They swallow hard at whatever look is on my face and nod. "I'll go check on her now."

"Do *not* tell her I sent you."

They blink. "Um. Okay."

I stand there for what feels like the longest fifteen minutes of my life. When the doctor emerges, it's everything I can do not to grab them and shove them against the wall until they tell me what I need to know. It doesn't escape my notice that they stay several steps out of reach.

They straighten their coat. "She's fine. She lost a little blood, but nowhere near enough to require a transfusion. We can do an ultrasound to check on the pregnancy if you'd like, but the heartbeat seems perfectly within normal ranges."

The heartbeat. My baby's heartbeat.

Later, I'll wade through the mess of conflicting emotions those words bring me. Right now, I only care about Callisto. "Thank you." I take a deep breath that does nothing to steady me and step back into the room. "All right. Let's go find your sister."

HERA

I'M IN A FULL-BLOWN PANIC BY THE TIME PERSEUS comes back into the room. Everything has gone so wrong. I might have been able to convince Persephone to listen to me, but that opportunity is slipping through my fingers with each passing second. If I admit my opportunity is already gone...

I have to talk to Persephone. I have to talk to her right fucking now.

I start fumbling at my IV. "I need to get out of here." This is all my fault. I should have figured out a way to meet my sister more securely. I should have at least had my team present, or tasked them with sweeping the area around us. I was so fucking careless and people got hurt as a result. People I care about.

They're going to get hurt worse before this is over if I don't do something, and fast.

Perseus crosses the room in three long strides and covers my hands with his. "Stop. What are you doing?"

"I have to see my sister." But not just my sister. I talked so much shit to Orpheus, but at the first sign of danger, he threw himself forward to protect me. Eurydice is never going to forgive me if he doesn't walk away from this. Fuck. "I have to see Orpheus, too."

I fully expect Perseus to tell me to stop, and sit still, and wait for the doctor to come back. Anything to shut me up until someone can show up to sedate me. But he just watches me for several heartbeats with those icy blue eyes and gives a short nod. "I understand, Callisto. We'll go see them right now. Give me a few minutes to figure out where your clothing is."

"It's ruined. The blood, you know." I'm speaking far too quickly. I recognize that, I understand it's a bad sign, but I can't seem to stop. "I already asked Imbros to bring me some spare clothing. Ze should be here shortly."

"Imbros. Right." He gives me another long look and then sighs. "Hold still. I don't want to hurt you by accident."

I watch in stunned silence as he digs around in the drawers until he finds a box of bandages and then expertly removes the IV from my arm. I can't find words when he's unclipping the heart monitors on my chest, as distant as if he were a nurse himself. The machine instantly starts beeping an alarm, but Perseus pushes a few buttons and it's silenced before it can draw any nurses or doctors from the hall.

I swallow hard. "You know your way around a hospital room?"

"Yes." He half turns away but seems to reconsider his abruptness. "You know who my father was. You know what he was capable of. Even before her death, my mother saw a lot of hospital rooms. After her death, I did, too." He looks around as if he didn't just drop truly horrific information as casually as commenting on the weather.

"I didn't know," I whisper.

"There's no reason you would have. I never visited public hospitals. What would people think, you know?"

People already believed the last Zeus was a wife killer. It didn't affect their apparent love for him or his social standing within the city. There's no reason to believe that finding out he was abusing his children would be the straw that broke the camel's back. Zeus still knew enough to hide, which speaks volumes. It makes me want to bring the former Zeus back from the dead so I can kill him all over again.

I don't tell Perseus I'm sorry. Those words mean nothing. I can't go back and change the past, and if he thinks for a second that I pity him, he'll resent me. It's not *pity*. I don't know what to call this feeling inside me. I would blame the damned parasite, but the truth is I'm growing increasingly sure the sensations inside me are not physical in nature. They're emotional.

Imbros bursts through the door and skids to a stop, zir

eyes wide. "I brought the clothing you asked for." Ze glances at Perseus. "Do you want to—"

Perseus snatches the clothing out of zir hands. "Either leave or turn around."

Imbros looks to me for confirmation, and while I don't fully understand what my husband is doing, I nod. Ze hesitates but finally turns zir back on us. I know it's a testament of zir lack of faith in Zeus that ze refuses to leave the room, but I don't comment on that, either. I'm not commenting on a lot of things right now.

Perseus sets out my clothing with regimented organization: dress, then bra, then panties, then socks, boots going on the floor. Then my husband, the so-called king of Olympus, goes to his knees before me. This isn't about sex—it would be easier if it was—and the shock holds me paralyzed while he takes one of my feet and slides the first sock onto it. He's gentle and firm and perfectly polite. As if he's a different person entirely.

While I'm still recovering from my confusion over this strange turn of events, he gets my second sock on and slides my panties past my feet. "Can you stand?"

"It was only a graze. I can dress myself."

"That's not what I asked you."

This isn't a battle I'm going to win. I'm so bloody tired; I don't have the stamina for another fight today. Or that's what I tell myself as I slide carefully onto my feet. I wobble a little, and instead of reaching behind me for the bed, I grip my husband's shoulder. He slides my underwear up my legs and into position. I find myself holding my breath the same way I did last night when he stroked my stomach. I am not ready to talk about it. I'm not ready to admit the only reason I allowed myself to get pregnant was so I could kill him. I'm sure as fuck not ready to admit that part of the reason I'm withholding this knowledge from everyone is because I... don't *want* to kill Perseus.

His hands linger on my hips, his eyes on my stomach, for a beat too long. I tense, certain he's going to make a comment, but instead he simply rises and snatches my sports bra from the pile of clothing. If he finds it strange that I'm wearing a sports bra instead of something more traditional, he doesn't comment on that, either. My older bras don't fit anymore, and the thought of dealing with an underwire makes my already achy breasts protest wildly. I can't buy new bras for the same reason I haven't bought new clothes: People might talk. There's no graceful way to put on a sports bra, but somehow he manages. And then all that's left is my wrap dress.

Except that's not all that's left. As soon as he ties the wrap, he nudges me back to sit and sinks down to put on my boots. I clear my throat uncomfortably. "I really can do this."

"I'm faster." That's almost logical, but how would he know if he's faster? This almost feels like care. But that can't be it. Our marriage is two comets crashing into each other, the devastation intense enough to end worlds. There's no space for quiet tenderness. I don't know how to deal with it, so I ignore it.

I clear my throat. "Imbros, please find out where my sister's room is."

"That won't be necessary." Perseus rises and takes my hand. "I have all the information. We can go there now. Orpheus was in surgery last I heard, but I think he should be out soon. We will find out more when we talk to Persephone."

My heart gives a strange sort of wobble. I don't understand this. He should be furious with me for meeting with my sister without the proper protections in place. If something happens to Persephone, Hades will rampage and his fury will be a thousand times worse than Circe or Hermes can gather. For that alone, my husband is deeply invested in keeping Persephone safe and alive. But keeping her safe and alive doesn't have to include sharing this information with me just because he knows I want it.

I am so confused. I even forget to take my hand from his as we walk out of the room and down the busy hallway to another, mostly identical room. One that contains my sister and a furious-looking Medusa. Persephone starts to sit up when she sees me, but Medusa plants a hand in the center of her chest and gently but firmly holds her in place. "Absolutely not. The doctor said you need to stay still."

"Medusa—"

"No. We're not doing this again. This is the second fucking time my general good nature has been used against me by the person I'm supposed to be protecting—which resulted in that person getting hurt. In *you* getting hurt this time. I let you sweet-talk me into attending this meeting, Persephone. And now I have to explain to my boss—your husband—why I allowed his pregnant wife to get shot. Lie still or I'm going to tie you to that bed until Hades gets here."

My sister's brows wing up and her chin lifts, a sure sign that she's about to lose her cool. I step forward before she can go nuclear. "Are you okay? I'm so sorry. I should have had better security. No one knew about our meeting but us, so I didn't think—"

"I'm okay." Persephone gives one last glance at Medusa and then reaches out for me. I have to slip free from Perseus to take her hand, but I do so without hesitation. She glances over my shoulder at him but wisely doesn't comment on his presence. "I know what we talked about, but surely these events prove that bending to our enemy's demands just means more people get hurt."

"No." I shake my head sharply. "That's not what today's events prove. If anything, they prove that you being the queen of the lower city and me being the queen of the upper city just put us further in danger." I almost keep speaking, but even in my strange state of mind, I'm aware of my husband listening in. If he knows I talked to Circe... If he knows I made a deal with her even after everything... he'll never forgive me.

Later, I'll worry about why I'm so concerned with my husband's forgiveness.

The door slams open before Persephone can formulate a response. The man who walks through is a personified storm cloud. Hades is a white man with shoulder-length dark hair, a closely trimmed beard, and a perpetual glare on his handsome face. That glare passes right over Perseus and lands on me. "You."

"Hades, I think—"

He points a harsh finger at Persephone. "No, little siren, I don't want to hear from you right now. We will talk about your propensity for putting yourself in danger for no damned reason as soon as we're safely back in the lower city." He turns back to the door and lifts his voice. "Let's get moving."

A team of three nurses come through the door with a rolling bed. I watch in something like awe as they transfer Persephone over despite her protests. It takes seconds. They even strap her down over her hips, careful of her stomach. "This is absolutely unnecessary, Hades," she snaps, batting at their hands.

"You. Were. Shot." With every word he speaks, it becomes more readily apparent that the Hades I've come to know is nowhere in evidence. This is the king of the lower city, and he is *not* satisfied. "So help me, Wife, if I have to gag you to get you out of the upper city and to safety, I will. Do *not* test me right now."

Persephone opens her mouth but seems to reconsider whatever she was about to say. Finally, she meekly folds her hands over her round stomach. She gives me a glance that's almost sympathetic. "I'll talk to you later."

Hades motions to the person closest to him, someone who appears to be the head medic for the team he apparently brought to the upper city to transport his people back. "Orpheus is out of surgery and in the recovery room. The second team needs to go to him. I want transfer initiated as quickly as possible without further harming him. Do whatever it takes."

Medusa shifts on her feet, looking distinctly contrite. "I'm sorry, Hades. It was just—"

"I will deal with you back in the lower city as well. See to my wife. Now." Everyone files out of the room except for Imbros, Perseus, Hades, and me. Hades turns to give me his full attention, and for the first time since meeting my brother-in-law, I have to fight not to take a step back. His voice is quiet, but somehow that's even scarier than if he were yelling. "I have stood by and allowed you to involve your sister in your little schemes and plots. No longer. You may be her family, Callisto, but I'm her husband. It's increasingly clear that you don't give a fuck about anyone except for yourself."

I can't speak. It feels like he's reached out and wrapped a

hand around my throat, cutting off my words, cutting off my air. It's not true. I love my sisters and my mother more than anything. I would burn the fucking world for them. I never wanted Persephone to get hurt. The entire reason we were meeting is to avoid that very outcome.

But I can't find the words to say any of it.

"That's *enough*, Hades." Perseus steps in front of me, not quite blocking my view of my brother-in-law but clearly conveying that if Hades wants to get to me, he'll have to go through my husband first. "We've all been making mistakes lately, so I think it's time for a little grace."

"You've had grace. You've abused it. Zeus. Hera. Stay out of the lower city. You are *not* welcome there." He turns and stalks out of the room, the door swinging softly shut behind him.

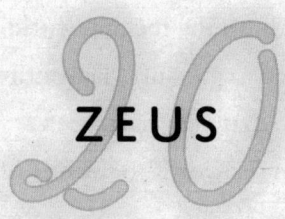

ZEUS

I WATCH CALLISTO DEFLATE BEFORE MY EYES. HER shoulders slump. Her head bows. The only sign of the woman I've come to know is her clenched fists at her side. We stand there in silence as Hades's team finishes up and whisks from the room. There's a disturbance in the hallway, likely the second team acquiring Orpheus. It happens so damned fast. Despite myself, part of me admires how effective he is. If there's a leader that I would have chosen to model myself after, it's Hades.

But that ship has long since sailed.

With how tentative and tumultuous things are between Callisto and me, I hate to bring up what we need to do next. Unfortunately, hiding from the truth won't make it less likely to kick you in the teeth. "Are you going to tell your mother? Or shall I?"

She lifts her head, her expression wan. "Do we have to?"

The look we share is full of so much acknowledged misery that I almost laugh despite myself. Only knowing I'll soon be on the phone with Demeter herself, explaining to her how two of her beloved daughters were hurt under my watch, keeps my lips from curving. "You know we do."

She tilts her head back and stares at the ceiling, obviously contemplating options that won't require the phone call. In that moment, I take the opportunity to survey her again. For all she told me, her wound is just a graze, for all the doctor informed me that both her and the fetus are fine, it's still hard to believe she's okay.

Likely because she's *not* okay. Getting shot is hardly a normal experience or without its trauma. Callisto showing even the slightest sign of buckling indicates that she's significantly more affected than she appears.

Finally, she says, "You tell her. If I do, then it'll become a fight, and I need my mother to listen when I see her next. I need her to see things my way."

See things her way. Her sister said several things before being whisked out of the room. I have questions about that—and the meeting itself. Callisto was very careful to ensure I had no knowledge of it, and she didn't even bring her trio of ever-present guards with her. That seems to indicate a level of secrecy that has nothing to do with her ongoing plans to murder me. I don't like it. I don't like it at all.

I cross my arms over my chest. "I'll call your mother and take the fall, on one condition."

"Oh, we're bargaining now?" She raises her eyebrow, seeming to settle a little bit more within her skin. "All right. Let's hear it. What's your condition?"

It's a risk, but everything we do these days is a risk. She already knows I feel enough for her to complicate things. And if she *doesn't* know, then it's because she's being intentionally obtuse. Everyone else fucking knows. "After this call, once we get the all clear from your doctor, you're coming home with me tonight. And you're staying there all night. Tomorrow, you'll accompany me to the countryside."

She narrows those pretty hazel eyes. "Not to stay in the countryside."

For all that her mother's scheming is enough to keep even the most composed person up at night, Demeter cares for her daughters deeply and would throw herself in front of a tank to save them. It would never come to that, of course. She has schemes within schemes within schemes, all designed to secure power and increase it. If a tank threatened, she'd bribe the driver and turn it on her enemies. If bribery didn't work, she'd find something to blackmail them with. She's formidable in a way even my father was wary of. There are few places safer for my wife than at her mother's side.

But I don't want Callisto so far from me. Selfish. Foolish. Pick your insult. It's all true and more. I'm a damned fool for her; despite all her murderous impulses, I don't want her to leave the city proper. "Not to stay. Poseidon thinks Circe might be planning something in relation to the mountains. It's possible she has knowledge of a pass through them that's been lost in Olympian history. I'm going to take some of Ares's people and look into it. You can use the opportunity to spend some time with your mother and Psyche."

"That's...thoughtful." It sounds almost like an accusation coming from her. She's not entirely wrong to be suspicious. If she's ensconced in her family's bosom, she'll at least be safe while I investigate the perimeter.

"Do we have a deal?"

She only hesitates a beat. "Yes."

Now for the truly challenging part. I pull out my phone and dial Demeter before I can think too hard about what's coming. I barely let her get a greeting out before I cut in. "There was an incident involving Persephone and Callisto. They're both fine and expected to make a full recovery."

"A full recovery." I've never heard three normal words sound so threatening. Not even my father could quite pull off the same level of polite menace. "I am going to need more details than that, dear Zeus."

I glance at my wife and then partially turn away from her. I may take the fall for this, but she's not fully free from blame. "They were meeting on the banks of the River Styx. There was a sniper. They and their two guards were all wounded but not severely enough to endanger their lives. The worst was Orpheus, who needed surgery, but he came through just fine and is well enough to be transported back to the lower city, alongside Persephone and Medusa. That was the first order Hades issued upon arriving at the hospital."

"He did what?"

Maybe I'm a coward, but if I'm willing to take the fall for my wife, I'm sure as fuck not for Hades. If I can throw him to the wolf that is Demeter in the process? All the better. Let *him* deal with her fury. "He charged in here and took both Persephone and her guards to the lower city. I'm not sure that any of them were actually discharged."

She's only silent for a moment. "And the extent of Hera's injuries?"

"She has a graze on her arm that required stitches and a few bumps and bruises, but she's otherwise perfectly fine. I'm taking her home and keeping her there tonight, but I will bring her out to the countryside tomorrow for you to spend some time with and reassure yourself that she'll make a full recovery."

"Very well. I'll see her tomorrow and get full answers then. In the meantime, I have a certain lord of the lower city to call." She hangs up without saying goodbye.

I turn back to find Callisto watching me with a strange expression on her face. Her lips curl the tiniest bit. "That was mean."

"If he's going to make dramatic statements and grand gestures, then he can deal with explaining why to Demeter." He's not going to be any happier with her than he is with the rest of us, and it's just as well. The safest place for Persephone is in the lower city behind that barrier. At least while it still stands. I have no doubt Circe has plans for it to be destroyed as well.

Personally, I could use Hades's help, but it's clear his priorities are his wife and the twin babies she carries. I can't fault him for that. Callisto doesn't even know that *I* know she's pregnant, and it's everything I can do not to package her up and ship her away—or lock her in a room until this is over. She'd hate me for either choice, but at least she'd be safe.

Except, no, she wouldn't. The first chance she got, she'd be knocking down walls and scaling the side of the building to go cause more trouble. My wife isn't one to be content on the sidelines. She'll be at my side instead.

Callisto sighs and starts to run her fingers through her hair, only to find it matted with blood from the cut on the side of her face. She winces. "I suppose a shower wouldn't be out of order."

Even with all my power, I'm no Hades to whisk her out of here despite the doctor's protest. I'd like my personal doctor to look her over just to be sure she's fine, but I already know she won't allow it. Until she tells me that she's pregnant, I have to tread carefully when it comes to her medical stuff. It takes another thirty minutes before I have discharge papers in hand and am able to usher Callisto into the black SUV I called to pick us up.

She slumps back against the seat in a way that makes my stomach twist. I'm a man of action. Give me an enemy to conquer, and I will dismantle it to the best of my ability. Give me a dispute to navigate, and I'll find the best way through, weighing the scales to ensure the fairest solution. But with my injured wife, I don't have the skills or the words to comfort her. I've never felt so inadequate in my life.

Ultimately, she takes the choice from me. We've only ridden two blocks when her eyes flutter closed, and her body goes limp, slumping down to rest her head on my shoulder. Panic flutters in my throat, but her steady breathing reassures me. She's had a horrific shock, and an injury on top of that, not to mention the increasing amount of stress every citizen in Olympus is feeling—particularly the Thirteen. It's no wonder her body shut down.

She's still sleeping by the time we park in the garage in our building. I don't hesitate to carefully scoop her up. Callisto is one of those women who's larger than life in everything she does, but she curls so sweetly into my arms that it makes me sick with need.

The need to be a completely different person. One who isn't the universally hated Zeus. One who she might want to marry for the man instead of the title. One who isn't emotionally stunted and unable to provide the support she obviously requires.

She stirs as I walk through the front door. "I fell asleep?"

"Yeah." I bypass the main living area and walk down the hall to the primary bedroom. I already know she won't allow me to put her to bed until she's clean, so I head into the bathroom and set her carefully on the counter. "Stay here."

It's a testament to her exhaustion that she doesn't immediately rip me a new one. She merely sits and watches as I start the shower and then pull the first aid kit from beneath the sink. Only then does she speak. "I'm bandaged up just fine."

"I know. But there's a chance that cut on your face might reopen once we get it wet. And we'll have to be careful of your arm."

"Perseus…"

Hearing my name—my true name—on her lips stills me. I'm helpless to do anything but meet her gaze. I don't know what I expect to see. I don't know what *she* sees, but she looks just as conflicted as I feel. She shifts uncomfortably. "I can't—"

I cut in before she can rip my heart out. Again. "I know this changes nothing. But just…let me take care of you tonight, Callisto. Please."

I can actually see the warring thoughts behind her eyes. My wife is perversely independent and hates me. And yet she nods jerkily. "Just for tonight."

HERA

I KNOW WHAT I *SHOULD* DO, BUT IT'S PERFECTLY AT odds with what I have the energy for. I *should* hop off this bathroom counter and walk away from the fragile new intimacy with my husband that I most assuredly did not ask for. But just because I didn't ask for it doesn't mean I don't crave it with a strength that scares me. All my life, one truth has been drilled into my head, over and over again.

I cannot rely on anyone but my family.

My mother would go to war for her daughters, even as she expects us to take some hits in the process. My sisters would go to unthinkable lengths to protect each other.

But the rest of the world? They cannot be trusted. They hate us for reaching for the shining power they decided was theirs by virtue of birth, for being country folk who dare come into the city and pretend each to be one of them. We may be nearly as rich as the Kasios family but we don't have a history littered with members of the Thirteen. Every Dimitriou has *worked*, unlike the legacy families who crouch in the center of the upper city. Vultures, every one of them. They scheme and backstab and have no problem trampling others to get what they want. They would have killed Persephone rather than let her rise as queen of the lower city. They *did* try to kill Eurydice. And Psyche, too. We've outlasted them all, through cleverness and strength and sheer perversity.

So the very idea of allowing my husband, holder of the hated title Zeus, to care for me?

Unthinkable.

But my body isn't quite obeying my brain's reluctant commands. Since our family moved to the city proper, I've been harboring an inferno of rage that will likely never be extinguished. How can it when nothing ever changes? Over and over again, I've comforted myself with the belief that I'm not like the glittering vipers—that my sisters aren't, either. That belief doesn't ring quite as true any longer.

Psyche turned their game back on themselves, resulting in Eros's mother being exiled. Persephone committed to a relationship with Hades that started as a way to ensure Zeus would never want to touch her again and ended with her becoming one of the most powerful people in the city in her own right. Even Eurydice, our precious baby sister, partnered with Eris to orchestrate Ariadne Vitalis betraying her father and her people. Through it all, I've schemed and manipulated and blackmailed as necessary to protect my family and secure my position of power.

I almost got my sister killed tonight with those schemes. I'm not that different from the legacy families after all. None of us are.

So I don't hop down off the counter and flee from my husband. There's no escaping the new truth nestled beneath my breastbone, a hot coal I want to claw out. I just sit there and shake as Perseus brings the shower up to a comfortable temperature and moves to stand in front of me. If he asked me if I need help, I would have choked on my own tongue before admitting that I do. But he doesn't ask.

He simply sinks to his knees in front of me as if it's the most natural thing in the world. Just like he did in the hospital. Except this time, there's no one else in the room with us. I'm not even sure where Imbros went, and that oversight should scare me. It will in the morning, but it doesn't feel like anything can penetrate the numbing agent of my new awareness.

I've failed. I've failed so spectacularly that it's almost laughable. It will be my sisters who pay the price for that failure—and my mother. Persephone loves Hades with everything she has. If something happens to him, I'm afraid it will break her. Not to mention she's in the same position I am, pregnant with his heir. That means if he dies, she becomes regent until their child is of age. Her children aren't any safer than her husband is. *She's* not any safer than her husband is. I refuse to allow my sister to be hurt. She's making the wrong decision, but if I could just talk to her, could just make her see reason—

At my feet, Perseus pulls off first one boot and then the other, quickly followed by my socks. He slides his hands up the outside of my legs, under my dress, to grip my hips. "I'm going to need you to stand. Can you do that?"

"Of course I can." I'm not so sure, though. Every part of me feels shaky, as if I'm held together by stubbornness and nothing more—and I'm all out of stubbornness. I ease off the counter and he tugs my panties down, waiting until I lift my feet to step out of them before he sets them aside in the growing pile of dirty clothes.

My dress is next, slid carefully over my head and dropped down next to me. The sports bra gets tangled around my neck, because of course it does. There's never been a graceful undressing involving a sports bra in the history of the world. But he eventually manages to free me from its confines and then I'm standing naked before him.

He surveys me with a critical eye, his attention lingering on the butterfly bandages on my shoulder and the dried cut on my face. "You're not supposed to get the bandages wet."

"You just got me naked and the shower's running. Figure it the fuck out. I'm getting in there and I don't give a shit about the bandages." The words are right, but the tone is wrong. It's almost pleading. I'm shattering before his very eyes and I don't know how to stop it. Normally, in the rare moments when weakness sets in, I have a private room to retreat to and no one to stand as witness. There's no opportunity for that now. It's come on too fast, and I'm out of control.

I don't see a way out of this. Both Hermes and Circe, have put me in an impossible position, trying to dismantle legacy titles that have existed since the founding of this city. No single person can do it. If they could, Hermes would have accomplished her aims long ago. She hasn't. She *knew* I would fail. Circe too. And still they let me flounder. Maybe they think it's funny. It doesn't feel very funny right now. It feels like despair.

While I'm spiraling, Perseus has come up with a solution. He kicks off his shoes and socks and pulls off his shirt. Even in my distracted state, I can't help the little flip my heart does at the sight of his bare chest underneath these unrelenting lights. Of the scars I noticed last time. Scars that tell a story, even though I don't want to witness it. And yet I don't stop looking.

He takes my arm and tugs me behind him into the shower, still wearing his pants. "This only works if you stand exactly where I tell you and do exactly as I say."

I don't have the energy to make a smart-ass comment or

push back. I merely nod and allow him to arrange me with my back against the tile wall, the water beating on my right side. At least for a moment. Then he takes the shower handle, adjusts the spray a little, and starts easing it over my body.

I jolt; I can't help it. "What are you doing?" I don't know why it didn't occur to me to ask when he came into the shower in the first place, but apparently this is a step too far.

"You promised to come home tonight and do what I say." He says it so mildly that I can almost convince myself there's ice beneath his words, just like there always is. Almost. It's not the truth, though. He's being gentle with me—*caring*, as if I'm made of spun glass and he's afraid of shattering me.

"Only part of that is true," I finally manage. "I never promised to do what you say."

"I know." His lips curve, just the tiniest amount, but on Perseus it's practically a boisterous laugh. "Can't blame me for trying, though." His expression falls back into more familiar, serious lines. "You can't shower without the risk of getting your bandages wet, and even if they weren't a factor, I wouldn't leave you in here alone. You look like you're about to collapse. Stand there and let me take care of you."

Take care of me. The very idea is absurd. I'm the one who takes care of the people around me. Not always in the way they would prefer, but a sharp cut accomplishes a whole lot more than a soft word, especially in our world. Perseus has been consistent since the beginning of our marriage, cold and distant and unknowable. Even now, he's awkward in his ministrations. His touch is tentative in a way I've never experienced with him—not even on our wedding night when we were new to each other. It's as if he's never done this before.

He's never done this before.

The realization rolls over me, sending my mind into perfect blankness. When would he have learned comfort? My mother may be a particular way with the public, but the moment she stepped through the door into our family home, she put down the Demeter persona and became herself. Still sharp, still ruthless, but warm in a way that had nothing to do with manipulation.

My husband doesn't do that. I had thought it was simply because I'm an enemy just like the ones outside the penthouse walls, but suddenly I'm not so sure. His home was hardly a refuge growing up. He would have learned there was no safe space. He was well and truly bereft of someone to comfort and hold him.

"Oh, Perseus." The words emerge as a sigh.

He pauses. "Are you okay? Did I hurt you?"

I press my lips together hard, but it does nothing to steady me. "No." I swallow past the lump growing in my throat, the burning in my eyes. "Don't stop."

"Okay." He gently tilts my head back, supporting my head with one hand, and brings the shower head to wash the blood from my hair. The look of concentration on his face makes my stomach flutter. He doesn't know what he's doing, but he's still doing it. For me. Because he...cares?

That can't be it. He hates me as much as I hate him. And I *do* hate him. I'm sure of it. The feeling might be a little less ragged than it was several months—or even a week—ago, but it hasn't gone away.

He's the instrument of so much pain, the representation of everything wrong with Olympus. A nepo baby handed a title that has been used to hurt people for countless generations. Just because *he* hasn't hurt anyone yet doesn't mean he won't in the future, given enough time and opportunity. His reign has hardly been without peril.

But even as I think of the words, they don't feel fully true. Not anymore.

I close my eyes and let my husband wash my hair. Having his hands on me like this, in warmth and *care*, feels so good that I let him wash my body as well. The silence between us is charged with all the things left unsaid, but I don't have the strength to cross that chasm. Not yet. It's not until he shuts off the water that some of my old strength comes back. Or maybe it's just desperation. I'm not going to be able to sleep, no matter how much my body needs it. I'm too aware of all the ways I've fucked up; my brain will not let me rest.

That's the only reason my hands fall to the front of his pants. Or that's what I tell myself as I palm his hard cock, a physical response he's obviously gone out of his way to ignore. Well, *I'm* not going to ignore it.

Perseus grips my wrist lightly. "That's not why I did this."

"I know." My chest is too full of all the things I can't say. All the things I don't know *how* to say. Perseus and I were doomed from the start. Our marriage will fail, will end in his death or mine. It's all but predestined, a fate written in the stars. From the moment I said *I do*, I knew it as truth. There's no space in our fate for softness and care. I don't know how to deal with the sudden pivot.

So I won't. Not tonight.

"Callisto. You were *shot*. Today. Mere hours ago." He doesn't release my wrist, but he does plant his free hand on the tile next to my face. "You need sleep. Not sex."

Maybe he's right, but sleep isn't going to come for me anytime soon. More than that, a desperation is rising within me. Some asshole shot me today. I could have died. I can still feel the possibility lingering close, the darkness at the edge of my vision. A promise of oblivion that never ends. Some people go to their deaths peacefully. I'm not one of them. I will spend every last breath fighting to stay alive, to remain with those I care about.

What better way to combat death than with the purest representation of life? The logic is a stretch by any definition of the word, but I don't care. It's a paper-thin excuse to take what I want—and what I want is my husband.

"I almost died today." The words come out halting, uncomfortable. "I need to feel alive, Perseus. I need *you* to make me feel alive. I need...you. Please." I'm not one to beg while still in my right mind, but I can see the stubbornness in the set of his jaw. He has a particular kind of comfort in mind, and it doesn't involve orgasms. Maybe that's why I keep talking. It's certainly not in a pathetic attempt to comfort *him*. "You've taken care of me. You're going to keep taking care of me. I promise not to pull any athletic moves that will mess with my stitches. I'll do whatever you say. I just need this. Please, Husband."

His hand twitches around my wrist when I call him *husband*. I've said it before, but the word has always contained enough derision to cut. Not this time. This time, I say it almost as if he's my husband in truth, the husband I would have chosen without duress.

Perseus narrows his gorgeous blue eyes at me. "You're testing me."

"I'm not. I promise."

"A trick, then."

If I let him, we're going to keep arguing all night. He wants this as much as I do, but he doesn't trust me. I've given him no reason to, and I won't in the future, either. But right now, my words are truth without any deceit behind them.

I wrap my free arm around his neck and press my naked body to his. I can't quite reach his mouth without him bending down, so I speak against his throat. "It's not a trick. I just need you. Will you deny me?"

His breath shudders out and he releases my wrist to press his hand to the small of my back. "No, Wife. I won't deny you."

ZEUS

I KISS MY WIFE. IT'S SOMETHING I'VE DONE A THOUsand times, but it feels different in this moment. It feels... intentional. Like a promise of something I don't know if I can fulfill. Callisto is hurt and obviously shaken, and a better man would wrap her up and tuck her in and leave it at that. But she opens for me so sweetly—*sweetly*—and I'm a goner.

I sweep her into my arms, careful not to jar her shoulder. "If it's too much, tell me to stop, and I will."

She lays her head on my shoulder and presses her hand to the center of my chest. "I know."

Two simple words, spoken without any hesitation, are nearly enough to dismantle me entirely. I set her down on the bed and shove off my pants. It takes a little more effort than it would otherwise because of the wet fabric, but I manage.

Callisto props herself up on her elbows and watches me closely.

I've barely touched her and the intimacy of being *seen* is almost more than I can bear. Despite myself, I can't stop from glancing at the light switch. She sees. Of course she sees. "You can turn the lights off if you want."

If *I* want. I turn back to her. "What do *you* want?"

She nibbles her bottom lip, the move so unlike my fierce queen that I can't help staring as if I've never seen her before. Maybe I haven't. We've been playing war games since the moment she came to me with an offer of marriage in exchange for my protection of her sisters. We've never been vulnerable with each other. Not in any way that truly matters.

Callisto shifts. "I want things I can't possibly have."

I'm a fool a thousand times over for the desperation rising in me as I process her words and search for meaning beneath them. "You want me."

"Yes." She shifts, her gaze raking over me before finally landing on my face. "I want you. But I can't have you. Not really. Even if we wouldn't eventually destroy each other, Olympus will destroy us both."

Her honesty draws me closer despite how much I hate her words. I climb onto the bed and stretch out next to her, mere inches away. As I search her expression, I realize I've never seen her look so…open. It makes me want to gather her to my chest and hold her tight, but I don't know if she'll allow it. I still can't help but reach out and smooth back her damp hair. "You have me, Callisto. You've had me from the start." A truth so stark, it feels obscene to say it aloud.

She shivers. "I like it when you say my name."

I'll say it forever if you let me. I know better than to speak that promise aloud. This moment hangs in the balance. She's scared and vulnerable, and tomorrow, when she's feeling more like herself, she'll hate me all the more for witnessing this moment of alleged weakness.

From the time I was a kid, I've been taught to lead, to manipulate, to *control*. I've never been taught how to protect. It's not a skill I truly understood I was lacking until recently, when all I want to do is protect my sisters…and my wife. They won't allow it any more than she will. If I were stronger, if I knew what the fuck I was doing, then maybe it would be different. Maybe they would trust me to stand between them and what's coming for us all.

Wishes are for the pathetic fools who don't have the power to make things happen.

I *hate* that my father's voice intrudes on this moment. I hate even more that he's right. I stroke my thumb over Callisto's cheek. Over and over again, we've brushed against the opportunity to pivot this marriage into something real, and over and over again, one or both of us has shied away from taking that first step. I wish I could believe tonight will change things, but I know better. Tomorrow, it will be back to war.

But that's tomorrow. Tonight, she's mine.

"I'll say your name as often as you like." I brush a light kiss to her lips. "Callisto." I kiss her again, deeper this time. She immediately melts into me, crossing the minuscule distance between us and sinking her hands into my hair. In this moment, we're not Zeus and Hera, the perpetually warring king and queen of Olympus. We're Callisto and Perseus, and if we aren't fully committed as wife and husband, we're *here*.

I grip her thigh and tug her leg up and around my waist. Closer. I need to be closer. I grab her ass and slide my hand down to press my fingers into her pussy from behind. She makes the sweetest little whimpering sound in response. I want to swallow it whole.

Callisto bites my bottom lip, raking it gently between her teeth. "That feels good."

"I'll always make you feel good." I don't know what I'm saying; the sensation of her wet heat clamping around my fingers is enough to short-circuit my brain. I like having her like this, pressed against me, pinned on my fingers, grasping at my shoulders with demanding hands. She kisses me harder but I don't pick up my pace, lazily finger fucking her.

She'll never be *mine*. I know better than to play possession games in the bedroom, but fuck if I don't want to growl against her mouth to remind her *I'm* the one making her so wet the sounds fill the room even over our moans and kissing. It's not that asshole Ixion driving her out of her mind, taking care of her when she needs it most.

It's *me*.

It's too much, but fuck if I care. "Come for me, Wife. You're so fucking sweet when you do."

"I need…" She shivers. "I'm so close."

I shift our positions just enough to wedge my leg between her spread thighs. It's a little awkward, but I'm able to guide her to grind against my thigh without sacrificing being able to reach the spot inside her that makes her go boneless and desperate.

"I've got what you need," I murmur against her mouth. "Take it."

She grinds on my leg, my fingers, her movements just as slow and sensual as everything has been since the moment I climbed into bed with her. I'm so hard, it's a miracle I don't come before she touches me. The agony of pleasure is worth enduring so I can feel the moment she clamps around my fingers, her back bowing. "*Perseus*."

Hearing her cry out my name when she orgasms breaks something deep inside me. I roll onto my back, taking her with me. Callisto lands straddling my hips, her eyes wide and wild. "Perseus, I—"

Fuck, I could get addicted to this. I pull my fingers from her and wrap them around my cock. "You can take more."

"I need—" Even as she protests, she lifts herself so I can position my cock at her entrance.

"Callisto." I have to stop, to focus on breathing, as she descends a bare inch. She's so fucking beautiful, it's unreal. The overhead lights in our bedroom lovingly caress her body, lingering on her fuller-than-normal breasts, on the faint curve of her stomach, on her strong thighs. They even manage to reach her perfect pussy as she takes my cock, inch by inch.

Watching my length disappear into her is something I've fantasized about more often than I'll ever admit. It's so much better in reality. Even with her orgasm slicking the way, she has to fight to descend on my cock. We've done this before, but I've never been able to drink in the sight of her in the process. The lights weren't off on our wedding night, but there was no room for this kind of intimacy.

"You can take it," I murmur. I grip her thighs, holding her wide as she rocks to take me deeper. "There you go, love. Just like that."

Her rocking hitches, and I have a beat to realize what I just said before Callisto plants her hands on my chest, her nails pricking my skin. "The way you watch me…"

Be careful. I ignore the internal warning. I can't think of anything but her right now. "How do I watch you?"

She sinks the last inch, sealing us together tightly. Callisto shivers and it feels so good, I can't stop my grip from spasming on her thighs. She slides her hand down her stomach to her pussy, creating a V with her fingers. She starts fucking me slowly, applying friction to either side of her clit. "Like you want to tattoo your name on my ass."

That surprises a choked laugh from me. "Not your ass, love." Damn it, I didn't mean to say it again. The word just keeps slipping out. "I'd do it right here." I shift my touch to cover her hand, pressing her harder against herself. She moans, which is a fucking mistake because my words once again get away from me. "So that every lover you take is constantly reminded of whose ring you wear."

"You are *such* a brute." The words come out slow and sensual. Callisto rides me with a steady rhythm as if she could go all night. She's beautiful enough to make my control shudder, lean and sharp and all too willing to cut the unwary. I've never wanted to feel the edge of a partner's blade the way I do with her. The little moments hurt, but the hurt means they happened.

And now here she is, flushed and fiery, coming back to herself, one stroke at a time. It's there in the way her spine straightens, the angle her chin tilts, in how she finally lets her eyes flutter shut and head fall back. Without her gaze challenging me, I can drink in the sight of her at my leisure.

I want to believe there's a future where *this* is how we are together. I love the thorns and viciousness, but I'm a greedy fucker because I want all of her. I want her fury and her strength and her trust and her vulnerability.

I want her...love.

Right now, she's giving me her trust, even though I don't deserve it. How can I when she was harmed under my watch? My gaze tracks to the bandages marring her golden skin. I should have been there to protect her.

Your family is your seat of power.

I tense, not wanting *his* voice here in this moment. Callisto feels it, because of course she does. In this moment, she seems just as tuned to me as I am to her. Her eyes open and she braces one hand on my chest so she can grab my chin. "Stop."

I freeze. "Stop?"

"Whatever you just thought about? Stop. It has no power right now." She shakes her head sharply and dips her hips, taking me so deep that I can't stop myself from moaning. Callisto smiles wickedly and this, *this*, is my wife. "Isn't it better here with me than wherever you went in your head?"

The question is so absurd, I can't help but laugh. I grip her hips and thrust up into her. "Everywhere is better with you."

She slaps me lightly, nowhere near hard enough to hurt. It makes my balls draw up. I dig my heels into the mattress and fight for control. Callisto, the little brat, clocks it. She does it again, this time to the other cheek. "You don't have to sway me with pretty words. I'm currently riding your long, thick cock, Husband." To demonstrate, she rolls her hips in a more exaggerated movement.

"Yes…" I grit out. "You're doing masterfully."

She laughs, clenching around me in the process. But even in the midst of this fantasy of a happy marriage, I can't help but notice the shadows plaguing me are reflected in her hazel eyes. Her smile dims, though she never loses her rhythm fucking me. "It can't last."

"Callisto." I love the way her eyes flutter when I say her name while I'm inside her. "Why not?" I pick up her rhythm, matching it and driving a flush across her entire body as another orgasm draws closer. "We are two of the most powerful people in this fucked-up city. We can do whatever the fuck we want."

"We…" She seems to force her eyes open. "We can't."

"Yes." I roll us and press her thighs wide so I can get just as deep as we both need. "Yes, we can." It takes a moment to find the tempo that has her thighs tensing against my palms and her nails clawing at my chest. "We can do anything together." I kiss her roughly. "Callisto." Another kiss. "*Wife*."

"Perseus, I'm going to…"

"Come for me," I growl against her lips, our ragged exhales so in sync it feels like they're one and the same. "Please, love, I want to feel it."

"Oh, *fuck*." She pulls me closer, and I'm only too happy to oblige to the prick of her nails against my ass. "You, too," she gasps against my throat. "Come for me, Husband. *Please*."

I'd had every intention of holding out, but in the face of my pleading, orgasming wife, I'm helpless. I move back to fuck her roughly, holding her thighs wide so I can ensure she doesn't shift on the bed and hurt her arm. A handful of strokes later, I give in to the pressure gathering in the base of my cock. I come so hard, my body clenches painfully in a shiver that's almost a spasm.

I roll to the side and carefully wrap my arms around her. Maybe she was right and we both needed the sex, but *this* moment grounds me more than anything else. I can feel her heartbeat, her breathing, the warmth of her skin. She's alive. She was hurt, but she survived. Something that clenched inside me when Ares got that phone call finally relaxes, just a little.

I press one last kiss to her lips. "Did I hurt you?"

"No." She smiles a little, looking soft and thoroughly fucked. "Thank you. I needed that."

"We both did." I am a fool for the hope that flutters inside me, fragile and unfamiliar and existing solely because of this woman. We made it through today. There is no guarantee of tomorrow, so I'll take my wins where I can. Here. Now. With my wife.

HERA

I LIE NEXT TO MY HUSBAND, MY BODY STILL THRUMming with the strength of my orgasm, my mind blessedly blank. In a little while, I'm going to have to start spinning and figure out my next steps, but…not yet. I'm not ready to leave this moment of curious safety.

It's not actually *safe*. I know that. He seems remarkably blasé about my attempting to murder him, but he wouldn't feel the same way if he knew I was working with Circe to save my family at the expense of the rest of the Thirteen and legacy families.

The thought makes me uncomfortable. Almost guilty. I'm not used to the sensation, so I start to turn away, but he presses his big hand to the center of my chest. "Don't run."

"I don't run from anything, least of all you."

Another man would laugh. Would make a joke of some

kind. Or maybe he would just grin. Perseus does none of these. Instead, he watches me with those oh-so-serious blue eyes. "Don't run," he repeats. "Please."

The temptation arises again to tell him...something. I have so many doubts about him and *us*, and yet I can't deny how safe I feel with him. I don't know how that equation works out, and because I don't know, I can't trust him with my sisters' and my mother's safety. If I confess what's going on with Circe, he's just as likely to toss me into some locked room as he is to work with me in pursuit of an actual solution—and if I'm locked up, I can't save them.

Not that I'm doing a bang-up job of saving anyone right now. Persephone has unilaterally told me no, and after the events of the day, there's no way Hades is going to listen to a single argument I make.

But even knowing how hopeless this entire situation is, I can't quite turn away from Perseus. I carefully cover his hand with mine, keeping it pressed against my chest. "It's late. I'm not going anywhere."

"That's not what I meant and you know it." He studies my expression. I have no idea what he sees there. "Did I tell you Hermes came to talk to me?"

I blink. "What?"

"She pulled her customary move of appearing without notice and disappearing just as quickly, but she stuck around long enough to issue some dire warnings."

My skin prickles. Is Hermes talking to all of the Thirteen? And if she is, what does that mean? She's been one of us long enough to know how unlikely it is to pressure any of the titles to step down. If they could be swayed by violence, they would have been so when the assassination clause became public knowledge and attempts on our lives became regular. Sure, Aphrodite and Hephaestus stepped down, but they were immediately replaced. The title still remains. What is Hermes prepared to do that could actually change that truth? "What dire warnings?"

He shifts to prop his head on his hand, his other hand still pressing lightly to my chest. "She said the Thirteen as a government structure is no longer working. As always, she seems to forget she's part of the Thirteen when it suits her."

My heart lodges in my throat. I know better than to hope, especially with this man, but I can't seem to help myself. I blame the hormones. But if Perseus *were* on my side...that could change things. That could change *everything*. "She's not exactly wrong," I say slowly.

"I know." Perseus closes his eyes and exhales heavily. "You don't think I know that? I saw every single thing my father did to hurt other people and how he used this title to do it. He's not the only one, either. I *know*, Callisto."

I almost—almost—reach out to cup his square jaw. Only sheer habit keeps my hand still. I don't comfort my husband, at least outside of sex, apparently. The thought should be ludicrous, but there's an ache blooming in my chest. I don't know how to combat my softening toward him. He's just as lost as the rest of us. I hate that I'm only now realizing this, and I hate even more that it shifts something inside me.

I don't want to kill my husband. But my new weakness doesn't stop there. I don't want him to die at all, not at my hand and sure as fuck not at someone else's.

I know what I should do. I should sit here silently and let him talk until he says something I can use against him. Even as little as he's confessed is enough to rock the foundations of Olympus even further. I can see the MuseWatch headlines now:

ZEUS WANTS TO RESCIND TITLES! CHAOS
Reigns!

The thought brings me no joy. And because it brings me no joy, I can't quite stop myself from shifting my touch to his forearm and squeezing lightly. "Then why not step down? Why not find another way?"

He opens his eyes, looking more tired than I've ever seen him. "There are thirteen of us. Even if I step down, even if Poseidon did, the others would simply move into that power vacuum and use it for themselves. In the best-case scenario, dozens of people die as the legacy families fight for the available titles. In the worst case, there's civil war."

I've watched him for months, cataloging every little micro expression. He's telling the truth—but not the full truth. "And what else?"

His flinch is almost imperceptible, but there nonetheless. "I started training to take the Zeus title from the moment I was born. It's my entire identity. I may have inherited the title before I was ready, but the fact remains that it's *mine*." He starts to shift back and now it's my turn to tighten my grip, to ask him without words not to run from me. He glances down to where I hold his arm and settles more comfortably against me. "Who am I if I'm not Zeus?"

I frown. I don't like his question, and I like even less the tone in his voice. It's threaded with something that almost sounds like despair. As if he can see the end of Olympus and he doesn't think he'll survive to witness it. As if he'll keep fighting anyway because he doesn't know how to do anything else.

I don't mean to move. I don't mean to say anything. I don't mean to react at all. And yet my body takes the choice from me. I shove him onto his back and climb up to straddle his stomach. "Stop that."

He raises his brows. "Stop what?"

"Poor little rich boy. Your father was a monster—no one will argue that—but this is Olympus. Monstrous parents are hardly a rarity. You're the most powerful person in this city, and only part of that power is because of your title. Your family has been here since the start. You're the ultimate legacy bloodline. Did Eris lose all her power when she rescinded the Aphrodite title?"

"She's Eris. What do you think?"

I think Eris is one of the most dangerous women in this city—and holding the title of Aphrodite *still* almost broke her. She won't admit as much, and I doubt Perseus would either, but there's no other reason she would have allowed the Aphrodite title to slip from her grasp. It wasn't the assassination attempt that shook her to her core. It's the fucking system, this fucking city. It chews people up and spits them out as fractured versions of themselves. Eris got out of the Thirteen before the system broke her, but only barely.

"This isn't working, Perseus." I don't mean to say the words, but just as my body took the choice from me, now my tongue and lips do. "I don't necessarily agree with Hermes's methods, but it doesn't change the fact that she's not wrong. How much evil has been done in the name of various members of the Thirteen? And I'm not talking about evil stretching back to the founding of the city. I'm talking about evil that happened in *our* lifetime while we were old enough to notice. Can you list it all? Because I can't."

He flinches again, and part of me hates how I'm hurting him with my words. How far I've fallen from my ambition to become a widow. Now I can't even handle delivering an emotional blow to my husband. Finally, Perseus says, "No. I can't list it all."

The admission settles between us. Something has shifted. It doesn't matter what my original plans were, or what his intentions were. There is only the way we are now. We crossed a line and now we can't go back. The worst part is how little I want to. "So the question remains—what are we going to do about it?"

He moves slowly, carefully setting his hands on my hips as if he's not sure of his welcome. "Even if I wanted to dismantle the Thirteen…even if it were possible…there's Circe to reckon with. She's not going to wait peacefully for Olympus to create a whole new power structure that might have a chance to stand against her."

There's only one solution to the Circe problem. There's always only been one solution. We just haven't managed to pull it off yet. "It's simple, really. We kill her and then forge a new form of government."

His lips curve the tiniest bit. "Your plan is spectacular in its detail."

"Hey." I lightly smack his chest. "The fact I'm sharing this plan with you at all is a step in the right direction. If there's hope for us, then there's hope for all of Olympus."

His smile dims, his blue eyes going oh so serious. His fingers dig into my hips, ever so slightly. "Is there? Hope for us?"

It's only then that I realize what I just said. What is wrong with me? I was so firm in my choices, so cemented into my plan. The last few days shouldn't have changed anything, and yet they've changed *everything*. I want to blame the parasite, but allowing myself even that amount of delusion is dangerous.

I could tell him. I could confess to being pregnant, could explain how terrified I am, could mourn the way that no matter how tightly I try to cling to control, it keeps spinning out past my fingertips. It's a sensation I'm sure he's experienced. Maybe there's comfort in knowing I'm not alone.

Except it would be a lie. He said it himself: He doesn't know who he is without Zeus. Wishing for a different way doesn't mean he'll actually put our words into action should the opportunity present itself. Even if we found and eliminated Circe today, his wishes would shift as soon as our enemy stopped looming large. As soon as it became easy to settle into what passes for normalcy in this city.

I don't know what hurts more about that future—losing him…or knowing I never had him to begin with.

So I don't tell him I'm pregnant. I just lean down and press a light kiss to his lips. "I don't know." It's the most honest answer I can give. I have no idea if there's hope for us. I don't think there is, but enough of me wants it that I can't shoot him down.

He strokes my hips as I straighten. "That's not a *no*."

My throat tightens and my eyes burn. Damn hormones. It's the only reason I'm fighting not to cry right now like some kind of sap. "It's not a *no*."

"I've given you great freedom since we were married. I knew you hated me, and that your feelings were unlikely to change." He sits up suddenly, bringing us chest to chest. "Tonight, you've given me hope, Callisto. Because I want you as my wife in truth, and if there's even a sliver of a possibility you'll agree to that, I'll fight until I have nothing left to bring it into reality."

Shock stills me and eliminates my ability to speak. *This* man is one I've only gotten a glimpse of, the one who shows up more and more as things go off the rails. This is not the ice king with a barrier around him to rival the one that used to surround Olympus, keeping me at a distance. I was grateful for the distance before. I'm not now.

I am well and truly fucked. "I hate you."

He strokes his hands up my back to grip the nape of my neck. "Say it again. Try to sound like you mean it this time."

Heat surges through me. Now's the time to shove away. Dawn is barely a hint in the sky visible through our windows, but there's so much to do and so many people depending on us. We can't afford to spend any more time in bed. I can't afford not to hate my husband.

Even knowing that, I lean in and speak my next words directly against his lips. "I hate you…most of the time."

He smiles slowly. "I don't believe you."

I kiss him. There's no other option to wipe the smug look off his face. Then my hands are in his hair and, fuck it, the world will go on spinning for another hour while we find what pleasure we can in each other.

While we find…comfort.

HERMES

"THERE'S NO SIGN OF HER."

I swallow down a sigh. I'm so bloody tired, I can barely see straight. I'm in the best shape of my life, but even someone of my unparalleled athleticism needs to sleep and rest occasionally. Rest has been in short supply lately. "Things are going a little better on my end. Hades isn't going to work with the rest of them. I made sure of it."

Atalanta hums a little under her breath. "Athena is furious Circe keeps evading us. Even I'm starting to get irritated. No one can be that good."

Circe is. She always was. Even when we were kids, her mind and ambition were fearsome things. As we grew up, those traits were refined by a life lived hard. She became ruthless. Unstoppable.

But I can't say as much to Atalanta. She's already giving

me worried looks when I speak with a little too much enthusiasm about Circe. Atalanta is a good woman, the best woman, but even with the struggles she's faced, she was born into a life of privilege. She might believe the system needs to shatter in order to be rebuilt, but she doesn't possess the deep desperation constantly clawing at my insides. "She's in the countryside. It's the only thing that makes sense."

"Poseidon did mention the possibility to both Demeter and Zeus. He's worried she'll come in through the mountains. It's a quick hike to the civilian camp from the foothills, but there have been no reports suggesting strange activity in the area. Though I don't know what would qualify as strange with the majority of the Olympian population there."

"I know." I rub my eyes. They feel so heavy. Everything feels so heavy. Damn it, I'm not going to get away without sleeping another night. "I'm going to crash for a few hours and see if things are clearer when I've got fewer cobwebs taking up space in my head."

"You can use my place if you want." The offer is a study in casualness. A step toward our path to something *more*. To spend my vulnerable time sleeping wrapped up in the fantasy of her, of what it would be like if it was *our* place and not just her place. It's absurd that I haven't even kissed Atalanta yet and I'm practically picking out wedding rings, but I live for the absurd. And what I feel for her *isn't*. It's soft and sweet with just enough hard edge to make things interesting.

And I can't have it. Not until we accomplish what we set out to do. Grabbing at a happy future too soon is a good way to end up pacified and making excuses to keep the status quo. We're so close. We can't afford to slip. "Next time."

Her voice betrays no hurt. "Next time. Get some sleep, Hermes."

"Never fear, darling. I'm the best sleeper to ever sleep." I keep the injected cheer in my voice until I hang up. Then I let my smile fall. I want what Atalanta's offering with a desperation that borders on frenzy. She's so damn interesting and intelligent and capable, and she smells so sweet. Sometimes I catch myself fantasizing about finding out if she tastes just as sweet as she smells.

Not tonight.

Not until this is over.

I fully intend to spend the night in one of the safe houses I have scattered about the city, but when I look up, I realize my feet have made a different decision for me. Blasted feet. I stand in front of the iron gate that leads into the first property I ever purchased after I became Hermes and got access to a truly spectacular amount of knowledge and wealth. I spent the next year getting it exactly perfect, recreating something that only existed in my mind—in *our* minds. A romantic little house surrounded by greenery.

Yes, the greenery here is half-fake, but I'm not a perfect person and it's pleasing to see plants and flowers even in the darkest part of winter. Or that was the theory. In reality, I haven't been back here since renovations were completed. I walked through the house and realized it was a tribute to a future I would never experience. A future spent with Circe.

I key in the code and slip inside, making sure the gate is closed behind me. It's late enough in the year that most of the live bushes have lost their leaves, but there are still a few dozen sharing their artificial brightness. It's strange to see them against their hibernating neighbors. Maybe I shouldn't have "planted" the fakes. Maybe…

Well, I made a lot of mistakes back then. I was young and foolish and part of me truly believed building this tribute to a dead woman would be enough to ease the pain of losing her. I was wrong on both counts. She's not dead, and it still hurts as much today as it did the moment Zeus came back from their honeymoon and announced Circe had passed. A loss opened up inside me when I heard those words and nothing I've done since has come close to filling it.

Maybe *that's* the reason I've held off on pursuing the interest Atalanta and I both feel. I don't have a whole heart to give her, and she deserves nothing less.

I key open the door and step inside, refusing to take the time to brace myself. Barely a week ago, I sent Ariadne and Icarus to this house to hide. Naturally, Atalanta was clever enough to follow them here, but she didn't catch them. An intentional mistake. I needed the Minotaur to help me with a tiny little task and he would have gotten unruly if something happened to his precious love or her brother.

I expect to see the dust disturbed and the house to feel like someone had been here recently—because someone was, in fact, here recently. What I *don't* expect was for it to be spotless.

The wooden floors gleam under my feet as I walk slowly down the hall. The first room—a parlor—is more of the same, the sheets covering the furniture nowhere in evidence. It looks just like it did the one and only time I walked through before closing it up for good.

"What the fuck?" But I know, don't I? Maybe I've always known.

I find her in the bedroom. Circe reclines on the bed, reading a paperback novel with two people clutched tight together on the cover, the woman's dress looking like something with claws got to it. For a moment, I'm convinced I wandered into another world, one where she wasn't ripped violently from me, one where *this* is our life—where she still reads those titillating novels and then kisses me as if she never needs to breathe.

She was very careful after her "death." Even after Minos dropped enough hints that his sponsor was someone I knew intimately, I still didn't quite believe it could be her. No amount of digging found digital evidence of her—no pictures, no social media, no government documents. I even tried to hack into several banking systems, but while I'm good, I'm not on that level.

I'm not prepared for her beauty. Oh, she was always gorgeous in the fresh-faced way young people tend to be, but it's been almost *twenty years*. The girl who I loved bears only a passing resemblance to the woman who idly presses a bookmark into her book and closes it carefully.

Her short hair leaves her face in sharp relief, giving me nothing to focus on but her big dark eyes and her model-like cheekbones and, gods, her mouth. It's as if the years have melted away what little softness she had and now her beauty is a weapon.

I belatedly realize I still haven't spoken, but the air has been sucked right out of my lungs. I can only stand there and stare.

She rises slowly, wearing a pair of leggings and a knit sweater that shows off her athletic legs and her lean body. And, damn it, her breasts press against the thin fabric, tempting curves that my hands know the weight of, despite my being sure time had stolen the memory from me.

"Circe," I finally manage, my voice mangled.

"Hecate." She moves around the edge of the bed and stops before me. In her bare feet, she's only a couple inches taller than me. She lifts an elegant hand, but stops short of touching my face. "The years look good on you."

"You too." Gods, I can do better than this. I'm no

longer just Hecate, victim of the whims of the powerful. I'm *Hermes*, for fuck's sake. There's never been a situation I can't find a way to backflip through—sometimes literally.

But standing here, held captive by her gaze, I'm not Hermes at all. I really *am* only Hecate, a woman with more dreams than I can contain alone.

Circe has new lines at the edges of her eyes, but they only enhance her beauty. She surveys me. "You know, when I realized *you* were the new Hermes, I hated you."

My mouth is so dry, I can't possibly dream of swallowing. "Hated, past tense."

"Yes, hated, past tense." Her full lips curve. "You were the one who taught me how to *look*. It didn't take long to figure out you were on a revenge mission." She glances around the room. "This house only further confirms it. You didn't miss a single detail, did you?"

"How could I?" I whisper. "Those dreams were all I had left of you after..."

"Yes. After." She cups my cheek the way she used to, all those years ago. "Join me. I'm so close to accomplishing more than we ever dared dream."

I almost say yes. That word, those three letters, dance on the edge of my tongue. I have to concentrate to swallow them back. "What is your endgame, Circe?"

She shrugs, so elegant that I want to fall to my knees and

weep. "Nothing more than what we always talked about. A dream, just like this house."

I knew it to be true the moment I realized who Minos's benefactor was. I just didn't want to believe it. I'm ruthless to a fault and I have blood on my hands—and will have more before this is over. But being Hermes, moving through circles previously closed to me, made me realize something I never could have imagined all those years ago, when the downfall of Olympus was just a dream shared in the dark space between my lips and hers.

The legacy families are just people. There are good ones and bad ones and petty ones and selfish ones. Some of them actually use their privilege to do good things. The system of the Thirteen must be abolished, but I don't have the stomach for wholesale slaughter. Some of those people have become my friends, even if they don't trust me much right now. Even if they weren't…there have to be lines.

Otherwise, we're just as bad as the thing we're trying to eradicate.

It kills me to take a step back, to put more distance between the love of my life and me. The next step feels like I'm being stabbed. "I can't. I'm sorry."

Her smile never dims. "I thought that might be your answer." She looks around the room again, but her gaze is distant in a way that makes me think she's seeing beyond these walls. "This place has changed you."

I shake my head sharply. "Losing *you* changed me. That's where it started."

"You could have me again." Her dark eyes go soft, just like they always used to before she'd kiss me. "I never stopped loving you—even when I hated you."

"I never stopped loving you, either," I whisper.

She closes the distance I tried to create, and I can't stop myself from inhaling, taking her spicy scent as deep into my lungs as I can. It's still the same, even if everything else has changed.

Circe kisses me. I make a sound that's part desperation and part protest, but my hands are in her hair and I'm pulling her close. *Gods, I missed you so much. I can't believe you're here. I can't...*

There's a sharp pinch at the base of my neck. I jerk back—or at least I try. My limbs aren't working properly. I stagger away from Circe, pressing my hand to my neck. My fingers come away with little drops of blood on them. "You..."

"Drugged you, yes." She ignores my attempt to flee and catches me around the waist, tugging me to the bed just as my legs give out. Then she lifts me easily onto the mattress and lays me out. She even makes sure the pillow under my head is properly placed. "There you go."

"But..." My tongue feels too thick in my mouth.

"Yes, that's a valid point." She shifts me onto my side,

facing her, and props one of the pillows against my back to keep me in place. "It will wear off in a few hours, but you'll be woozy for another few after that."

"*Hours.*"

"Yes, sweet, hours. It's one of my little concoctions." She crouches next to the bed, putting herself in my fading line of sight. "I can't risk you developing a sudden case of heroics. I meant what I said, Hecate. I never stopped loving you, and it'd break my heart to kill you. Don't make me." She presses a soft kiss to lips that I can't feel. "I'll be back for you when it's all over. Wait for me."

I try to call her back, to tell her not to do this. In all my scheming, I never even considered that things could play out this way.

I pass out before the first word leaves my lips.

HERA

THE SUN IS WELL ON ITS WAY TO ITS PEAK IN THE sky by the time we manage to leave our penthouse apartment. We don't speak much, but we don't have to. Even though nothing is resolved and everything outside our bedroom is terrible, I can't deny that something changed between Perseus and me. It started before we had sex, before I was shot, before we started using each other's real names instead of our titles. Maybe it started even earlier than that. I don't know. I'm having a hard time *thinking*.

Guilt is a live thing inside me. Circe's threat continues to rattle around inside my mind. I forgot. Yes, it was only for a little while, but forgetting at all is downright unforgivable. She's clearly working within some kind of timeline. She's not going to wait for me to get my shit together, especially when it's becoming increasingly clear that I *don't* have the right words or a convincing argument to make my family step down.

I text Ixion to let him know the plan as we step into the elevator. I should have updated him hours ago to ensure he and the others could meet us here before we left. There was plenty of time to make that happen, to shatter the strange peace Perseus and I have floating between us. Except...I didn't.

As a result, when Perseus holds open the door for me, there's no one to remind me I'm more than capable of taking a second car so I don't have to spend hours longer in his presence. There's no one to look on disapprovingly at the way his hand presses lightly to the small of my back. There's no audience to how I hesitate the tiniest bit to relish the connection.

I slide into the back seat and he follows me in without hesitation. The second the door closes, his woodsy scent surrounds me, bringing to mind all the delicious things we were doing to each other just a short time ago. I shift in my seat, my body hot and restless. Damn it, *no*. I have to focus. The devil on my shoulder may be whispering that we have hours before we arrive in the countryside, but there's work to be done.

Zeus doesn't need the reminder. He gives my hand a squeeze and releases me to pull his phone out. Headphones are next, and then he might as well be on another planet for all the attention he pays me. There is relief in that. His self-control ensures I don't have to rely on mine. And if it irritates me, well, that's a small enough price to pay.

My phone vibrates in my hand, a call coming in from Ixion. I sigh. This isn't going to be pleasant. "Ixion."

"With all due respect, Hera, it's very challenging to protect you if you aren't communicating your plans with us. This is the second time in twenty-four hours you've gone off without a guard. Do I need to remind you what happened just yesterday?"

My spine straightens instinctively. "Check your tone, Ixion. I may be deeply grateful for your loyalty, but you work for *me*. If I choose to take a calculated risk without your presence, that is *my* choice. You aren't in charge."

"You make that abundantly—" There's a scuffle on the other side of the phone and then Imbros comes on the line, zir tone perfectly even and absent of any of Ixion's irritation.

"What Ixion is trying to say," ze starts, "is that we take our jobs very seriously and we worry about you. When we heard you had been shot, we were deeply concerned. Before you contacted me to bring you clothing, we had to get information about your status secondhand from Ares."

My anger threatens to drain away, but I hold on to it with both hands. I have too many people to worry about right now, I don't need more. I *can't* have more. "You can meet me at my mother's current residence in a few hours. I have my husband's full security detail with me, so I'll be safe enough in the meantime."

"Understood." There's a strange note in zir tone, but I can't quite divine it before we hang up. It's just as well. I don't have it in me to manage that trio's emotions. Even wanting to says something I'm not prepared to examine. There's a lot I'm not prepared to examine these days.

I glance at Perseus, but he's deep in conversation with someone. It only takes a few sentences for me to realize it's Poseidon. He's filling the other legacy position in on our plans to follow up on the possibility that Circe has infiltrated the countryside by way of the mountains.

I could tell him she's actually in the city and not the countryside, but even with my ill-fated meeting, I think his instincts are right. If Circe had enough people to cause a true problem, she already would've done it instead of offering veiled threats. Either she's waiting for backup or something else is going on. It doesn't hurt to be thorough.

I can't stall any longer. As much as I'd like to call Persephone, I can't risk Perseus hearing what I have to say. So I take a deep breath and I text my sister.

> **Me:** I'm sorry about yesterday. But I need you to reconsider.

Bless my sister. She doesn't make me wait long for a response.

> **Persephone:** I said what I said, and I expect you to respect it. I understand that you're worried about us, but we have things well under control.
> **Me:** Except you don't. There are enemies in the lower city right now. If you had things under control, they'd already be dead.

Before I can talk myself out of it, I send her two of the videos Circe sent me. One of her and one of Eurydice. I don't send the threats against Psyche and our mother. There's nothing Persephone can do about either, and worrying about them will distract her from what she needs to be worrying about—herself.

> **Persephone:** What is this?
> **Me:** Exactly what it looks like. They're close to you. There's no doubt Circe will continue being a threat. If you want me to stop worrying about you, then take care of it.

My phone rings but it's not my sister calling. It's Hades. Fuck. I glance at Perseus, but there's no avoiding this call. "Hades."

His deep voice comes on the line, rife with tension. "How long have you had these pictures?"

That horrible guilt worms inside me. I shift uncomfortably. "A couple days. But the threat—"

"I have participated in your mother's power games without complaint for months. Nothing has been accomplished except to exasperate the issues we already suffer from in Olympus. The enemy is in our city, targeting my wife and children, and you, our supposed ally, are not relaying relevant information in a timely manner."

The guilt gets worse until I'm choking on it. "I had things under control."

"Clearly, you didn't. Do you have any actual useful information, or are you going to continue trying to terrify my pregnant wife?"

Anger flares, beating back the worst of the guilt. "She might be your wife, but she was my sister first," I snap.

"True. But which of us has taken better care of her?" While I flounder in the face of that question, my jaw working but no sound coming out, he continues. "I'll deal with the threat against Persephone and Eurydice. Have no fear of that. Instead, you should be worrying about the rest of Olympus, Hera." The emphasis on my title, instead of my name, stings as much as anything else he said.

Worse, I deserve it. "If you'd just step down—"

"Don't be naive. That may work with your mother, but it

won't work with *me*. Circe won't allow the risk of the legacy titles rising against her in the future. She has to kill all three of us—which means she has to kill Persephone, too. It doesn't matter what you do, because *that* truth will not change. Stop dancing to Circe's tune." He hangs up before I can come up with a response.

It's just as well. I have no response. The only assurance I have of my sister's safety is Circe's promise to not kill her if everyone steps down. In hindsight, Hades is right. I'm being incredibly naive. I let hope tint my vision until all I could see were the possibility of roses. Not the truth.

Fuck.

I slump back into my seat and close my eyes. There's a way through this, but I can't see the path. Circe on one side and Hermes on the other, both working toward the total destruction of Olympus as we know it. To date, Hermes hasn't directly threatened my family, but the threat exists all the same. I have no doubt Hermes is capable of murder, should the situation call for it, and Circe has already proven she's all too willing to kill her way to the top.

But it's not just those two I have to worry about. Even if Perseus was willing to step down, *he* wasn't part of Circe's offer. She won't let him walk away…which leads me to wonder if she'll let *me* walk away if I insist on keeping the baby. Without thinking, I press my hand to my stomach. *You can't have my baby, you bitch. I'll kill you first.* Except

I don't know how. Every time I turn around, I'm being outplayed and outgunned. I'm just as helpless as every Hera who's come before me. I'm fucking *failing*.

"Breathe, Callisto."

I glance over as Perseus laces his fingers with mine and squeezes my hand slowly, a silent command to match my breathing to the increasing and decreasing pressure of his palm against mine. Damn him, it helps. Within a few moments, the panic recedes enough for me to think clearly. Mostly.

"What if we don't survive this?" The question slips out despite myself.

"We will." He tugs me until I slide across the seat and tuck myself against the side of his body. If his holding my hand helped, the contact of his body against mine helps even more. His breathing is steady. I close my eyes and press my head to his chest, letting the slow beat of his heart soothe me even though I don't deserve it.

"Circe is too good. She's always ahead of us no matter what we do. I don't see a way through."

Perseus wraps a tentative arm around me and strokes his free hand through my hair. "We don't have to see a way through as long as we keep moving. She hasn't struck again, which means she's waiting for something. We just have to figure out what it is and eliminate the threat—just like we did with the ships."

As if it's so easy. As if Hermes and Circe aren't running laps around us no matter what we do. But I want to believe the lie, so I don't point out that we've been several steps behind from the very beginning. Instead, I sit there as my eyes get heavier and heavier, until sleep takes me despite myself.

Sometime later, Zeus presses his lips to my forehead. "Wake up. We're almost there."

Embarrassment heats my cheeks. I can't believe I fell asleep on him, in the middle of the day, no less. I keep my gaze down as I slide back over to my side of the bench seat and comb my fingers through my hair. To distract myself, I pull out my phone to see if I've missed any messages. There's one from Persephone telling me that everything's going to be okay, a false reassurance if I've ever read one. But what stops my breath in my lungs is the text from an unknown number.

Unknown: Clock's ticking, Hera. You're working too slow. Seems like someone has to offer you a little incentive to pick up the pace.

I read the message again and again, but the text doesn't change. A clear threat if I've ever seen one. But from who? I would assume Circe, but there's no denying Hermes is a major player at this point as well. It could be either of them.

I look up as the car pulls through the dirt road passing through all the tents. It appears exactly like it did yesterday, but everything seems leached of color. Fear is a live thing inside me. I've never failed so spectacularly as I have in the last few days. I can't convince my brother-in-law to step down. I can't convince my sister there's a real threat despite her being *shot* yesterday. I can't even convince the husband I'm starting to believe might actually be falling in love with me.

How the fuck am I going to convince my mother?

ZEUS

STEPPING OUT OF THE VEHICLE IS LIKE ENTERING A new and mostly unfamiliar world. This city of tents is filled with my people, yes, but there's nothing normal about any of this. People move about, intent on one job or another, not paying the slightest bit of attention to me. Back in the city, before Circe became such a threat, I couldn't walk down the street without people stopping me to ask to take pictures or to sign something of theirs. Even before I inherited the Zeus title that was true. Because I was always going to claim it.

That title Hermes wants me to relinquish. Hera, too.

My wife follows me out of the car, and I can't stop myself from placing my hand on the small of her back as we walk together toward the particularly large tent that must house her mother. This, at least, is expected. Demeter does nothing halfway.

Two armed guards—both women—stand one on either side of the entranceway, but they nod us through without hesitation. I catch a slight furrow in Callisto's brow. "Were they here last time you came out?"

"No." She frowns harder. "Something must have happened in the last twenty-four hours."

I wait for her to crack a smile or draw the obvious conclusion, but she just keeps looking around as if she's never seen this place before. "You and Persephone were shot yesterday. That's more than enough motivation to add some security measures to protect your mother and Psyche." And Eros, I suppose. But he's never had a problem with taking care of himself—and Psyche as well, for that matter.

My life would've been significantly simpler if I had married Psyche instead of Callisto. She's just as cunning as their mother, but Psyche is invested in playing the game. Callisto only touches on the game in order to break the entire system.

And yet I wouldn't have it any other way. I can't imagine sharing my bed with the soft and apparently sweet Psyche, instead of having it be a battleground the way it is with Callisto and me.

This is no doubt another indication of what a shitty leader I am. I should always be thinking about what's best for the city—not for me personally. My father had it backwards, and his actions drove a division between the upper and lower city that I'm not sure can ever be fixed. When he ordered the fire that killed Hades's mother, he sowed the seeds of war. And then he did it again when he attempted to murder Circe, toppling the first domino that brought us to this place.

Callisto steps away from me pointedly. "I'm going to go speak with my mother and sister. Are you heading straight to the mountains or do you have something to do first?"

It's a clear dismissal if I've ever heard one, and there's a part of me that wants to push back against it. We've finally made true progress in our relationship. I'm loath to give up an inch of it. "Ares should be here shortly, and then we'll head out into the foothills to see if there's anything to find. Wait for me? We'll drive back to the city together."

She opens her mouth like she might argue, but finally nods. "I'll be here when you're ready."

Even with her reassurance, it's ridiculously difficult to turn around and walk out of that tent. I check my phone, finding a message from Ares with the information about where she'll meet me, so I head there directly. Walking through this transitional city is strange to the point of being surreal. People are on their phones, but they're also hauling great buckets of water. There is a massive row of portable toilets at the edge of camp, and I make a wide circle around them.

To have created even this much infrastructure in such a short time is a true testament to Demeter's skill. There is a reason she was voted in by the entire population of Olympus.

The way she continues to be superb at her job truly speaks to the type of person she is. Cunning and ruthless to a fault, yes, but also competent and caring about her constituents.

I find my sister and her two partners standing on a low hill about a hundred yards from the edge of the camp. Ares is dressed in her new usual, fitted pants that look almost military and a long-sleeved shirt. She even has a shoulder holster and a gun. I don't think I ever saw my sister with a gun before she claimed the title, but she took to it like a fish to water. The two men flanking her are Achilles and Patroclus, former competitors for the Ares title, now her lovers and...boyfriends? It seems a silly title for two such imposing figures.

Patroclus is athletic but built a little bit leaner than both myself and Achilles. He has square-framed glasses and is scrolling through a tablet. He is a white guy with short dark hair. On the other hand, Achilles is even taller than I am and built like a tank. His light-brown skin is on display because he's only wearing a T-shirt and pants, his hair cut even shorter than Patroclus's.

Ares turns to face me as I come to stand next to her. "How is Callisto doing?"

When I first became Zeus, and then Eris and Helen ascended to Aphrodite and Ares in the months following, I firmly adhered to only calling them by their titles. Helen, on the other hand, has refused to follow suit. It used to irritate me, but now I find it strangely endearing. "She's recovering. It was only a graze, not nearly enough to keep her out of the action."

"Hades is refusing to answer my calls, but I'm assuming Persephone survived just fine. Otherwise he'd be over on our side of the river causing more havoc than Circe."

"Callisto talked to both of them this morning." Not a medical update, specifically, but at least I have the information from the hospital yesterday. "Persephone and the twins are fine. Medusa suffered only minor injuries, and Orpheus is expected to make a full recovery." I glance at the men. "What did you find?"

Achilles makes a face. "You're not going to like it."

"We figured out the shooter's position," Patroclus cuts in, steady as always. "From there we were able to search the cameras in the area and triangulate their identity."

Helen clears her throat. "Perseus... It wasn't Circe who shot them. It was *Hermes*."

There's a rushing in my ears, so loud I can barely think past it. "Say that again."

"She was wearing a hooded sweatshirt, but it's her." Patroclus flips his tablet around to show a screenshot of a woman who is clearly Hermes, even though she's dressed nondescriptly and has her head down. "Note the bag on her back. That's the rifle."

I can actually feel my blood pressure rising. I've tolerated

Hermes's ridiculousness because it seemed relatively harmless, at least until Minos showed up. But ever since then, she's proved herself to be just as dangerous and ruthless as Circe is. "Where is she now?"

Helen huffs out a breath. "Your guess is as good as ours. We've been trying to track her down even before this, but with little success."

Hermes shot my wife. She endangered our unborn child. She could have killed Callisto. I clench my fists. "When you find her, I'll deal with her personally."

My sister reaches out a tentative hand and squeezes my shoulder. "We'll find her, Perseus. Callisto is with her mother right now, and there's nowhere safer. We'll figure it out."

Every time someone says that, I believe it less.

But no matter how much I want to turn around, march into that tent, and take my wife home, there's a reason we're out here, and we need to see it through.

I force myself to survey the mountains. My father wasn't fond of the country, so we never spent much time outside the city limits. Maybe there's beauty to the ragged peaks stretching high into the sky before us, but all I can see is the possibility for ruin. "Poseidon suspects Circe might be utilizing some little-known mountain pass."

"Yes, I read the report." Helen turns to face the mountains as well, her shoulder nearly brushing mine. "I wish I had better news, but we don't have the manpower to search this area in any kind of effective way. Even if there weren't the evacuees to assist with and a city to search, we're too inexperienced with this type of terrain. We almost lost someone earlier today because they didn't see a crevasse and nearly fell in. I suspect we could search the mountains for years and not find every secret they hide. There might be a pass, but we are unlikely to find it."

She's right. It's just not what I want to hear. We have maps of the mountains, but they're ancient. For as long as I can remember, and at least going back several generations, Olympians have mostly ignored the peaks to the west and north. There are specific crops and herbs that grow in the lowlands, but once you reach a certain elevation, it's only rock. And that rock is sheer and impossible to scale. Or so we thought.

I sigh. "What about drones? They should be able to see more than we would on the ground."

"Yes, but you have all hands on deck searching for Circe in the city. We only have so many hands, Perseus." She glances at Patroclus and Achilles and steps a little closer to me so she can lower her voice. I appreciate her attempt at privacy, but they're standing near enough that there's no way they don't hear. "We already know that Circe is in the city. She's got maybe twenty people, tops. All we need to do is find her—"

"But that's the problem. We can't find her." I scan the

mountains, but there's nothing to see. The day is cold and cloudy, mist covering the top peaks from our sight. "She's smart enough to know she can't take the city with so few people. She'll have another way."

Helen curses under her breath. "She's only one woman. I understand that we've suffered losses, but she's human, not some supernatural boogeyman who will pop up when we least expect it. We just need to be prepared."

I want to believe that. Truly I do. But evidence supports one truth: being prepared isn't enough. I nod in the direction of the north. "Walk with me."

She worries her bottom lip but nods. "Achilles. Patroclus. Would you mind getting the search parties put together? We're running out of daylight, and I don't want to spend the night out here."

Neither one of them looks too happy to let her walk off with me, but I'm her brother. Even if we haven't always seen eye to eye, I've never wished her harm. Yes, she would've married the winner of the Ares title if I had my way, but after seeing both Achilles and Patroclus perform in the trials, it was all but guaranteed one of them would've won if Helen hadn't. Except she *did* win—because she was the best—and fuck if I'm not so proud of her that it makes me a little ill.

We start to the north, skirting the edges of the foothills. I wait until we're well out of hearing range before I speak. "What do you think of the Thirteen?"

Helen shoots me an alarmed look. "What kind of question is that?"

"Before she shot my wife, Hermes came to see me." Easier to focus on Hermes as the source of the topic than the careful conversation I had with Callisto in the privacy of our bedroom. Helen and Hermes used to be friends, before their relationship buckled under the weight of Hermes's treachery. I relay everything Hermes said before she disappeared. Helen looks more and more concerned the longer I speak.

She barely waits for me to finish before she cuts in. "It won't work. The legacy families would never allow the Thirteen to cease to exist. And what would she set up in place of it? A democracy? That's not easy to accomplish, and it's just as likely to be rife with corruption as our system."

"If there were term limits, it would prevent a lot. As members of the Thirteen, we hold our positions until we step down or die, and the number of people who have stepped down is minimal. Most keep the positions until their deaths."

"I'm aware," she snaps. "Are you actually giving this credence? You were trained to be Zeus from the moment you were born. You'd walk away from that?"

"Eris did." I speak the words we've so carefully danced around for months. After Eris stepped down from the Aphrodite title, we never spoke of it again. Not her and me. Not Helen and me. From the expression on my sister's face,

I suspect they haven't, either. I press forward. "She's happier for it."

Helen glances over her shoulder. I follow her gaze to where we can still see the silhouettes of her partners standing on the hill we left behind. "I fought so hard to become Ares. I almost lost so much."

"I know."

"Even if I were willing to hear Hermes out and entertain this idea, that doesn't remove the threat of Circe. We have to deal with her before we can do anything else."

She's right. It's the proper priority—not cowardice. Or that's what I tell myself as I nod. "Agreed. We'll shelve the conversation until this conflict is resolved."

We keep walking for some time in silence, curving to the east with the mountains. We reach the edge of the encampment and are about to turn back when I catch sight of something strange. I grab Helen's arm and tug her back a few steps. "What is that?"

"What is... What are those people doing?" Helen slides back alongside me, her attention narrowing on the pair of women skirting away from the tents, heading into the foothills. They walk with purpose and no urgency...exactly how someone would if they were looking to fit in. My sister frowns. "The citizens are under strict instructions not to wander because it's so dangerous for people who aren't familiar with this area."

"Let's find out." I start down the hill, taking an angle so we don't lose sight of them. The hills are deceptive, as Helen said, and that makes it hard to navigate—or follow someone.

The change that comes over Helen is truly impressive to behold. She was already deadly serious, but even the way she moves changes as she slips down the hill next to me on soundless feet. "I'm taking lead. Stay behind me."

"Helen—"

"Come on."

I decide not to waste time arguing and follow her, albeit less silently. Our father taught all his children how to be predators simply by existing, but there are different flavors of that and Helen has always leaned toward the physical. It's how she won the Ares competition.

We move forward carefully. If the hills were less deceptive, the two women would have lost us immediately, but the moment they're shielded from sight of the camp, they turn toward the mountains. I want to keep them in sight, but Helen grabs my arm and keeps me back until they disappear from sight.

"What are you doing?"

"The ground isn't frozen solid." She nods behind us, drawing my attention to the faint outline of our footprints. "With everything close to the camp trampled, there's no way to know who's coming or going, but there can't be many tracks out here. We've been focusing our efforts to the north and south, assuming Circe wouldn't be so brazen as to send her people this close to the camp." She makes a face. "That was a mistake. I'm sorry."

"She's done nothing expected from the moment she arrived." I bump my shoulder against Helen's. "Now you've joined the rest of us in being outsmarted by her."

"Yeah, well, fuck that." She waits a beat and then moves forward to where we saw the two women last. Sure enough, there are footprints in the dirt, faint enough that I wouldn't have noticed the signs if I wasn't looking for them. Helen draws her gun and looks at me, expression serious. "We don't shoot them if we don't have to."

I do the same, a horrible stillness settling over me. "Right. We need the information they have."

She nods and starts forward, moving faster this time. I shadow her footsteps, ice layering over me in waves. By the time we crouch on the crest of a low hill and look down on the four women grouped together, nothing can touch me at all. I'll do what needs to be done, and if I have nightmares about it later, it's a small enough price to pay for enacting my duty. As we watch, they crouch down around a device, speaking in low voices. None of them appear to have weapons, but surely they must. "We split up and come from both sides. I'll take point and distract them, and you come up behind to stop any heroics."

My sister gives me a long look. "That's more dangerous for you."

I know. A danger I'm willing to take on to spare her. "Go."

I wait two eternal minutes and then slip down the side of the hill and come at them from the side. The blond with a head full of curly hair and light-brown skin sees me first and shoots to her feet. I already have my gun out. "Hands up."

For a moment, I think they won't obey, but Helen steps forward from behind them, her gun drawn as well. "Try to be a hero, end up a martyr."

The women exchange a look I can't read and slowly raise their hands. I nod at my sister. "Pat them down."

She makes quick work of it, tossing away two guns and four knives. She also pulls out zip ties from her jacket and fastens their hands behind their backs, one by one. It takes seconds. Helen places her hands on their shoulders and guides them to their knees, and only then does she give me her attention. "Demeter needs to know, but I don't like the idea of marching them back like this."

She's right, and not only because there are four of them and two of us. The last thing we want is to cause a panic. "Call in Achilles and Patroclus and transport these three back to the city for questioning. I'll take this one to Demeter." I jerk my chin at the blond, who glares up at me with a fury that makes my skin prickle.

For a moment, I think Helen might argue, but she finally nods and pulls out her phone. While she calls Patroclus, I crouch before the blond. "This is the beginning of the end for you and Circe. We have you right where we want you."

If anything, her fury seems to grow. "Yeah, I guess you do."

Helen hangs up. "They'll be here in five. They aren't far off from our position now."

It's the longest five minutes of my life. I want nothing more than to rush back to Callisto and whisk her to the city. I don't care if she hates me; I'm shutting her in our penthouse until we get to the bottom of exactly how many of Circe's people have infiltrated the civilian camp.

The moment Achilles and Patroclus arrive, out of breath and damn near sprinting, I slip out of my coat and drape it over the blond's shoulders, pausing to zip it up. It looks odd, but it's less eye-catching than the zip ties. I haul her to her feet. "Let's go." The sooner I deliver her to Demeter, the sooner I can get my wife to safety.

HERA

I DON'T BOTHER TO TRY TO FIND PSYCHE BEFORE hunting down my mother. As much as I value Psyche's perspective, she's not in the position of having a direct connection to a title—thank the gods. I need our mother to listen to me, and I need her to do it now.

Besides, if I see Psyche, she's going to want to finish our conversation about my pregnancy, and I have no more answers now than I did a few days ago. My feelings just get more complicated with each hour that passes. No matter what happens, I have to ensure there's a world for my little parasite to grow up in.

The surge of protectiveness sets me back on my heels and has me pressing my hand to my stomach despite my determination not to give any indication of anything being different. It's strange how quickly things change.

I find my mother presiding over what I can only term as a war room. There's a massive round table she must have hauled out here from the country house, so large it takes up half the space. On it is what appears to be a very accurate representation of the encampment and its resources. My mother is speaking softly with one of her advisors, a white person with a shock of red hair whose name escapes me.

The moment she sees me, she waves them away with an impatient flip of her fingers. "Come here right this instant and let me see you." She rounds the table as I walk to meet her and then her hands are on my shoulders, turning me this way and that as she examines me critically. Her expression falls and she pulls me into a tight hug. "Gods, I was so worried about you. I've spoken with Persephone, but our conversation was too brief to get all the details. What happened?"

This is the moment. That text message from an unknown number is a grim reminder of how high the stakes are. My mother loves power, but I'm about to wager on the hope that she loves us more. I wish I could be certain of how those scales will balance. "We need to talk."

She eases back to take my shoulders again. My mother is smart, and she takes one look at my face and nods slowly. "Of course." She releases my shoulders and takes a step back, resuming her Demeter mask. Even out here, she's wearing a floral wrap dress, committing fully to the bit. Earth mother, beloved by all. There was a time, so far back that I can barely remember it, where she favored jeans and simple shirts. We had a working farm, and my mother isn't the type to sit back while others do the labor for her. She's always led by example, and those years were no exception. She had no problem getting her hands dirty.

She still doesn't, to be honest, but it's a different kind of dirt that she deals with now.

"I'm listening," she says when I take too long to speak.

I haven't been fully honest with anyone in so long that it's hard to push past the instinctive resistance. It would be so easy to blame Hermes for all of this the way I did with Perseus and take that angle.

It won't be successful with my mother. She has worked alongside Hermes in the Thirteen for a decade and change. The others tended to see Hermes as she presented herself: the court jester, the petty thief who breaks into people's houses because it amuses her. My mother never could figure out what was beneath the trickster persona, but she knew there was something. She respects Hermes. I don't know if she will after this, but *Hermes* isn't the one sending me pictures of my family in the sniper's scope.

Any less direct threat will be too easy to brush off.

I take a deep breath and it shudders around the edges. "Mother, we're in trouble."

To her credit, she doesn't point out the tent we're standing in or the civilian encampment we can hear through the thin walls of fabric. "This isn't about the shooting."

"It is." I take another ragged breath. "But not only that." I suddenly want nothing more than to dump this entire problem into her lap. I may be my mother's daughter, but even at my most ruthless, I can't measure up. It never really bothered me, not when we go about things in different ways, but failure after failure has left a horrible taste in my mouth.

And the stakes have never been higher.

I meet her hazel eyes, so similar to my own. "The Thirteen are going to fall. I don't know if Circe will be the one to do it, or if Hermes will, but the writing is on the wall. Maybe it has been for a long time."

"That's defeatist thinking."

"No, that's reality. Hermes waylaid me on my trip back to the city. All this time, she's been working to dismantle the Thirteen. She wants to set up a new form of government in Olympus. One that is determined by the people instead of by lineage and politicking and backroom alliances. Circe sure as fuck seems to want the same thing, albeit through a significantly bloodier path."

My mother's brows rise with every word I say, until they disappear beneath her fringe of bangs. "You don't seem nearly as angry about the idea of a new form of government as I would expect."

"I hate this city. I always have," I say flatly. "I've been

the most vocal about my distaste for how things are run. That doesn't mean I want the Thirteen put to the sword, metaphorically or otherwise. If the outcome is inevitable, then we need to take the path to ensure our family is safe."

"The legacy families will revolt before they allow even a modicum of power to slip from their grasp. And even if Hermes—or Circe—somehow managed to pull this off, those positions would still be filled with legacy families the same way they are now. They have too much power and money and influence for it to be otherwise." But even as she speaks, she wanders around the table, her hazel eyes speculative. "What she's after is a fool's dream. Look at any other government in the world, and you'll see they're just as corrupt as we are. The rich see after themselves and everyone else suffers for it."

I blink. "Since when have you concerned yourself with governments outside of Olympus?" Up until recently, the barrier ensured that while we have trade alliances, they're limited. The only people who could bring ships—or people—through the barrier were descendants of the original Poseidon. It's only been three days since the barrier fell. The rest of the world hasn't yet realized we're no longer separate and protected, but when they do, we're going to have bigger problems than just Circe.

My mother gives me a sharp look. "All knowledge is worth acquiring. There's a lot of good information out in the world, and it would be absolutely silly to ignore it just because we can't have active alliances with other countries."

I imagine she's utilized more than a little bit of that knowledge to further her own goals. My mother has never met a tool she's unwilling to use, and knowledge is only one component of the equation. I clear my throat. "Even with the hurdles, changing the government might be a wise move to regain the goodwill of the people. Their faith in the Thirteen has fractured beyond repair. They deserve to be represented by leaders they choose."

"Are you sure this sudden change of tune has nothing to do with your not wanting to be Hera or married to Zeus?" She crosses her arms over her chest. "It won't work the way you're imagining it, and even if it could, there would be chaos in the changeover. You're not thinking things through, darling."

I drag my fingers through my hair, fighting to remain calm. This is my *one shot* and I'm fucking it up. I'm not Psyche or even Persephone with the right words to accomplish my goals. Usually, I go with pure viciousness, but that won't work with my mother. "I could say the same of you. Why are you so resistant to the idea of being voted in? That's how you acquired the title of Demeter. You don't think you could win another election?"

She scoffs. "Of course I could. That's not the point. It's about stabilization, which is something we've been lacking for nearly a year now. Look around us." She motions widely, even though there's nothing to see but the opulence of her tent. "The entire population of Olympus is living out of tents in the mud on land that sat fallow for nearly a decade before I purchased it recently. They aren't happy. They won't put up with this for long. We have to find a solution so they can go back to their homes before we can even consider a project of such scope."

She's not wrong, but the Circe problem won't resolve itself unless the government problem does. Even if Perseus is right and there are people secretly coming in through some mountain pass, we still would have registered a standing army. It's not here.

That's not comforting in the least. Circe doesn't seem to be of the mind that she needs a government in place to take over for the old one. She wants the Thirteen gone in a permanent way, and if there's a plan after that, none of us will be alive to worry about it. "Mother, I need you to listen. I—"

"We need to leave." Perseus shoves through the tent flap, his expression all storm clouds. Behind him, he drags a blond woman with a furious expression on her handsome face. "Now."

"Zeus. How lovely of you to finally join us out in the countryside. And who is this?"

He shoves the stranger forward and pulls his coat from

her shoulders, revealing that her hands have been zip-tied behind her back. "We found four of Circe's people going over maps in the foothills. They've infiltrated the encampment. Ares and a small team are taking the other three back to the city, but this one is for you to question."

"I...see." My mother's tone is all sweet honey, nearly hiding the poison beneath. It's a testament to her stress that it's even showing up at all.

"Poseidon told you to post sentries to ensure no one could surprise us from the mountains." His tone is low and dangerous. "I would like you to explain to me how these people have been coming and going without you knowing about it."

My mother frowns, but not even I can be certain if she's lying or not when she says, "I have no idea what you're talking about."

"Because there were no fucking sentries!" he roars. "You wouldn't have noticed anything, and now we have no way of sifting them from Olympian civilians without causing a full panic. There are no cameras in this encampment, and creating a smaller, more organized version of the camp on this table isn't going to tell you which of those people out there are our citizens and which are the enemy's." He holds out his hand to me. "It's not safe for you to be here, Ca—Hera. We're going back to the city immediately."

True to form, my mother doesn't panic. She taps her

fingers to her lips and surveys her table. "I don't think it's wise for you to leave. You'll be exposed on the road back. Better to stay here while we figure this out."

"We'll be safer in the city." Perseus shakes his head sharply. "Once we've questioned the other three, I'll send along a report with all the information we acquire."

"That's not necessary with this captive in front of us. We'll question her and we'll find them." She twists to face me. "But my point remains. We have Eros and plenty of guards here. Stay. Please."

I'm still processing my mother saying *please* when my husband cuts in. "I am more than capable of seeing to my wife's safety." Each word is so cold it's a wonder they don't crack in the tension between all of us.

I step closer to him and lower my voice. "She might be right. It's not a good idea to leave in the midst of all this. *You* should be here overseeing the search—and you should let people see you doing it. It would do a lot to restore the people's faith in you."

"I know." He says it so simply that I'm sure I mishear him. In the moment of my confusion, he takes my hand and pulls me close, wrapping one arm around my waist as he angles us toward the doorway. "But gaining goodwill from the people won't matter the slightest bit if something happens to you. Your trio of guard dogs aren't here to watch your back, and I don't trust any of my people enough to send you with them alone. We're returning to the city where I can establish your safety before we do anything else."

While I will be left behind to chew my fingernails ragged and worry about all the people I love.

All the people I love...

I shove the thought—the possibility—down deep and lock it away behind dozens of chains. It's the hormones, the parasite, the stress of the situation. I love my sisters. I love my mother. I tolerate my brothers-in-law. There is no scenario where loving my husband ends in anything other than tragedy.

Zeus has to die. He's brought nothing but terror and pain to this city. And Perseus has proven he won't relinquish the identity of Zeus, even if it kills him.

Even if it kills my heart in the process.

I'm reeling so much from the loss I can see barreling toward me that I don't realize Perseus has stopped until I run into his back. "Perseus?"

He's so tense he's practically vibrating. "Let us pass."

I shift sideways enough to see that the guards watching the doorway have entered the tent and now block our exit. Neither of them look at *us*, though. Their gazes are trained over our shoulders...at my mother.

"No," I whisper. I turn slowly to face her, my heart not wanting to understand what my brain has already comprehended. "Tell me you didn't."

My mother is just as poised as ever, sympathy practically oozing from her immaculate pores. She smiles sadly as she moves to the blond stranger and pulls out a tiny knife to cut away the zip ties. "I'm sorry, honey, but the writing is on the wall. You know I'll always do what's best for you—and this city. Even if it hurts a little in the process."

"Mother, *please*." My voice breaks on the last word. "Don't do this."

"It's already done." She motions to the guards. "Take them."

HERA

27

EVEN AS THE GUARDS MOVE TO APPREHEND US, there's a part of me that still doesn't want to believe it's come to this. My mother—my fierce, ambitious mother—has always done what she feels necessary to ensure the longevity of our family. It's why she was so committed to one of her daughters marrying a Zeus, the better to weld our lineage to a legacy title. Two, honestly, since Persephone married Hades. If she could have found a way to snag Poseidon in the mix, no doubt she wouldn't have hesitated.

To betray Zeus now? To betray *me* now?

Perseus steps between me and the guards. "If you touch her, I'll kill you myself."

My mother sighs. "No one is going to harm my daughter. *You*, on the other hand, are a different story." She glances at the blond Perseus brought in. "Are you well, Antigone?"

The blond smirks. "Yeah. He was as gentle as a lamb."

Mother nods and motions to the guard again. "Subdue him, please."

Fear unlike I've ever known takes hold of me. I grab my husband's arm. "No. Don't hurt him."

Another of those sighs, as if I've disappointed her. "I realize you're enjoying your time as Hera, but the work you've done with the orphanage has garnered you enough goodwill that you could hold office if that's truly your desire. When this is over, you won't need him."

Hold office. When this is over.

Somehow, even in my quick processing of this betrayal, I still hadn't grasped the true depth of it. I take Perseus's hand. I don't know what else to do. "What did Circe threaten you with to make you betray Olympus?"

"You know me, darling. I don't deal well with threats." Mother shrugs. "Circe came to me with an offer. I saw value in it. The people have done the rest."

"The people…" Perseus murmurs.

"No one is happy in Olympus. Not really." The light voice comes from deeper in the tent. Even knowing who's coming, it still feels like a blow to my body when Circe walks up to stand next to my mother. She's wearing jeans and a knit sweater, which should make her look more approachable, but there's nothing approachable about this woman. She smiles, sharp and cutting. "Demeter hasn't forgotten about the people she serves, or that leadership *is* service. Pity that you have."

Perseus moves in a surge, stepping quickly to the side and pulling me behind him, keeping me between his body and the side of the tent. "Traitor."

"History will say otherwise." My mother doesn't look particularly happy, but she's clearly set on this path and there isn't a damn thing anyone can say to divert her from it. She brushes a hand down her sleeve. "We are holding a vote next week to dismantle the Thirteen and set up new representatives for the population."

"Representatives that you'll no doubt be part of," Perseus snaps.

"I've always been a representative of the people." She doesn't rise to meet his anger. "Unlike you and the others, *I* was voted in."

He's brimming with rage and practically vibrating with a need to act, to attack. If he does, we're both going to end up dead. More than that, no matter how angry I am at my mother right now, she's still my mother. I don't want her hurt. Maybe locked up for a few years until she learns to stop using people as pawns, but not hurt—certainly not dead.

I press my hand to the center of his back and strive for calm. "And what of the legacy families? They'll never stand for it."

Circe smiles, a cat with the cream. "Funny thing, that.

Olympus has lost its connection with its roots. When the Thirteen were originally created, there were only three legacy positions—intentionally. The founders always meant for the best and brightest to hold the other positions—not for them to be recycled through a handful of families with too much money and power. If anything, we're returning the city to what it was meant to be."

"That's not an answer."

"I know." She comes around the edge of the table and leans against it. "Those families have contributed to the rot choking the city and its population. After the trials, that won't be an issue any longer."

"Trials…" Perseus is retreating into himself. I hadn't realized how much he'd let his ice-king persona fade around me until it forms around him, so thick that I'm distantly surprised his back remains warm against my palm. He straightens a little. "I'm sure these trials will be fair and just."

"As fair and just as the legacy families and the Thirteen have been." Circe's smile never falters. "Killing you in the dark would be satisfying for me, but I would never dream of being so selfish as to deny all of Olympus the same satisfaction."

Mother shoots her an unreadable look and holds out her hand. "Callisto, come here. The guards will take Zeus to his cell to await trail."

At that, I laugh, harsh and grating. "No trial for me, then?"

"Everyone knows Heras hold no power," Circe states blandly. "Why punish another victim?"

I stare at her for a long beat. "Why bother to threaten me and my family if you were already working with my mother?"

She shrugs. "It's smart to hedge one's bets. Demeter is too clever to be a sure thing, and if you could have accomplished your aims, it would have resulted in the same thing. Victory." She flicks her fingers at me. "There's just one last element to consider. I meant what I said, *Hera*. You can leave Olympus and keep that little cluster of cells, or remove the cells and stay. I don't particularly care which option you choose, but you will choose."

My mother's eyes go wide. Her surprise only lasts a heartbeat before she has her charming earth mother facade back in place, but it's there. "You're pregnant."

Perseus is stone against my touch. My whole body goes hot and then cold. I didn't want him to find out like this. "I'm sorry I didn't tell you," I whisper. For him, only for him. When he gives me no response, I meet my mother's gaze. "Yes, I'm pregnant."

Mother's gone pale. "You didn't tell me."

"I didn't tell anyone."

Circe looks between us, her careful smile still firmly in

place. "Very well. I'll honor whatever your choice, but I'm not in the mood to deal with schemes when I'm this close to victory. If you keep it, you'll occupy a cell with your husband until the trials. Once they're concluded, I'll have you escorted out of the city and you can go on your merry way."

"Why not just kill me and ensure I don't take a page from your book and return with an army?"

Her smile broadens. "You can try. But I think once you have that baby, you'll find your priorities shift. It would be a shame if something happened to the little one because of their mother's vengeance."

Threats, threats, and more threats.

Perseus still hasn't said anything. Why hasn't he said anything? I hate how lost I feel in this moment. This is what I wanted, isn't it? My husband dead. My family safe. But the thought of terminating the pregnancy, no matter how intently I considered it at first, fills me with a sense of loss I can't put into words. The thought of losing *Perseus*? Circe knows nothing of vengeance if she thinks I'll stand by and allow it to happen.

This man who was never supposed to be mine in any permanent kind of way. This husband I've hated with a fury that filled me to the brim and beyond. This lover who's shown me nothing but respect and care in his own way, even when we hurt each other with our sharp, broken parts.

He's *mine*. And I love him.

"I'll have your answer now," Circe finally says.

"I'm not terminating the pregnancy." The words are out before I can consider the wisdom of announcing it so firmly. But this woman isn't one to leave things to chance. If I agreed to the other route, no doubt I'd be whisked away to a waiting doctor within the hour.

My mother flinches. "Callisto, please listen to reason."

"Like you have?" I reluctantly let my hand drop but Perseus reaches back to lace his fingers through mine. He squeezes my hand in the same slow rhythm he did in the car. Reminding me to breathe. Helping to keep me from panicking. Against all reason, it works. I lift my chin. "I've made my decision. I'll see it through. I learned from the best, after all."

"So be it." Circe motions to the guards. "Take them. Antigone, see that it's done properly."

"With pleasure."

Mother actually lifts a hand before she catches herself. She glances at Circe and I can actually see the machinations taking place behind her hazel eyes, so similar to mine. These guards aren't hers; they belong to Circe. Which means this power dynamic isn't nearly as equal as they're presenting it.

Did Circe offer my mother a similar choice to the one she offered me? I'd wager good money she did.

Not that it excuses my mother doing *this*, but as

Antigone takes me roughly by the shoulder, ignoring Perseus's snarled displeasure, I hold Circe's gaze. "This won't end the way you want it to. You won't win."

She laughs, high and light. "Sweetheart, I already have."

ZEUS

I DON'T FIGHT THE GUARDS AS THEY MUSCLE US out the back of the tent and to a series of low buildings I hadn't noticed in my walk-through with Helen...

Helen.

She should be on her way back to the city now, but she has no idea Demeter betrayed us. She'll report whatever findings to the woman... I twist to look behind us, earning a shove from the taller guard, a woman with a short shock of bright-red hair and a scar down the side of her face. They don't say a word, but they don't need to. The threat is clear. If we dig in our heels, they'll drag us to our destination. Violently.

If it was only me... But it's not only me. I have Callisto to watch out for, my pregnant wife walking next to me with a shell-shocked look on her face. If Demeter's betrayal surprised me, it seems to have devastated her.

The low buildings have obviously been constructed in a hurry, the smell of the sawdust lingering in the air. Another series of guards—all women—ring around it, each hardened in a way I don't know how to put my finger on. It's clear these are more of Circe's people. Whether that means she doesn't fully trust Demeter or something else remains to be seen.

We're shoved into a dim room with only a small window high on the opposite wall, and the door is slammed behind us. Antigone takes a few extra seconds to rattle the lock, checking it and reminding us that there's no easy escape. I waste no time going to Callisto and pulling her close. She resists for the barest moment, and then her arms are around me and her face is against my chest.

I rest my chin on her head. "You should have taken the deal."

Her nails dig into my back through my shirt. "I'm sorry I didn't tell you I'm pregnant."

"I already knew." There's no point in hiding anything anymore. "I figured it out a couple days ago."

She pulls back enough to look up at me, searching my expression. I don't know what she sees; I barely know what I'm feeling right now. Callisto worries her bottom lip, looking unsure for the first time in our marriage. "I originally only let it happen so I could kill you and act as regent until the para—baby grew up."

"I know," I say gently.

"You know about the pregnancy. You know about the assassination attempts. You seem to know a lot." Her mouth twists into something that's almost a smile, but she doesn't quite pull it off. "It's a wonder you didn't toss *me* off the balcony."

How can she say that after everything? I frame her face with my hands. "I would never hurt you, Callisto." Even with our current dire circumstances, I appreciate the way she shivers when I say her name. There's one last untruth hanging between us, and I want it gone. "I haven't been with anyone else—not since we agreed on the engagement and marriage."

She stares up at me. There's so much going on behind her pretty eyes. She worries her bottom lip. "I...haven't, either. I know you think Ixion and I... But we haven't. It's only been you."

I had already decided that it didn't matter, but hearing her confession after giving my own delivers a cruel kind of hope. We're trapped and have been outmaneuvered by our enemies, and yet I've never been surer of what I'm feeling. I frame her face with my hands. "I love you."

"I love you, too," she whispers. She closes her eyes. "Too little, too late. No matter what Circe told my mother, these trials are a sham. She's going to kill us all. The Thirteen, the legacy families, anyone who might threaten her power."

I hug her closer again. I wish I had a solution or a clever plan to get us out of this, but even with everything she's done,

I didn't see the betrayal from Demeter coming. If it hadn't put my wife firmly in the crosshairs, I might even admire Demeter for being so savvy. It's a clever play, no matter how ruthless. "That was always her aim."

Callisto sniffles a little and slips from my arms. "Damn hormones. I hope my mother has a plan for Persephone. She's not one of the Thirteen and *we* aren't a legacy family, so putting her on trial won't go the way Circe wants. Persephone is all but universally beloved and she's visibly pregnant. That will inspire sympathy." She shudders. "There will be an accident. That's the only way."

I can't stand being this close to her and not touching her. I catch her hand and lace my fingers through hers again. "We'll figure it out."

"*How?*" Callisto gives a ragged laugh. "If you didn't notice, we're in a cell in the middle of what is essentially an enemy camp. Circe has integrated her people with ours, and while we may have the majority, she's right about the greater population not being happy. We can't count on any help from that direction. Hades has even more reason to stay behind the barrier in the lower city, and the rest of the Thirteen couldn't even unify to vote to act when Circe was on our doorstep. With Hades, my mother, and us out of the equation, there's no way they'll manage it now. We're fucked."

"When you put it like that, it does sound bad."

She blinks. "Did you just make a joke?"

I can actually feel the ice cracking around me. It only happens with her. It's only ever happened with her. "A small one."

She shakes her head slowly, a grin pulling at her lips. "Now is not the time for jokes, Husband."

"Might as well go to the gallows laughing, Wife."

"Of course you would have gallows humor." She chuckles a little before her smile fades away. "We're in trouble."

"I know."

"I don't see a way out."

I hate to admit it, but... "I don't, either."

We stare at each other for a long moment. "Well...shit." She walks to the wall opposite the door, tugging me behind her, and slides to the floor. I follow her down, close enough that we're pressed together from shoulder to thigh. I wrap my arm around her and we sit in silence as the light through the small window changes. By the time it's dark enough that I can't make out her features clearly, I still don't have a plan or answers.

We are well and truly fucked.

I don't realize I've shut my eyes until Callisto goes tense beside me. "Do you hear that?" she whispers.

"Hear what?" But as soon as I voice the question, I register the faint sound of a scuffle outside the door. It sounds like a fight. Has Circe decided that she won't risk a trial for Callisto? Surely she noticed the way Demeter hesitated, ever so briefly. It would be hard to frame an attack in a locked cell as an accident, but I'm sure she has some fiction ready to spin. "Get behind me."

"Perseus?" For once, even as Callisto questions me, she obeys, slipping between me and the wall. I move until we're just to the side of the door. If someone comes in here with the intent of violence, they'll be looking ahead, not in either direction.

What will you do, fool? You have nothing.

I have my hands, my body, my determination that no one will lay a single finger on my wife. We're in an impossible situation, with no way out, but I'm not about to stop fighting.

The sounds on the other side of the door cease. For a moment, I wonder if it was nothing, but then the door swings silently open. I tense, ready to spring.

"If you jump me the moment I walk through the door, this is going to be quite the botched escape. I'm hardly at my best right now, thanks to a little friendly poisoning. We don't have time for heroics. We have to move."

Hermes.

"What trap is this?"

"No trap." She speaks quietly and quickly, and even though I can't actually see her, she sounds absolutely exhausted—a condition I didn't know could affect *her*.

"Did you say *poisoned*?" Callisto whispers.

"I did, in fact. Don't worry, I'm fine. You don't survive in Olympus without building up an intentional immunity to a whole boatload of poisons." She laughs faintly. "Or maybe I'm just a paranoid type of person. Anyway, there's a shift change in seven minutes. We have a lot of ground to cover and very little time to do it. Are you coming or not?"

I open my mouth to argue, to point out that she wants the same thing as Circe, that she's no doubt leading us out of a cell and into certain death.

Before I have a chance to, Callisto takes my hand and squeezes. A silent urge to listen to Hermes, to take this opportunity. No matter how strange. I suck in a breath and squeeze back. She's right. Even if Hermes is somehow competing with Circe on who gets to kill us, she's offering an opportunity to escape. It's more than we had ten minutes ago. "We're coming."

"Then hurry up."

I keep hold of Callisto's hand as we slip out into the night to find the pair of guards on the ground, bleeding out from what appears to be several stab wounds. Hermes stands just to the side of the door, dressed fully in black with her braids fastened away from her face. She motions with the bloody knife in her hand. "Let's go."

I have so many questions, but they can wait until Callisto isn't in immediate danger. I pause to urge my wife in front of me and then we follow Hermes as she takes a nearly direct route to the edge of the camp. Not the same way we came in, though. Instead of heading toward where the majority of the cars—and Demeter's tent—are, she veers south.

The tents here are mostly dark, the hour late enough that no one has reason to be up and about unless there's a job involved. I keep alert for guards, but either Hermes has dispatched them already or there weren't many to begin with. The latter actually makes the most sense. Whether or not Circe has made her plans clear to the people here, she's obviously intending to manipulate on promises instead of relying on violence. A large number of armed guards undermine the fantasy that she's a savior instead of a conqueror.

She's certainly *capable* of force, but she's smart enough to know that route would cause the majority of the civilians to balk. Instead, she's allied herself with one of the most popular members of the Thirteen and no doubt will start her reign by promising to take care of the people historically overlooked by the Thirteen.

"Hermes," I say softly.

"Not yet." She moves so surely, weaving through the tents with no discernible path, and yet we reach the edge of the camp in less than thirty minutes. She's taken us opposite of the main road, far to the south of where most traffic in and out of the camp is.

Hermes picks up her pace, forcing us to do the same. I keep a close eye on Callisto. She doesn't appear to be flagging, but she's had one shock after another, and she was shot *yesterday*...by Hermes.

"Hermes."

She turns to walk backward and motions for me to keep it down. "We're not quite far enough yet. The sound carries in the hills, especially on clear nights like this."

"How would you know?" Callisto asks softly.

"These are my old stomping grounds. Ancient, really." Hermes tilts her head back, weaving a little on her feet. "I should have wondered why Demeter wanted *this* land specifically, but I wasn't using it and selling it seemed to make sense at the time. I didn't think…" She swipes a hand through the air. "It doesn't matter. I have an off-roader just over the next hill. We can talk once we're clear."

It takes everything I have to keep my peace until we breach the hill in question and walk down the other side, finally losing sight of the camp. I release Callisto's hand and move past her, grabbing Hermes's shoulder and spinning her around. "We talk *now*."

She grabs my hand and hits the pressure points to force me to release her. "All you do is talk, you fool."

"Better that than shooting *two pregnant women*." I clench my fists, wanting nothing more than to remove this damned threat to the woman I love.

"You talk and talk and talk, and you don't *listen*," she hisses. "If I wanted them dead, they'd be dead."

"Orpheus required surgery," Callisto snaps. "That was a bit more than making a point."

Hermes shrugs. "What do you care? You hate him." She

relents almost immediately. "Besides, that was an accident. I didn't expect him to valiantly try to throw himself on top of you to save you."

"For fuck's sake, stop playing games and speak frankly. *What do you want?*"

She shakes her head slowly. "I've *been* speaking frankly. I want the Thirteen abolished and a new form of government set up—one that represents the people fully, and not just a select few blessed to be born into the right families. I want to live in a city where a man can't snatch up a person off the street, force them into marriage, and then murder them on their honeymoon…without a single fucking consequence." She sucks in a breath and moderates her tone. "But what I don't want is to see all those people murdered simply for being born into a privileged family. Doing that is no better than how *he* lived."

There's no question which *he* she refers to: my father.

She's not done, either. She meets my gaze boldly. "You were just as much a victim of him as anyone else. You've fought to be a better man than he was. You have a wife you love. You have a baby on the way. Is holding a title you never wanted worth losing all that?"

I told Callisto that I don't know who I am if I'm not Zeus. It's the truth. But the last forty-eight hours have rocked my worldview down to its very core. I never thought I'd have a chance at love, never thought the future might be full of hope instead of dread.

I look at my wife. She's got her emotions locked down tight, but I've spent months watching her every micro expression. She doesn't believe I'll choose her over Zeus. Why would she? I've given her no cause to trust me, not when it comes to this. "If I'm not Zeus, then you're not Hera."

She presses her lips hard together for a long moment. "I only became Hera to protect my family. Instead, it certainly seems like it just put them further in danger."

As loath as I am to speak this vulnerability in front of Hermes, I have to know. "If I'm not Zeus and you're not Hera, what reason do you have to stay?"

At that, her calm cracks a little. She looks like she wants to shake me. "Perseus, are you really going to pretend like I didn't tell you I love you a few hours ago? That means something to me."

"It means something to me, too," I say softly. Her words are hardly a guarantee for the future, but right now we have no guarantee at all. I wrap my arm around my wife and turn back to Hermes. "I'm assuming you have a plan."

"Of course I do." She grins, looking a little like her old self again. "We're going to the lower city."

HERA

THE LESS SAID ABOUT THE TRIP BACK TO THE CITY, the better. Riding on an off-road vehicle was an adventure as a child and an excuse for freedom in my early teens. It's significantly less comfortable as an adult. I cling to the harness holding me securely in my seat as Hermes hurtles through the night at speeds that mean a mistake will likely be fatal.

Of course, even allegedly recovering from a poisoning, she doesn't make mistakes. She's Hermes.

She fucking shot me...but then she rescued us.

I don't know what to think. I don't know what to feel. Our circumstances have swung from vaguely hopeful to full despair to nebulous in a way I can't quantify. Perseus loves me. He wants a future with me, even if our titles aren't in play.

Unfortunately, the barriers between us and that possible

future are high and thorny. Circe. My mother. Possibly the entire population of Olympus, or at least enough of it to be the majority. How can we possibly survive?

First, we have to survive Hades. He's not going to be happy to see us. Just yesterday, he explicitly told me that I'm not welcome in the lower city. He has no reason to offer us refuge, especially when we are bringing this level of bad news.

There's nowhere else to go, though. We could abandon the city but...I can't walk away from my family. Perseus sure as fuck isn't going to walk away from his.

As soon as that thought strikes me, I grab his hand. "Helen?"

His expression is grim as the wind whips his hair back from his forehead. "She went back to the city, so she should be safe enough for now. Even if Demeter fabricated some reason to call her back, she wouldn't come tonight. I'll call her as soon as I get to a phone."

If she returns to the countryside to make her report, she'll be taken, just like we were. The thought makes me sick. I *like* Helen. She might be a Kasios, but she has fought for everything she has. It's admirable. "Hermes!" I call. "Do you have a phone?"

"Couldn't risk it," she calls back. "Not until we're safely back in the city."

I glare at the back of her head. That's not how phone taps

work, at least not to my knowledge, but it's possible there's tech I'm not aware of. It's happened before. Even so...I don't trust Hermes. I doubt I ever will.

I'm actually surprised when the lights of Olympus appear in front of us, backlit by the rising sun. Hermes doesn't bother to stop at the city limits. She just drives us right in, cruising through the eerily empty streets to the Juniper Bridge. She pulls to a stop in the middle of the street and unbuckles herself. "Might as well walk from here. We can't get through without Hades's permission."

"Not even you?"

She glances over her shoulder at me. "Not this time."

It's only in the growing light of the early morning that I realize how tired she looks. Or maybe sick. I frown. "What's wrong with you? Is it still the poison?"

"Nothing so mundane. I'm suffering from a broken heart." She says it blithely but doesn't quite manage to pull off an unbothered tone.

For the first time, I wonder who Circe was to Hermes. At one point, I thought they were working together, but I was clearly wrong. Even so, there's history there. The way she spoke about what the last Zeus did... There was too much in her tone. It's personal, not a theoretical tragedy that happened to someone else.

Perseus takes my hand as I climb out of the back seat and we turn as one to face the bridge. "Now what?" I ask.

"Just a moment. She should be here any..." She visibly brightens. "There you are."

Atalanta walks around the corner of a nearby building and crosses to us with long strides. She's wearing her customary cargo pants and fitted long-sleeved shirt with heavy boots. Her face is a mask of concern. "Where were you? I couldn't get ahold of you, and when I went to the house—"

"Long story, no time." Hermes doesn't glance at us, but there's new tension in her spine. She's hiding something. The fact that she's not doing it well is more a testament to how *off* she is right now, like an instrument slightly out of tune. "I need your phone. The spare."

Atalanta hesitates. She clearly wants to question Hermes more fully but finally fishes a phone out of her pocket and passes it over. Hermes turns to us. "Call Helen after you talk to Hades. You'll only get one shot at this. By now, Circe knows you're gone, and she'll send her hunters after you. If you don't manage to convince Hades to let you into the lower city, you'll die."

I notice what she's very carefully not saying. Perseus does, too. He says, "You're not coming with us."

"Even if I were welcome there, I can't do what's necessary if I'm hiding behind a barrier destined to fall. It won't protect you forever, but it will slow Circe down enough for you to have a chance to come up with a plan. I highly suggest you stop fucking around and actually make one. I won't be able to haul your asses out of the fire next time." She turns back to Atalanta. "Let's go."

Atalanta nods and looks over her head at me. "Good luck. You're going to need it." She turns and they walk away together, leaving us and the off-roader behind.

"I don't understand her," Perseus mutters. "Working to the same end goal, except for a singular difference, doesn't exactly exempt her from being on Circe's side."

Once again I'm struck by the realization that there's history there—potent history. "She helped us this time, so it doesn't really matter what her goals are, does it?"

He makes a face like he wants to argue but finally shrugs. "Do you want to call Hades or should I? We can't stay out in the open for long."

Considering the *last* time I was on the River Styx I ended up getting shot, I'm inclined to agree. I look down at the phone. "Did you mean it? You'd actually walk away from the title?"

"Callisto." He presses his fingertips to my chin, lifting my face to his. For once, my husband is not a mask of ice, giving away nothing. His eyes are warm and worried and filled with so much love it takes my breath away. "I don't know if Hermes's plan is the right one, but I almost lost you yesterday. If Circe has her way, I *will* lose you." He caresses my cheek with his thumb. "I don't know who I am if I'm not Zeus. That much is true. But I'd like to survive this, to have a chance to find out—with you, if you're willing."

A few days ago, I would have laughed in his face. It's stunning how quickly things have changed between us. My lungs feel too big for my chest. I lean in to his touch. "I'm willing. More than willing."

His lips curve a little. "Even if it means giving up your quest to kill me?"

"Especially then." I've never been so thankful for failure as I am in this moment. I inhale slowly. "You should be the one to call Hades. Be honest. No posturing. No bullshit. Tell him what you intend and what Circe plans."

He presses a light kiss to my forehead. "Okay." He takes the phone, pauses to tug me closer to one of the bridge's large pillars, takes a deep breath, and dials. A pause. "Hades, it's… Perseus. I need you to listen to me until I finish. We don't have time to fuck around."

Twenty minutes later, Hades himself arrives to escort us across the bridge and into the lower city. His expression is forbidding and intense, his dark gaze scanning our surroundings as he ushers us into the waiting SUV.

None of us speak during the short drive to his residence, or the even shorter trip up to his study, where Persephone, Eurydice, and the rest of his inner circle wait. My sisters come to me in a rush, pulling me into a tight hug. "We were so worried," Eurydice says.

"Psyche isn't answering the phone. Neither are Eros or Mother." Persephone takes my shoulders and surveys me. "It's bad, isn't it?"

"Worse than bad," I whisper. I'm so exhausted I'm in danger of weeping. More than that, there's relief to be back with at least some of my family, to be able to share the burden of holding down the future for us. "I'm sorry about yesterday."

"I know." Persephone hugs me again, her round stomach pressing to mine. "Now, bring us up to speed."

Perseus and I sit on the couch and he reclaims my hand as he repeats everything he told Hades over the phone, pausing for me to provide input where I need to. In the end, it takes little time at all to lay out Circe's plan, our mother's treason, Hermes's alternative.

Through it all, Hades is a vault. He only sighs once we've finished. "I suppose it's too much to hope that you're lying."

"They're not," Charon says from his spot in the corner. He holds up his phone. "I just got a text from my contact in the camp. They're mobilizing to return to the city, with Circe and Demeter at their head."

"Fuck." Hades pinches the bridge of his nose. "Call the rest of the Thirteen. All of them except Demeter. Extend an offer of sanctuary, conditional on their following the laws of the lower city." He glances at Persephone. "I'm sorry, little siren, but if your mother—"

"No, I understand," she cuts in, looking sick. "We can't trust her. Not with our people."

"You mean to offer sanctuary?" Perseus frowns. "But you hate the Thirteen."

"Yes, I do." Hades leans back in his chair. "But apparently Hermes and I have something in common. I can't stand by and allow them to be murdered after a farce of a trial. I may understand Circe's anger, but being harmed doesn't excuse intentionally harming others."

I'm so tired that I feel physically ill, but I can't help asking, "What about Hermes's intention to dismantle the Thirteen and allow the population to vote?"

He shrugs. "We'll cross that bridge when we come to it."

It makes sense to worry about later, but I have to wonder if part of his nonchalance is because he knows his people love him and would vote for him in a heartbeat. No matter what has happened in the upper city over the years, *Hades* has always ensured his people were taken care of. He's a true leader, and if we survive this, he'll remain so until the day he steps down. Maybe he'd even welcome this change if it came without a threat, because it means his children will have a choice in their futures.

Perseus releases my hand to wrap his arm around me. I hadn't realized I was weaving a bit until he bolsters me. "What do you need from me?"

"Nothing at the moment." Hades's gaze also falls on me,

something almost sympathetic in the depths. "Eurydice will show you to a pair of the guest rooms."

"We only need one."

Hades narrows his eyes. "There's no need to pretend with *me*, Zeus. I know better than most what your marriage is."

"What it was," I say slowly. "Not anymore. We only need one room."

My brother-in-law doesn't look convinced. It's my sister who says, "Are you sure, Cal?"

"Yes."

She and her husband exchange a look. "So be it. Eurydice?"

My baby sister has grown so much in the last year. She's strong and steady as she rises and motions us to the door. "This way."

She leads us up a set of stairs to a luxuriously appointed en suite. I want nothing more than to collapse facedown, but my sister shoots Perseus a look. "We need a moment." It's not a request.

He nods. "I'll get the shower going."

She barely waits for him to disappear into the bathroom before turning to me. "You don't have to stay with him."

"I know." I can't help pressing my hand to my stomach, to the faint curve there. "A lot has changed with us. I... love him."

Eurydice's eyes go wide. "*What?*"

"I know." Despite everything that's happened, I let out a laugh. "Shocked the fuck out of me, too."

"As soon as you get some sleep, rest assured that we *are* catching up on everything that's happened." She pulls me into a quick hug. "I'm glad you're okay."

Then she's gone, closing the door softly behind her. As much as I want sleep, Perseus is right—a shower will help tremendously. I find him leaning against the counter, waiting for me. He looks up as I walk into the bathroom. "How are you? Really?"

My chest tries to close and my eyes burn. "I can't even process what just happened, how my mother…" I swallow hard. "And Psyche is still with her."

"Circe has no reason to hurt Psyche—or Eros, for that matter. Neither holds a title and threatening Psyche would be guaranteed to turn your mother against her." He holds out a hand. "Come here."

I let him hold me, let him strip me slowly out of my clothes, let him tug me into the shower that's my preferred temperature, let him guide me so my stitches are well away from the spray of water. I stare up at him as he washes my hair, his face a mask of concentration. "I really do love you, you know."

He smiles slowly, so warm that I can't help leaning in to him, wanting to soak the heat right into my soul. "I love you, too, Wife. No matter what the future holds, that won't change."

"What happens now?" I whisper.

"Now, we finish our shower and get as much sleep as we can." His smile fades, replaced by steely determination. "Tomorrow, the battle for Olympus truly begins."

ACKNOWLEDGMENTS

This book has been such a long time coming. I know it's been a marathon, not a sprint, and I deeply appreciate all the readers who have stuck around since *Electric Idol* introduced the idea of Zeus and Hera. I've said this in various places before, but I really wanted their love story to be messy and at least partially reflective of their myths, which meant we all had to wait for their happily ever after. I promise I was in as much agony with the waiting as you were! I also promise that every single post I saw of people losing it over the wait fueled me! Thank you!

As you can imagine, this wasn't the easiest book to write. When you anticipate something so strongly, doubt creeps in (yes, this is a *Hadestown* reference, endlessly, forever). I can only write the story my soul wants, and I hope y'all enjoyed reading it as much as I enjoyed writing it. If Zeus and

Hera were different in private than you imagined them after reading the rest of the series… Well, I hope you understand. I'm just telling the most authentic story I possibly can, but it's only my singular contribution to the constantly growing thread stretching back to when these myths were first passed around orally. That thread will continue to stretch on long after I'm gone, and I find peace in that. If my Zeus and Hera weren't to your tastes, there have been and will be others. Maybe you'll be the one to write them and bring them to life in a completely different way!

My deepest appreciation to Mary Altman for being the best editing partner an author could ask for throughout this series (and beyond!). You weathered through no less than three truly unhinged emails of a neurotic author who was sure that *this* would be the answer (none of them were). If the edits on this book went smoother than nearly any other in the series, it's because of the work you've put in to push me to better my craft. I never doubt that I can come to you with the wildest ideas and you'll "yes, and" me, which is the greatest gift an author can have. Also, when people are mad at me for *Shattered Gods*, I'm going to recall the conversation we had at Book Bash in 2024, where you said, "Okay, but what if [character] dies?" and it was too perfect and hurt too sweetly to deny. I'm crying, they're crying, we're all crying! Thank you for never letting me take the easy way out when there's a stronger thread to pull.

All my thanks to Pam Jaffee, my fearless publicist. You wrangle the herd of cats that is me, keep me alive on tour, and listened to me talk about the end of this series—and this book, specifically—on a particularly harrowing winter drive on the *Midnight Ruin* tour. We lived! I wrote the book! We're doing it! Thank you for being this series' biggest cheerleader and putting up with my ADHD chaos. Also, like, it's not to be overstated how you lovingly bullying me into Delta lounges has made traveling so much less painful. You're the best!

Thank you to the team at Sourcebooks: Diane Cunningham, Diane Dannenfeldt, Stephanie Gafron, Emma Grant, Heather Hall, India Hunter, Bret Kehoe, Kelly Lawler, Nia Saxon, Julie Schrader, Todd Stocke, Katie Stutz, and Michelle Wozny.

A very specific shout out to all my Patreon members. You've been so amazing throughout this series, and your early enthusiasm for the teasers for this book are fuel that kept me going. I appreciate you all so very much.

A particular thanks to Jenny Nordbak for being my partner in crime (and by crime, I mean books!). Whether it's fielding twelve texts the moment you wake up or listening to me ramble on about this book as I was writing it, you've been such a wonderful influence to go harder and more fearless in all things. You never doubted that I could pull it off, and that confidence kept me going even when I was in the weeds of plotting.

I tend to write books in conversation with other media, because that's how my brain works. There wasn't one specific piece that spawned *Tender Cruelty*, but I hold endless love for the books where the author wrote enemies to lovers and didn't pull their punches. Reading them makes me want to be better and go harder. Special shout out to Amber V. Nicole's Gods and Monsters series (Dianna, my queen), Laurell K. Hamilton's Anita Blake series (I always forget how much she *hated* Jean Claude, but my god she did), Tigest Girma's *Immortal Dark* (yes, this came out after I wrote the book and no, I don't care because it's S-tier enemies to lovers and everyone should read it) and basically all of Kresley Cole's Immortals After Dark series.

And, of course, no acknowledgments would be complete without Tim. Yes, I know you're reading this looking for your name. Hey babe, it's 9:11 (yes it is, shhhh, I win). We have this bicker-ment at least once a month, but I wouldn't be able to do this without you. You hold down the household, keep everyone alive and fed, and don't divorce me for buying increasingly difficult-to-hang art for our walls. Yes, I could run the dimensions by you first, but where would the fun be in that? I love you beyond words, which is saying something because this bitch always has something to say. Thank you for always having faith in me, even when I don't have faith in myself. You've never once doubted that I could do the damn thing and, look at that! I'm doing the damn thing!

ABOUT THE AUTHOR

Katee Robert (she/they) is a *New York Times* and *USA Today* bestselling author of spicy romance. *Entertainment Weekly* calls their writing "unspeakably hot." Their books have sold over two million copies. They live in the Pacific Northwest with their husband, children, and two Great Danes who think they're lap dogs.

> Website: kateerobert.com
> Instagram: @katee_robert
> Threads: @katee_robert
> TikTok: @authorkateerobert

COURT OF THE VAMPIRE QUEEN

THREE POWERFULLY ALLURING VAMPIRE MEN AND ONE QUEEN TO RULE THEM ALL.

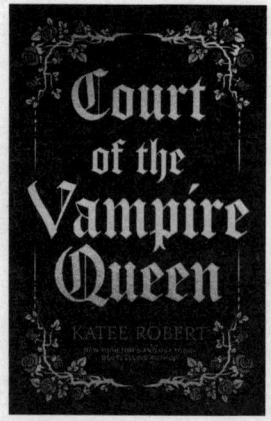

All Mina ever wanted was to escape her father's control. Half human, half vampire, she lived eternally torn between two worlds, never fully experiencing the pleasures of either—until her father chose her as the pawn in his latest political move, gifting her to the darkly powerful and dangerously seductive Malachi Zion.

Malachi is not a vampire to be trifled with. But the longer Mina spends with him, the more she realizes he's not the monster she first thought—and as fear bleeds into lust, then trust, then something more, Malachi opens Mina up to a world she never knew could be hers for the taking: including the love of Malachi's two closest friends and companions. Now surrounded by all three men, Mina may finally have the power to face down her father and take back the life—and crown—that by all rights should be hers.

"Addicting [and] delicious."

—*Oprah Daily* for *Electric Idol*

For more info about Sourcebooks's books and authors, visit:

sourcebooks.com

DESPERATE MEASURES

ONCE UPON A TIME, I WAS A SHELTERED PRINCESS. NOW HE OWNS ME, BODY AND SOUL.

One night and my entire life went up in flames. All because of him. Jafar. As my world burned around me, he offered me a choice: walk away with nothing but my freedom…or rise to his challenge and win my fortune back.

I bargained. I lost.

Now Jafar owns me, and even as my mind rails against him, my body loves the delicious punishments he deals out. It's almost enough to believe he cares. But a gilded cage is still a prison, and I'll do anything to obtain my freedom. Even betray the man who captured my heart.

"Deliciously inventive."

—*Publishers Weekly* STARRED review for *Neon Gods*

For more info about Sourcebooks's books and authors, visit:

sourcebooks.com

LEARN MY LESSON

ONCE UPON A TIME, I WAS A PRINCE.

A single night with Megaera and I'm willing to do anything to save her from Hades, the man holding her captive, victim to his every whim. A bargain with the devil himself seems a small price to pay in order for Megaera to go free... Until I learn that she's exactly where she wants to be.

She's Queen to Hades's King.

And I'm the fool that walked right into their trap. The same fool who desires them both as much as I hate them. I can't resist Megaera's touch—or stop from being drawn to Hades's dark desires. By the time I realize just how deep a game he's playing, it may be too late...For all of us.

For more info about Sourcebooks's books and authors, visit:

sourcebooks.com

THE SEA WITCH

ONCE UPON A TIME, I MET A MAN WHO STOLE MY HEART.

In my desperation to reunite with him, I have nowhere to turn but the Sea Witch. Ursa is as beautiful as she is dangerous, and the one person my father warned me never to let close. But she's all crimson lips and pretty lies, and I'm convinced despite my fear. It's a simple enough plan, if not for the faint of heart. An auction to sell the one thing I possess of any value—myself. The money will free Alaric and then we can finally be together.

Except nothing is simple at all. Ursa is playing at games I can only begin to comprehend. And Alaric? The man I thought I loved might be just as much a villain as the woman I can't help but be drawn to. When playing in the darkest depths of love and lust, it will be everything I can do not to drown.

For more info about Sourcebooks's books and authors, visit:
sourcebooks.com